A Note on Dray Prescot

Dray Prescot is a man above middle height, with brown hair and level brown eyes, brooding and dominating, an enigmatic man with enormously broad shoulders and superbly powerful physique. There is about him an abrasive honesty and indomitable courage. He moves like a savage hunting cat, quiet and deadly. Reared in the inhumanly harsh conditions of Nelson's Navy, he has been transported by the Scorpion agencies of the Star Lords, the Everoinye, and the Savanti of Aphrasöe, the Swinging City, to the unforgiving yet rewarding world of Kregen, four hundred light years from Earth, under the Suns of Antares.

Here he has made his home and has struggled through triumph and disaster, acquiring titles and estates on the way, which he views with a cool irony. Determined to relinquish the burden of being Emperor of Vallia when that island empire is once more united and at peace, he plans to hand all over to his son, Drak. Now the Star Lords have set to his hands a task in the exotic southern continent of Havilfar, but, as usual, the meaning of the mission is veiled from him. To prevent a league headed by Vallia's bitter foe, the Empire of Hamal, from succeeding, Prescot has played in the deadly game of Death Jikaida. He has been sorely wounded.

Prescot records his story for us on cassettes and each book is arranged to be read as complete in itself. Now the future lies before him as he determines to return home to Vallia, and to Delia and his family and friends. But Kregen is not like this Earth.

Hurled once more into headlong adventure, Prescot must battle for his life—and sanity—but, this time, his struggles do not take place in the streaming mingled lights of the Suns of Scorpio, nor even in the fuzzy pink and golden radiance of the Seven Moons of Kregen. . . .

"He could not break that skeletal grip."

A FORTUNE
FOR KREGEN

by

DRAY PRESCOT

As told to
ALAN BURT AKERS

Illustrated by
RICHARD HESCOX

DAW BOOKS, INC.
DONALD A. WOLLHEIM, PUBLISHER
1633 Broadway
New York, N.Y.   10019

FIRST PRINTING, DECEMBER 1979

1 2 3 4 5 6 7 8 9

 DAW TRADEMARK REGISTERED
U.S. PAT. OFF. MARCA
REGISTRADA. HECHO EN U.S.A.

PRINTED IN U.S.A.

Table of Contents

List of Illustrations

Chapter One

On a Roof in Jikaida City

There are more ways than one hundred and one of stealing an airboat and this was going to be way Number One. Just walk up to the craft, step aboard, and take off—first making sure she was not tethered down.

That was the theory.

The guard stepped from a shadowed doorway on the first landing and stuck a glittering great cleaver under my nose.

"Stand where you are, dom, or your head will go bouncing down those stairs you've just walked up."

Light from the lamp held in the hand of a bronze cupid at the head of the stairs struck sparks from his eyes. All he could see of me must be a silhouette. The muffling mask of gray cloth over my face and head and the dull baggy clothes were unrecognizable.

"Why, dom," I said. "You're making a mistake—"

No doubt he understood me to be attempting exculpation. When I lowered him gently to the carpet with my left hand gripped in the fancy front of his uniform, and, my right hand tingling just a little, took away that murderous cleaver, he slumbered peacefully—but he'd wake up understanding the mistake I had pointed out to him well enough.

Stepping carefully over him I went on up the next flight of stairs. This hotel, a veritable palace in the Foreign Quarter of Jikaida City, was occupied by the great ones of the world who came here to play Jikaida without affiliation to the Blue or the Yellow. On the roof rested the only flying boat in the city. That airboat was my ticket out of here and, because it was owned by a man from Hamal, and Hamal was at war with my own country of Vallia, it was morally quite proper for me to steal the craft.

7

Well—morals take the devil of a beating when there's a war on. There are, to be sure, far too many wars and battles on the world of Kregen, four hundred light years from Earth, but I was sincerely doing what I could to lessen the number.

The time was just on halfway between midnight and dawn. The hotel remained quiet. The carpets muffled my tread. There must be a few more guards about and, sentry duty being what it is, there were bound to be one or two having a quiet yarn up on the roof, one eye on the airboat.

The quicker I got out of Jikaida City and, if the Star Lords permitted, back to Vallia, the better. A caravan across the Desolate Waste to the east would be far too slow for me in my mood. Vallia was in good hands, that I knew; but I still felt the need to get home. Also, knowing the way fate— which is a poor second best in any confrontation with the Star Lords—has the nasty habit of hurling me headlong into adventures that are none of my seeking, I fancied I had a few sprightly moments in front of me before I reached home. Well, by Vox, that was true.

As I stole up the next flight of stairs sounds floated down from above. I frowned. There was laughter, and high shrieks, and a tinny banging. A small orchestra was playing and trying to make its music heard over the din. I went on and came out onto the top landing. In the corner the small door that led onto the roof was unguarded. I had only to cross the stretch of thick pile carpet, open the door, close it carefully after me, and creep up the stairs, my sword in my fist. . . .

More confounded theories.

A door opened and a man staggered out. He wore only a blue shirt and he was highly excited, his arms draped over the shoulders of a couple of sylvies half-dressed in tinsels. He roared, his head thrown back, warbling out a song whose words were unintelligible and whose tune was unrecognizable.

The wall at my back felt flat and hard. I pressed in as though trying to burrow through into the room beyond.

Beyond that suddenly opened door the lamplight glowed, spilling out and casting shadows over me. The noise in there racketed away and now the orchestra, no doubt having made up its mind to be heard, howled and shrilled and scraped. Men and women shrieked with laughter and shouted over the music, determined to be heard. The clink of bottles and the crash of overturning glasses added a genial blend of bibulous accompaniment. The man and the girls staggered past, screaming with laughter, to disappear into a darkened room along the corridor.

Lamplight fell across the carpet in a butter-yellow lozenge.

To reach the door leading onto the roof it was necessary to pass that lozenge of light.

The orchestra and the people—all grimly determined to be heard—redoubled their efforts. The racket coruscated. The door remained open and people passed and repassed—or staggered and restaggered—from side to side. Another man came out. He crawled on hands and knees. A slinky little Fristle fifi rode his back, alternately hitting him with a slipper and giving him sips of wine from a glass. Most of the wine—it was a light straw color—soaked into the carpet. They were both yelling their heads off. I shoved another inch or two into the wall.

Somebody else reeled out of the door, tripped over the man on his knees and the fifi, and collapsed, howling with laughter. His wine went all over them. He had been drinking a deep red wine, and the color blazed up in the lamplight.

A voice yelled over the din.

"Hey, Nath! C'mere, for the sake of Havandua—these Hamalese have me—" The rest was lost in a gurgle.

The fellow who was being ridden by the girl stood up. He reeled. The girl clung to him, her naked legs wrapped about him. Making no effort to throw her off he went barging back, and the chap who had fallen over him lurched up, shaking his head from side to side and chuckling foolishly.

He looked at his empty glass, made a solemn clucking noise, and wandered off toward the open door. He hit the wall beside the door, bounced, shook his head, took a grip on himself and navigated back into the room.

Somebody shut the door.

Oh, yes, by Krun. They were all Somebodies in there. . . .

Letting out my breath I eased from the shadows and started for the door. My hand was on the latch. I was pushing the door open—when the light sprang into being again at my back.

A girl's voice, all giggles and hiccoughs, said, "Leaving already? You Hamalese are too solemn! Come and have a drink."

Without turning, I said in as light a voice as I could muster, "You should try telling that to a Bladesman in the Sacred Quarter of Ruathytu."

A man's voice, heavier than most, said, "Hamalese? I don't—"

There was nothing else for it.

I went through the opened doorway, slammed the wood at my back, and shot the bolt across. No time to catch a breath. It was up the stairs hell for leather and out onto the roof under the stars of Kregen.

The airboat was there—tethered down, of course!—and with a canvas cover thrown across her slim lines.

The first chain ripped free. The second chain was in my fingers. The scrape at my back sounded clearly. In an explosion of movement I dived sideways, recovered, hauled out my sword.

The two guards were in nowise chagrined that they had failed to surprise me. She of the Veils floated free of cloud wrack then and showed them to me—as the moon showed me to them.

A banging started below as the party-goers hammered on the door I had bolted.

The guards bore in, their swords held in the professional fighting man's grip. They wore the fancy uniform of employees of this establishment, a riot of ruffles and bronze-bound armor, the whole outlined in black and yellow checkers. They knew what they were about. They anticipated no real trouble from me. The gray cloth mask over my face would hearten them rather than not, for they would take this as a sign of one who wished to remain unknown in the shadows, and unwilling to face a fight.

And, by Zair, they were right!

The wounds I had taken in that last fight on the Jikaida board were nowhere near properly healed. I was still weak. Yes, I could wield a blade and give some account of myself. But to engage in protracted swordplay, I knew, was beyond my present powers. This night's doings had been intended as a quick and furtive entry, a fast snatch of the airboat, and a remarkably smart getaway.

These two hulking guards had no intention of allowing me to carry on my plans for another moment.

As I say—so much for theory.

With the nerve-tingling scrape of steel on steel, the blades crossed.

Now—now these two were fair swordsmen. They earned their hire by standing guard. And, also, it was perfectly clear they would kill me as a mere part of earning that hire. That was their job. There was no great panache in it, not a sign of lip-licking enjoyment in their work. They just went about the business determined to prevent me, a masked thief, from stealing the airboat they were paid to protect.

As I say, they were fair swordsmen. After a few passes I knew, weak as I was, that I had the mastering of them both.

The blades screeched and rang as I fended them off, and pressed, and retreated, luring them on to the final passage that would settle this thing. But—but they were just men earning their daily bread. They were doing what they did for purely economic reasons. Their morality encompassed my death as a thief so that they might earn their daily bread, in the same way that my morality encompassed stealing this airboat in order to fly back to Vallia.

I could have slain them both; run them through in a twinkling.

enough misery in two worlds without adding villainy to it and

Many a superior swordsman of the darker persuasion would have done so and thought nothing of it. There is calling it heroism. These two guards went to sleep after a flurry of blades and a rapid double thump—one, two—from the hilt.

The delay they had caused, slight though it was, had undone my plans and earned their hire.

Men boiled out from the stairway onto the roof, so I knew they had broken down the lower door. Some of them wore shirts, some of them wore trousers or breechclouts, and although very few were possessed of all items of clothing, they all possessed swords. They set up a howl as they saw me, a dark, masked, mysterious figure just stepping back from two unconscious guards. They charged, screeching.

I recognized the tone, the mood, the feeling of their yells.

Anger, of course—but, chiefly, a high delirious excitement, a sudden passion for the chase, the game, the feeling that in a spot of action would come the highlight of the evening's entertainments.

The chains tethering the flier remained fast locked.

Now there was no time to act as I have acted in other places and other times in circumstances not too dissimilar.

I ran.

The roofs of the hotel presented a bewildering jumble—a jungle of tiles and cornices and chimneys and spires.

Away we all went in a rout, and they were hallooing and yelling and prancing about back there, waving their swords, their naked legs flashing in the fuzzy golden and pinkish light of She of the Veils. Kregen's largest moon, the Maiden with the Many Smiles, lifted over the edge of the world and shone pink and rose down through shredding clouds. There would be plenty of light. As I ran and skipped from roof to roof I reflected that, by Vox, there would be far too much light.

This quiet, cautious, carefully planned exercise had turned into a right old shambles.

The fellows chasing me back there were not all apims, not all Homo sapiens like me. Among them the wonderful variety of diffs of Kregen was well represented. A loose slate which made me slither down a prickly roof almost did for me; with a convulsive lunge I hooked my fingers around the guttering and managed to hang on. Below me the gulf yawned. Far below, far and far below, light spilled across a cobbled courtyard as a door was opened. A voice bellowed up.

"What in the name of Vilaha's Tripes is going on up there?"

The pack yelled and caroled and they were creeping out along the roof ridge toward the spot where I had slipped. They looked like a ghostly dance of death up there, silhouetted against the moon radiance, for some of them pranced out balancing as though they walked a tightrope. Others got down on their hands and knees and shuffled along. Only one had the hardihood—or foolhardiness—to slither down the tiles.

He came down rather too fast.

He started to scream as he picked up speed, sliding down the roof. His flailing hands sought for a grip, and scrabbled against the tiles, and slipped. He hit the guttering and it broke away with a groan, and dipped down. Only a bracket near me held the end of the guttering. It hung down like the snapped yardarm of a swifter, smashed in the shock of ramming.

The fellow was screaming now, clutching desperately to the

angled guttering, and slowly—slowly and horribly—he was sliding down the guttering toward its splintered end.

In a few moments he would slip off the end, make a desperate and unavailing snatch at the guttering, and fall to the cobbles beneath. He'd go splat.

His death meant nothing to me, of course.

I got my other hand up to the secured guttering and hooked a knee. I looked up. His comrades were still yelling up there and most of them did not even know he had fallen. They were running on to get to the end of the slate walkway along the ridge. There was not much time.

The leather belt around my waist was thick and supple; it came off in a trice and I gripped the end and threw the buckle end around in an arc. It swung like a pendulum.

"Grab the belt, dom!" I shouted.

His white face looked like the head of a moth, in the moon-dappled shadows. I could see his mouth open; but he was too far gone to scream. His eyes were like holes burned in linen.

He made a grab for the belt on the next swing, and missed, and jerked back as the guttering groaned and inched down.

"This time, dom," I shouted. "You will not miss."

The brass belt buckle glittered once and then vanished into the shadows. He made an effort, the humping, thrusting strain of a too-heavy horse attempting to leap a too-high barrier. The brass belt buckle was grabbed; just how good a grip he had I did not know. My own pains were beginning to make me think I might not be able to hold him when his weight came on the line. There was only one way to find out.

The guttering screeched, rivets pinged away, and the guttering fell.

The man swung, like a plumb-bob, dangling on the end of the belt.

Scarlet pain flowed over my body, from my arm and shoulder where Mefto's sword had cut me again and again, and down into my very guts. I shut my eyes for a moment—and held on.

With a clanging roar like fourteen hundred dustbins going over a cliff the guttering hit the cobbles.

The man swung and dangled.

Presently I started to haul him in. He came up, gasping,

his face like the ashy contents of those fourteen hundred dustbins, his eyes black and bruised in the fleeting pink light.

"Get your knee—over—the damned guttering."

He wore a gray shirt. His knee was skinned raw. But he got it over. Better a bloody knee than the squash on the cobbles.

With his weight half on the guttering alongside me I transferred my grip to his shoulder and half-pulled half-twisted him to safety. He lay there panting. His body heaved up and down with the violence of his breathing.

The yells of his friends receded. Only three were left up there on the slate walkway. I ignored them.

"You're safe now," I told him. I spoke sharply, to brace him up. "Brassud!" I said. "Get a grip on yourself."

"You—" He gasped it out, shaking now, looking down at the gulf and that distant rectangle of light from the open door, and back to me. "You—why?"

"I'm not an assassin. Get your breath back."

"By Krun!" he said, which told me he was Hamalese. "I'd never believe it—not even if—"

"Believe. And give me my belt back. Unlike you, I wish to retain my trousers."

And he laughed.

The night breeze played along the roof. The man below yelled again, coming back out the door with a lantern. The men up on the roof answered him, shouting down. There was a deal of confused yelling.

"Can you make your own way along the guttering? You'll be safe when you reach the gable end—the ornamentation there is profuse, if in bad taste."

He stared at me. He was a young fellow, with dark hair cut long and curled, and with a nose rather shorter than longer, and with eyes—whose color was imponderable in that light—which, it seemed to me, stared out with forthright candor. He had a belt fashioned from silver links in the shape of leaping chavonths, and a small jeweled dagger; he had lost his sword. He regained control of his breathing.

"I think so." He screwed his face up. "And you?"

"I—" I started to say.

"Stay here. I shall make my way to that zany lot and tell them nothing of your presence. Then, when we have gone, you may get away."

"You would truly do this?"

"Yes. And I give you my thanks. Lahal and Lahal—I am called Lobur the Dagger." He laughed again, and I saw he had recovered himself and was much taken with this night's adventure, now that it had, miraculously, turned out all right and not with his untimely death. "I do not expect you to make the pappatu—"

"I think not. In the circumstances."

"By Havil, no!"

The noise from his comrades had passed over and the three who had remained on the slate walkway above our heads had gone. The man and his lantern below were visible, just, at the far end of the building. The jut of a dormer window obscured him. We were alone under the Moons of Kregen, sitting on the gutter of a roof, talking as though we shared tea and misciles in some fashionable hostelry in the Sacred Quarter.

"There were three of your friends on the roof above—they are gone now—but I think they saw you did not fall."

"Friends? Oh, yes, friends."

He was clearly getting his wind back and setting himself for the scramble along the gutter. I am sure the thought stood in his mind, as it stood in mine, that there was every chance another section of guttering would give way under his weight.

There was no point in urging him to hurry. I fancied the hunt would bay along the next roof and courtyard. But, all the same, I had no desire to sit here all night.

The opportunity to gather information ought not to be overlooked and he might well be in the frame of mind to say more than in other circumstances he would allow himself.

"You are Hamalese. I hope you have enjoyed your Jikaida here. Do you return home soon?"

We were sitting side by side on the edge now, dangling our feet over emptiness. He laughed again.

"Jikaida! No—I have no head for the game. I wager on—on other things. As to going home, that rests on the decision of Prince Nedfar, and he is, with all due respect, besotted on Jikaida."

"Most people are, here in Jikaida City."

"And live well on it, too—" He cocked his head on one side, and added, "Gray Mask." He laughed, delighted at the conceit. "That is what I shall call you, Gray Mask. And the

people here know well how to take our money. The whole
city is full of sharps and tricksters."

"So, Lobur the Dagger, you believe I am not of the city?"

He looked surprised. "Of course not! Didn't think it for a
moment. Who, here, would know aught of the Sacred Quarter of Ruathytu?"

So either he had heard my quick remark to the unseen girl
at my back, or had been told. So, he must think I was
Hamalese like himself, perhaps a wandering paktun, a mercenary. This could be awkward or could be useful.

I spoke with more than a grain of truth as I said, "Ah, yes.
What I would give to be able, at this very moment, to be sitting on the roof of that sweet tavern of Tempting Forgetful-
ness in Ruathytu instead of here, on The Montilla's Head."
And then I thought to prove myself a very cunning, very
clever fellow indeed. I added, most casually, "But the commands of the Empress Thyllis are not to be denied."

He drew a quick breath. He cocked an eye at me. "Prince
Nedfar—who is the Empress's second cousin—is here on
state business. This is known. But a second embassy?" He
sucked in his cheeks. "I do not think the prince knows—or
would be pleased if he did know."

Well, that wouldn't worry me. Any confusion I could sow
in the minds of the nobles of Hamal I would do and glee in
the doing. If this Prince Nedfar, who had come here to talk
of alliance with Prince Mefto, grew angry at the thought he
was being spied on at the commands of the empress then I
would have struck a blow, a small and near-insignificant blow
it is true, against mad Empress Thyllis.

So, quickly, I said, "The Empress is to be obeyed in all
things. That many of these things are such that an honorable
man must recoil cannot affect their consummation. I have no
grudge against the prince."

"But you sought to steal his airboat." He shifted at this and
looked hard at me. "And by Krun, Gray Mask! That would
have stranded me here in this dolorous city!"

"Mayhap, Lobur, you would have come to a delight in
Jikaida."

"Hah!"

The time had run out and I began to entertain a suspicion
that he kept me here talking so as to detain me for his
friends. They'd be back, soon, hunting over the back trail.

Yet I fancied I might sow a little more discontent and, into the bargain, reap more information, for which I was starved. The risk was worth taking.

So I said, again in that casual way, "Many men murmur at the empress. You must have heard of plots against her. And, anyway, things go badly for Hamal in Vallia, do they not?"

He hitched around and as the guttering gave an ominous groan, stilled immediately. His pride would not allow him to take any notice of that menacing creak from the rivets and brackets.

"Aye, I have heard of plots." This was good news—by Vox! excellent news! He went on, "And we do not prosper in Vallia. They are devils up there—I have heard stories that are scarcely credible. They have a new emperor now, the great devil Dray Prescot, who was once paraded through Ruathytu at the tail of a calsany—"

"You saw that?"

"Yes. By Krun—the man is evil all through and yet, and yet, I felt a little——" He paused and hawked up and spat. We did not hear the splat on the cobbles far below. "Enough of that maudlin nonsense. If I could get my dagger into him I would become the most famous man in all Hamal."

"Indubitably."

"But the chance is hardly likely to come my way."

"No. And I think it is time we moved off. Much as I am enjoying this conversation——"

"Yes, Gray Mask, you are right. I owe you my life. I shall not forget." He looked at me. "You will not give me your name?"

"If you were to call me Drax, I would answer."

"Drax?"

"Aye."

"Hardly a Hamalese name——"

"What did you expect?"

"No. No, of course, Drax, Gray Mask, you are right."

We had been sitting thus and talking companionably for a time, and he was sitting on the side nearest the broken guttering and farthest from the gable end that was our goal. He inched back and leaned against the tiles, making ready to pass behind me. I got myself two very secure grips. As he eased himself sideways he could easily give me a sudden and treacherous kick and so spin me out into the void.

He saw that instinctive movement as I secured myself. When he reached the other side he stopped.

"You thought, perhaps, I might push you over?"

"The thought was in my mind."

In the pinkish glow of the moons his face darkened. "You impugn my honor! D'you think I would—"

"No."

"I owe you my life." He suddenly trembled, and I saw the tremor pass through him as a rashoon shudders over the waters of the inner sea, the Eye of the World. "By Krun! When I was slipping down that damned gutter—sliding to the end to fall and squash—I tell you, Drax, Gray Mask, it was awful, awful. I thought—and then—"

"If we ever meet again we will drink a stoup or three together."

"Aye! That we will."

We spoke a few more parting words, and then we gave the remberees, and he edged his way cautiously along the gutter, making each step a careful probe for weak spots, until he reached the gable end. He vanished in the shadows of sculpted gargoyles and zhyans and mythical beasts. A macabre, a weird, little meeting, this conversation on a roof. But I had learned a little and I hoped I had sown a few seeds of doubt.

Damn the Hamalese! And double damn mad Empress Thyllis. But for her and her megalomaniacal schemes we'd have had Vallia back, smiling and happy, after the Time of Troubles by now.

The moment Lobur the Dagger disappeared into the twisted shadows I started along after him. There was no point in waiting. If he intended to betray me then the quicker I got in among them the better. Hauling him in had taken its toll of my feeble strength. Yes, yes, I had been a stupid onker in thus chancing all when I was not physically ready; but I needed that airboat on the roof. The voller that belonged to Prince Nedfar.

Looking down over the next courtyard from the concealment of that garish profusion of sculpture I could see no sign of Lobur or his cronies. The shadows lay thickly. The moons shafted ghostly pink light down and painted a pale rose patina across the lower roofs and walls. Around me LionardDen, the city of Jikaida, lay sleeping.

Very well.

Despite my physical weakness, despite all that had happened—was not this the moment to strike?

On that I started to climb up the gable end, handing myself up from stone beast to stone beast, working my way back to the slate walkway along the ridge.

Once up there I would retrace my steps to the roof where the airboat lay.

Maybe I would again be unsuccessful. Maybe there would be so many guards, so many obstacles, that I just would not be able to overcome them all. But that made no matter. I do not subscribe to the more stupidly florid of these notions of honor, particularly of rampantly displayed honor. But, here and now, there was a deal of that juvenile and exhibitionistic emotion mingled with the shrewdly practical idea that they'd be off guard up there. This was a chance.

Climbing along the roof back the way I had come, I knew the chance had to be taken.

Chapter Two

Gray Mask Vanishes

The kennel containing the two stavrers I had passed in something of a hurry showed up ahead in the moonlight as I leaped—not too nimbly—up onto the coping. The stavrers had been aroused by the uproar. They stretched out to the full extent of the chains fixed to collars about their necks. Chunky, are stavrers, fierce and loyal watchdogs, with savage wolf-heads and eight legs, the rear six articulated the same way, and they can charge with throat-ripping speed. After a distance they flag; but that stavrer charge, bolting all fangs ready to rip and rend, is quite enough to protect an honest man's house.

Now these two set up a fearful howling.

Two helmeted heads popped up over a nearby roofridge among that jungle of roofs. Two arrows were loosed at me. They were not Bowmen of Loh shooting at me—chances are that I would not be here talking had they been—and I went flying down into a leaded gulley between tiled slopes and so scrabbled along like a fish in a stream trap.

This was all beginning to get out of hand. A guard jumped down from a chimney pot and tried to take my head off with his axe, and I ducked and got a boot into his midriff, and he went yowling away, holding his guts. The axe clattered down over blue slates and vanished into emptiness.

Other men were shouting, there was the shrilling sound of whistles, and more barking, from stavrers and other kinds of domestic animals nicely designed to rip the seat out of your pants, or to rip off other more important parts of your anatomy. Feeling incredibly like a fool, and beginning, also, to feel the humor of the situation breaking down all the silly anger, I went charging down a roof slope, came around a chimney corner and saw the uplifted coping of the roof whereon rested the airboat.

Any hope of stealing the voller vanished instantly.

She lay there bathed in the light of many lanterns. The men had turned out—some still without shirts or trousers, but all with swords. There was one young fellow there, with wide black moustaches, turned out as though for Chuktar's Parade—fully accoutered in harness and with shield and thraxter at the ready. His helmet shone under the lights of the moons.

So I debated. The debate was very short.

The stavrers were baying at my heels, the guards were massed in front, the moons were casting down more and more light as they rose—the Twins, the two Moons of Kregen eternally orbiting each other—had been early this night, and The Maiden with the Many Smiles and She of the Veils were late. The light would strengthen in rose and gold until the first shards of light from the twin suns, Zim and Genodras, illuminated the horizon. Then this exotic world of Kregen would be revealed in radiance of jade and ruby and the light would increase and burn and any fellows foolish enough to be hopping around on the roofs of high-class hotels would get all they deserved.

Home—rather, back to the tavern at which I was lodging for the moment—seemed to me the order of the day—or night, seeing that the day's orders would be so uncomfortable.

Mind you, if in retrospect I make it seem all light-hearted and if, truly, I did feel that light-headedness then, do not misunderstand me. I was raging with anger and frustration. Oh, yes, my island empire of Vallia, cruelly beset by predatory foemen, was in good and capable hands. I could go gallivanting about having adventures for as long as I wished; but I felt the deep tide drawing me back home. I had to get back to Vallia and make sure, make absolutely sure, that all was well. That I intended to hand it all over to my lad Drak as soon as possible was merely another reason for return. He was there, in Vallia, and I had not the slightest inkling what he was up to.

And, too, my half-healed wounds must have contributed to that feeling of light-headedness, as though this was all one gigantic jest.

So, bitterly angry, and stifling my laughter, I hopped off

the roof down onto the next one and scuttled like an ancient crab along the ridge and slid down a drainpipe to the courtyard with its arbora trees. They are called this because their flowers look much like arbora feathers. If I thought I was on ground level I was seriously mistaken.

I remember I was thinking that I'd just let all this fuss blow over, and rest up a bit and get my strength back, and then I'd be back here to The Montilla's Head and this time I'd really lay my avaricious paws on Prince Nedfar's airboat. But really.

A door made from sturmwood and the bottoms of old bottles ahead looked promising, the roseate moonlight catching in the bottles and whirling hypnotically. I eased across with a quick glance aloft and then the door opened and disaster walked out—rather, disaster reeled out, shrieking and yelling.

The girl—she was a kitchen maid—was not apim but one of those charming diffs with the faces of apim infants, all soft, rounded curves and chuckles and dimples, permanent babyfaces, naïve and simple and delightful. The men folk have harder faces, it is true, but they, too, carry that hint of undeveloped childishness about them. For all that, the men have tough, muscle-hard, brawny bodies. The womenfolk have been blessed with female bodies that are marvels of curve and symmetry, sensuous, fascinating, endlessly alluring, intoxicating to any man—whether apim or diff—who shares our common heritage. This race of diffs—I once used to miscall diffs beast-men or men-beasts, halflings, not understanding—are often given the name Syblians; although the name they give themselves, not wishing to be confused with Sylvies, is Ennschafften.

The drunken lout chasing the girl was calling, in between hiccoughing and belching, yelling to her to stop.

"Mindy, miundy," he called, staggering out of the door, his shirt tangled around his waist, his face enflamed with drink and passion, his eyes fairly starting out of his head. "Miundy, mindy—wait for me, you little—come back—or I'll—" And he staggered against the doorjamb, and bounced up, reaching out after the shrieking girl.

Now in these and similar situations a fellow had best keep out of the way until he knows exactly what is going on. Many an upright citizen stepping in to rescue a maiden in distress has been turned on by what seemed victim and attacker, both contuming him with insults for coming between a family squabble of man and wife. So I waited quietly in the shade of the arbora tree. The scent was delicious, and I breathed in—thankful, I may add, for the rest.

The Sybli caught her foot in a gray old root of the tree and she stumbled forward three or four paces, off balance, her arms spread out to try to save herself. She wore a tattered old blue and yellow checkered dress, badly torn as to bodice and skirt, and her feet were bare. She almost saved herself, and then she lost her balance and fell.

The man laughed and staggered forward. He was apim, a big, husky, full-fleshed fellow who knew what he wanted— and took it.

The girl Mindy tried to rise and gave a gasp as her ankle twisted under her. Her face showed babyish terror. The man leaped forward and she kicked out. I felt like giving a cheer as he yelped and reeled back, cursing.

"Never, you beast, never!" she cried. Her body was shaking.

"You will or I'll—"

She bit him as he came in again, sinking her sharp teeth into his hand. He let out a fearsome yell. It was quite clear that this secluded courtyard was soundproof and that with all the hullabaloo on the other side of the hotel this fellow was perfectly confident that the girl's cries would not be heard.

She bit hard. He managed to drag his hand back and he stuck it in his mouth. He did not look so drunk or so amorous now.

In the confusing lights of the moons reaching ghostly pink and gold fingers into the courtyard the girl tried again to draw away. Her baby-face glistened with terror.

"You leave off, Granoj, you hear! You keep away—"

Granoj shook his head, took his hand out of his mouth and leaped on her. She kicked and struggled and screamed and I slowly straightened up from leaning against the tree. He wore a sword, a thraxter, the straight cut and thruster of Havilfar, and he was probably a soldier off duty, judging by the belt and his boots.

And then, so swiftly I was almost too late, his mood changed. He saw, clearly, that the girl Mindy was not going to do as he wished, and he turned ugly. And, too, she had hurt him. She had kicked him shrewdly.

"I'll show you, you stupid Sybli! You can't make a fool out of me—"

He ripped his sword free and swung it up. That he was going to strike her with the blade was crystal clear.

I stepped out, with a sigh, and caught his arm.

"This has gone far enough," I said, and I tried to put the old snap into my voice.

But I felt that treacherous light-headedness, I felt the weakness, and with an oath he stepped back, having not the slightest difficulty in breaking my grip on his arm.

"You rast! You first—and then the girl!"

With that, he charged full at me, the sword upraised.

My own thraxter cleared the scabbard with what seemed to me agonizing slowness.

He was bull-strong, enraged, the drink lending him a reckless passion. He swung and chopped and hacked, and I had to dance a right merry little jig evading his savage attacks. The girl stopped screaming. The swords rang and clashed. He forced me back, and I felt the tree at my back, and I could not retreat any farther. And he laughed and taunted me most vilely, and rushed in. His words boiled around, his sword flickered cleverly, and he used a swordsman's trick that is well-known in fighting circles, and he would have had me had I not known the trick.

Without thought—for thought was too laggard now—my own sword arm did what a sword arm must do if it wishes to retain a body from which to hang. and this Granoj staggered back, suddenly, and as he staggered back so he pulled free of my blade. That steel glimmered darkly wet. He put a hand to his side, and he looked down, and lifted the hand, and the blood dripped, dripped. . . .

So Granoj fell.

Whether or not he was dead I did not know. I felt the weakness on me, and I staggered and the Sybli was at my side and I thought she would berate me, and attack me for the deed. She put her hand around my waist, and held me, and said, "You must hurry, jikai! You must go away from here, quickly, and go with the thanks of Mindy the Ennschafftena. Hurry!"

The walls of the courtyard wavered like curtains in a

breeze. The whirlicue stump ends of the bottles of the door gyrated at me. I choked up phlegm. I fancied my wounds had opened and were bleeding again.

"Yes—must go—you are—all right—"

All the frivolity of the night's proceedings had turned nasty and ugly.

Death beat his black wings—as the quondam poets say—and I was feeling like one of the warmed-over corpses served up fresh from the Ice Floes of Sicce. If I did not get away, and me with a gray cloth mask over my head, I'd be done for.

"I am all right, jikai—hurry, hurry—there is a wicket and stairs—the Street of Candles—there will be no one there now—my thanks—"

Staggering, sword in fist, hardly seeing, I was steered toward the little wicket in the corner. She threw open the gate and the slimy stairs led down, little used. I started at the top and the next moment I was at the bottom and with a pain there, too. I clawed up to my hands and knees and looked back. I could just see her outline.

"Remberee, jikai—again my thanks—hurry!"

The wicket shut with a flat slap, like curtailed applause.

An arched opening gave egress onto the Street of Candles. No one was about, as Mindy the Sybli had promised. The shuttered doorways and windows added a ghostly note of desolation. A stray gyp went whining along, his brown and white coat wavering through the shadows. First things first. I wiped the sword on the gray cloth mask and then carefully folded it, bloodstains inward, and thrust it into my shirt. Clues . . . clues . . .

Then, sword scabbarded, all of Jikaida City going up and down and corkscrewing around me, I lurched off. By the time I had reached an avenue I recognized and could take my bearings the city was coming alive and the thin radiance of Zim and Genodras pulsed warmly in the sky to the east.

Chapter Three

"Now you've done slallyfanting around, Jak," said Pompino, crossly making his most cunning move in the Game of Moons, "perhaps we can get down to some serious thinking about getting out of Jikaida City."

"Oh, aye," I said, "I've done slallyfanting around for a time."

The bed with its yellow sheets was cool and wide and the loomin flowers and the flick-flick on the windowsill splashed bright color into our room. Pompino's move received my expected counter. He still disdained Jikaida and Jikalla, and was most wary of Vajikry, which, as people who play it thoughtlessly discover, is an unforgiving game. He would have indulged in King's Hand, but we were one die short and you cannot play good games of King's Hand with only four dice. As for Skull and Crossbones, you can enjoy so fearsome a mental bloodletting in that unholy game that I had cried off as being too weak.

We were settled into a reasonably priced and comfortable tavern in the Foreign Quarter. At the lady Yasuri's expense, I might add. I mended. She had pursed up her lips and told us that if we stayed at The Plume and Quill we would attract less attention than if we baited at her Star of Laybrites. As The Plume and Quill catered to the superior tradesmen of foreign parts who visited Jikaida City to do business, I didn't quite follow her reasoning; but she was paying. The lady Yasuri was the reigning Champion, and the Mediary Games had begun, and day by day they played Blood Jikaida, and, every now and then, Death Jikaida.

Pompino, who was, like me, an agent of the Star Lords, had berated me silly for getting mixed up in the schemes of other people, when we should be bending all our energies to doing what the Star Lords wanted. I didn't argue. I was as weak as a kitten, and the wounds had opened and the doctor, a shriveled little needleman with a brusque way with him, had cautioned me to stay in bed—or else. With a sniff he packed up his bag and his balass box of acupuncture needles and took himself off. His bill, too, would be paid by the lady Yasuri.

He had said, this Doctor Larghos the Needle, "I did not have the felicity of seeing the Death Jikaida in which you fought, young man. But I have heard of marvels." He shook his head. "It was said no man in all the world could best Prince Mefto the Kazzur at swordplay."

"I did not best him—"

"I know, I know. But he is minus his tail hand now, and there are only two places in Kregen that I know of where he may have a new hand graft. And he may not know of them."

"I hope the cramph doesn't!" said Pompino, most menacingly.

"Would you tell me of them?" I was thinking of Duhrra.

"No. Idle questions deserve sharp reprimands—"

"It was not an idle question."

He glanced at me, still stuffing his medical kit away, a glance that said eloquently that, as I had not lost a hand I had no need of the information. He probably thought I was making conversation. "The nearest is in the Dawn Lands and is rumored to exist in the country of Florilzun." He snorted. "But try to find that country on any map—try to find it. Hah!"

So I was left to look at the loomin flowers and get well.

Pompino was wearing a smart pale blue lounging robe and he took from a pocket a small brush and started to preen his Khibil whiskers. His sharp foxy face was engrossed. Because he was a Khibil, a member of that race of fox-faced diffs who are keen and smart and superb fighting men, he rather fancied himself. I did not mind. He was a good comrade although setting too much store by his understood duty to the damned Star Lords, the Everoinye, whom he thought of as gods.

To me they were just a pain, superhuman entities who eddied me about Kregen on a whim, and who might, if I rebelled, hurl me back four hundred light years to Earth.

"Had you stolen the Hamalese airboat and taken off, Jak, do you think the Everoinye would have allowed you to depart?"

"I do not know."

"But you had to try?"

"Yes."

"And you will try again as soon as you are well?"

"If that cramph Prince Nedfar has not quitted the city by then."

I had told him just enough about my escapade to answer the most obvious inquiries. I had not mentioned Lobur the Dagger. Pompino, who was a shrewd fellow, imagined I hailed from Hyrklana, a large island off the eastern coast of the enormous southern continent of Havilfar. I had been a kaidur in the arena in Huringa, the capital of Hyrklana, and could pass myself off as a member of that nation without trouble. But Pompino would wonder why a Hamalese—even one whose life I had just saved—had made no greater demurral about letting me away scot free.

Pompino himself, who came from South Pandahem, hated all Hamalese with the vigor of any man who has seen his country overrun and despoiled.

In the quiet backwater of The Plume and Quill I lay abed and mended. Being situated in the ▒▒▒▒▒ Quarter the tavern was outside the hurly-burly that continually bustled in the twin cities, Blue City and Yellow City. Jikaida dominated all. Jikaida, that greatest of board games of Kregen, was here played with fighting men, played in blood and death. To be of the Blue or to be of the Yellow, to win—and not to think of losing—these were the vital facts of life here.

"I," said Pompino, who like Lobur the Dagger had no head for Jikaida, "am thoroughly sick and tired of this city and Jikaida! By Horato the Potent! What in all Kregen has that stupid woman Yasuri got that we must protect her at the orders of the Star Lords?"

Maliciously, I said, "You question orders from the Star Lords, Pompino?"

He jumped. His foxy face bristled. "No! Of course not. Who said so?"

And I laughed.

Slowly, I mended. Slowly, my strength came back. Truth to tell, I recovered full health and strength far more quickly

than anyone could who had not bathed in the Sacred Pool of
Baptism in the River Zelph of far Aphrasöe. All the time I
lay there, uselessly, I fretted over Vallia, and over Delia, Delia, Empress of Vallia. Was our son Drak doing the right
things? Was Delia well? Oh yes, I fretted. But I had had an
assurance from the Star Lords, delivered by their spy and
messenger, the gorgeous scarlet and gold raptor called the
Gdoinye, that Vallia did not succumb to her enemies and
that Delia thrived and was well. This, I had to believe.

To do anything else would not only make me go off my
head, make a lesser man of me—it would destroy me.

One day when I had demolished a whole vosk steak, a
heaping pile of momolams, an equally heaping pile of
steamed cabbage, had wolfed down a handsome squish pie—
with a mental genuflection to Inch standing on his head—and
was popping palines into my mouth, Pompino bustled in.
And, I may add, that was the third such meal of the day and
the time only just gone the bur of mid. He started without
preamble: "Jak, tell me what you know of Moderdrin, the
Humped Land."

"The Humped Land? Never heard of it—wait a minute." I
chewed a paline, savoring the flavor, feeling the goodness refreshing every part. "I heard a couple of rat-faced fellows—
they were gauffrers—arguing in a tavern about going to a
place that might have been Moderdrin. I paid them no attention, minding my ale, for Dav was yelling for his stoup—"

"Yes, yes. But you know nothing of the Land of the Fifth
Note? Moderdrin?"

"No. What of it?"

"Gold, Jak, that's what of it."

I sniffed, and popped another paline. The yellow berry
tasted just as good as the last. Never satiated on palines, no
one ever can be, an impossibility. Palines had sustained me
on my very first visit to Kregen. They tasted just as good
now.

"You may scoff. Gold, jewels, treasure—unimagined
treasure—"

"Just lying around for you to stroll along and pick it up?"

His foxy face twisted up in fury at my obtuseness and his
whiskers quivered.

"There is more. More than gold and treasure—there are

magic arts to be won—secrets that wizards would give their
ibs for—sorceries that will transform your life—"

"So?"

His eagerness switched into a comical surprise.

"So—what?"

"So—when do you start?"

"Who says I am going? There is danger—well, there must
be danger, else everyone here would be rolling in wealth and
all be as clever sorcerers as any Wizard of Loh."

"The point is, Pompino, my fine friend. You have two
counts against you. One is you want me to go with you. And,
two, you don't know if those onkers of Everoinye will let you
go."

His concern was genuine.

"Jak! Jak! How many more times? I pray you, do not contume the Star Lords so! If they punish you—"

"Yes, you are right."

His punishment would be of and on Kregen. My punishment would be off Kregen and back to Earth as quick as a
gigantic blue Scorpion could whisk me across the interstellar
gulf.

"So you had best tell me all about it."

The telling was brief. All he really knew was that the
Humped Land lay to the south and west of LionardDen, that
brave men and bold might pluck its treasures, and he was
meeting a man who would tell him more later that night at a
tavern of ill repute on the edge of the Foreign Quarter. The
tavern was called Nath Chavonthjid, after a mythical hero,
and was situated very close to a poor quarter of the city
where nightly riots brought out the watch with thwacking
staves, and sharp swords, too, on many occasions.

"And are you fit enough to come with me?"

"Aye," I said, giving a deep groan. "I suppose so."

"It could make our fortunes and give us magical powers—"

"Or leave us rotting in a ditch with a dagger in our backs."

"I think you scoff too much, Jak the Nameless!"

"You are right, Scauro Pompino the Iarvin!"

The long green tendrils of the flick-flick plant on the windowsill licked out and scooped up a couple of fat flies which
had been buzzing about, and slipped them neatly into the
waiting and open orange cones of the flowers. All Kregans
are aware of the symbolism inherent in the flick-flick.

Pompino laughed.

"Yes, I am right. And tonight you must not scoff. This fellow—he calls himself Nathjairn the Rorvard—is mighty prickly and only lets us into his plans—"

"For red gold, Pompino?" At the Khibil's abruptly upflung head, and the quick stab of his hand, I nodded. "Aye! He will take your gold for this great secret—and what will you get out of it?"

"I have asked questions—" He was mighty stiff about the imputations to his shrewd practicality. "Such a land exists. Expeditions do go there."

"Do they return?"

"You have heard of this famous sorcerer of Jikaida City, Naghan Relfin the Eye? Where did his powers come from, seeing he was but a poor saddler five seasons ago?"

There was truth in the remark. This sorcerer, Naghan the Eye, lived sumptuously, performed magics for large sums of money, and did have real, if indefinable, powers.

"You suggest Naghan the Eye obtained his necromantic powers from somewhere in Moderdrin, the Humped Land?"

"And there is the rich merchant on Silk Street who was ready to enlist to play Death Jikaida when he vanished from the city. He returned with a caravan of wealth—from the south and not the east, over the Desolate Waste."

"No doubt he went with a rascally gang of drikingers, common bandits who robbed honest men—"

"Not from the south and west."

I looked at Pompino. Maybe he had another reason for this fol-de-rol about magics and treasures to be picked up. "You suggest, do you not, my Pompino, that instead of attempting to steal the airboat, instead of going with a caravan across the Desolate Lands to the East, we strike southwest in order to put this city behind us? Is this not so?"

"You are too clever for me, Jak. Yes and no. We cannot move if the Star Lords do not permit it. And there *is* magic and there *is* gold to be won in Moderdrin. I believe it. Yes, we could do far worse."

If we went far enough to the southwest, got over the Blue Snowy River, and continued on we'd come eventually to Migladrin. I had friends in Migladrin. And, of course, if we turned west and carried on, we'd come to Djanduin. I never forget I am King of Djanduin, although, and deliberately

with the troubles in Vallia, I had allowed the fragrant
memory of Djanduin to attenuate and grow frail. There was
no denying the warm feeling that shook me as I thought of
Djanduin, and the rip-roaring welcome that awaited me there,
the times we could have. . . .

The superb four-armed fighting Djangs and the clever gerbil-faced Djangs of Djanduin would not forget me, their king,
and this I knew with a humility that came fresh each time.
Inch had passed on the messages. King of Djanduin I was,
and I would be remiss in my duty if I did not visit that wonderful land very soon.

But, now, until the Star Lords discharged us from our duty
to this tiresome lady Yasuri, I was going nowhere. And, truth
to tell, Yasuri was not so tiresome, not after what she had
been through and was now reigning Champion, Queen of the
Kazz-Jikaida board of Jikaida City.

I said, "We will see this Nathjairn the Rorvard tonight,
Pompino, your new friend, and we will measure his words."

The upshot was that all Pompino's avaricious dreams of
quick wealth and superhuman powers vanished like smoke in
a gale.

Dressing ourselves with some thought—for we were going
into a shadowy borderline where the Watch would venture in
strength and not at all if they didn't have to—we donned
simple drab-colored clothes, of which we had a supply, and
strapped up our brigandines, and hitched on our weapons.
The feel of steel about me came with not so much a shock as
a kind of surprise; I had skulked abed too long.

The twin suns were just sinking as we walked quietly along
the avenues and headed for the poor quarter where the inn
was situated. Far and Havil, they call the red and the green
suns in the continent of Havilfar. It is a point well worth
remembering. The Jikaida players were packing up their
boards in the sidewalk restaurants and taverns as we went by.
The brightly painted and intricately carved pieces were being
laid tenderly away in the velvet-lined balass boxes. Pompino
looked at me, and his foxy face bristled brilliant and russet in
the last of the light.

There was no need to ask him what he was thinking.

Perhaps, this night, we two would be laid to rest in the velvet-lined balass box.

The inn called Nath Chavonthjid leaned against the evening, and the leaded windows spilled yellow light upon the rutted path. A miscellany of animals was tied to the hitching rail. We walked in. I know my hand rested on my thraxter hilt. The fumes of wine reached us and, mixed with them, the stink of dopa, that fiery liquor of Kregen guaranteed to drive a fellow fighting mad. Nobody with any sense has any truck with dopa, as nobody who values life touches kaff, the virulent Kregan drug that wafts to a heaven and a hell.

"Nathjairn?" said the portly Rapa behind the bar, his beak twisted askew from an old fight. He wiped a flagon on his apron and nodded to where men in leather aprons were hauling something toward the rear door. "There he goes, may Havil take him into his care."

We walked across.

Nathjairn the Rovard was being carried out, sightless, his throat a single crimson wound from which the blood dripped thickly.

Chapter Four

I Refuse to Fight in Kazz-Jikaida

Pompino switched his wooden sword about and thunked me prettily on the shoulder. I nodded to him, saluted and disengaged. The flagon of ale invited from the table and I drained it all down thirstily. In these practice bouts I had hitherto always attempted the difficult task of fighting with the object of losing with superior skill, that is, of seeming to give of my utmost and yet contriving to let the other fellow win. This is, as I have remarked, difficult.

Pompino took a swingeing draught of his own ale, and wiping his reddish whiskers where the foam clung, said, "I don't see how you lasted half a mur against Mefto the Kazzur, Jak. I really do not."

"He is the best swordsman I have ever met, Pompino. But, I repeat, he is nowhere near the greatest."

"You make the distinction?"

I threw the rudis onto the bed and pulled a chair forward into the space we had cleared for the practice bout. Fighting men must practice their art. If they do not, and grow slack, the fierce clangor of battle is no time to find out they are out of practice.

"Oh, yes. Swordplay is more a matter of the spirit."

"Horato the Potent is my witness you speak the truth. But how may a man attain to greatness without this spiritual quality?"

"He cannot. Witness Prince Mefto—"

"I could wish it in my heart you had slain him."

I did not wish to pursue a sore subject. "I shall make another attempt on Prince Nedfar's airboat."

He nodded. "I shall come with you—"

34

"And, my Pompino, you have heard no more of the Humped Land?"

He swore, a resounding oath that rattled the rafters.

"No. Men talk about it, slyly. But Nathjairn was prepared to take an expedition out. Now another one may be seasons—"

"We could always strike out southwestward ourselves."

"All men warn against such foolishness."

"The dangers are not so great as across the river and among the great lakes."

"True. Unless we go with an expedition, it is foolish to think of it. We go by caravan across the Desolate Waste, or we take the voller—and that may be the best answer."

LionardDen, called Jikaida City, was cut off from the rest of the continent of Havilfar. Vallia always called me, that beautiful island always would; and I missed Delia badly; but she had her own life to lead with the Sisters of the Rose. I confess Pompino's wild talk of treasure and sorcery intrigued. And that brought up another question.

I gave him a look as he refilled his flagon.

"You were all for going home to Tuscursmot in South Pandahem. You had, you said, spent enough time parted from your wife—"

"True." He drank and wiped his whiskers. "But the old girl will survive without me. We rub along. And while there is gold and wizardly powers—why, dom—just think of it—"

"Having heard of the Humped Land, now we must wait until someone puts an expedition together—is that it?"

"You mean—you'd go?"

I twirled the rudis. The heavy wood was dented and splintered from the force of our blows. The flick-flick plant satisfied another small segment of its appetite, and a fly vanished from the ken of men. "I may—I do not know. I am in more than two minds. But all is mere conjecture while we must care for the lady Yasuri, under the orders of the Star Lords."

"True. Damned true."

If a weathervane may be blown by the winds of heaven in any direction, then I was a weathervane, right enough.

"Y'know, Jak," said Pompino, carrying on a thread of thought begun by our remarks. "It is strange the Everoinye, if they are so tender for the welfare of the lady Yasuri, allow us to stay here, instead of at her hotel, the Star of Laybrites."

"The Star Lords are a bunch of onkers, of get onkers, and deserve to be stewed in their own juices." At his stricken face, I added, hurriedly, "Yes, yes, my Pompino, I know. But they have understood me, over the seasons. They know what I think of them. Until they prove themselves as being as good as humans, I cannot take them seriously as gods."

"You—" His reddish whiskers bristled, his dark eyes stood out, he looked as though he would choke. "Jak, Jak! They'll strike you down."

"Not them. That's not their damned way."

"Their ways pass the understanding of mortal men."

"If a being, an entity, cannot show the same decent qualities one expects of a fellow human being, why should any man be expected to worship and give praise to such a being?"

"I do not know. No one knows."

A knock at the door heralded the chambermaid, a little Fristle fifi with brown fur and a delightful smile, who told us the landlord had a visitor for us.

"Show him up," said Pompino, and we laid aside the wooden swords and took into our fists steel thraxters.

But it was only Onron, the lady Yasuri's Rapa coachman and chamberlain, decked out in a fine new livery, who told us with some condescension that the lady wished us to accompany her to the play this evening.

"The play?" said Pompino, laying aside his thraxter. "Since when has the lady ever wanted us to go with her to Jikaida?"

"The play, I said, you imbecilic Khibil!" The Rapa fluffed up his red tribal feathers, his beak polished and shining.

Pompino started up, bristling, but we sorted it out.

Between some members of some races of diffs there does exist an immediate, top of the head, instinctive antipathy, varying in intensity from diff to diff, that has over the seasons become formularized and lacking any intensity of conviction. The slanging becomes mawkish or merry, not taken seriously, a peg to hang a mental hat on, a way of release from other tensions, a little banter to lighten up the day.

In that spirit the Rapa Onron could say with a spit, "They should send you both to Execution Jikaida. That would make you skip about, believe me."

"I," said Pompino, "have no wish to hear another word about Execution Jikaida. We don't admit foul smells in here."

Before he could add the obvious and, perhaps, liken Onron to some particular stink, I butted in and got the details, as Pompino would have done after a little more enjoyable wrangling.

As popular entertainment, the theatre lagged a long way after Jikaida in Jikaida City. But there were playgoers in the city who demanded and obtained the best plays, and tonight's offering at Dottles Playhouse was to be given by a traveling company who had just come in with a caravan across the Desolate Waste. Pompino and I prepared for the evening, at the lady Yasuri's instructions wearing brigandines under our lounging robes, and with thraxters belted to our waists—well, they went outside the robes, for no sensible Kregan willingly parts with his sword unless he knows that the company he will keep and the haunts he will frequent will prove friendly.

The play was to be a great and famous old favorite of all those Kregans who love true theater and not the mindless singsong baubles dished up on the popular stage. We were to see *Jögen*, Part One, which comes from the fifth book of *The Vicissitudes of Panadian the Ibreiver*, the sublime cycle of plays by Nalgre ti Liancesmot. I was looking forward to it, and even Pompino, whose tastes were attuned more to the mass media—to use that oft-abused much later descriptive—gave his opinion that *Jögen* was always worth seeing and that he hoped this newly arrived company were of some quality.

There was the obvious aphorism to quote him—from Panadian, to be sure, "The empty grave proves the armor's worth." To which, it is interesting to remember, a later playwright, En Prado, adds the rider: "The gallows dangle proves the armor's faults."

There is debate over the latter, and as we went with the jostle of the crowd toward the theatre, Pompino was attempting to sway me to the school of thought which says that En Prado really wrote armorer's faults and not armor's faults. Either way, as we went in under the mineral-oil lamps' flare to find the lady Yasuri, either way makes sense. It is a pretty point of a particularly fascinating and useless kind of academic lore.

The fellow who tried to slip a dagger into my ribs so that he might more easily steal my purse was jabbed away with a fist in his mouth and then a boot in his guts. The crowd parted around him, and only two women squealed. Pompino wanted to put a knife between his ribs.

"Leave him be, good Pompino. He but practices his trade—and poor pickings he will get tonight, with a broken tooth and a bruised mouth marking him for a brawler."

The would-be thief picked himself up. His clothes were neat as they must be for his trade here. "By Diproo the Nimble-fingered," he spat out, spraying blood. "You are damned quick."

"Schtump!" shouted Pompino angrily. "Clear off!"

He went away, then, as the theater's hired guards stalked across to sort out the disturbance. I noticed the thief walked with a limp, and felt sorry for him, and then we pressed on into the lighted area where people waited and we saw the lady Yasuri.

She saw us too, and her little body drew itself up. Her lined old nutcracker face had mellowed wonderfully of late; but her nose and her tongue were as long and sharp as ever.

"You are late, you famblys."

She wore a deep-maroon cloak over a severe black bomba-zine dress, as we had first seen her. Her small body was decked with gems so that she glittered like a stalagmite. She was continually being looked at and pointed out as the reigning Jikaida champion, and she lapped up the fame and the applause. I shook my head. She had cared for me wonderfully after the final game in which she had taken the championship; but it had only been because I'd fought a crazy man's fight that she had won. It was clear that she owed me. It was also clear to me that she was now more wealthy than ever. And, with equal clarity, it was borne in on me that I could no longer tolerate the acceptance of charity in lieu of payment.

Pompino started to bumble about being held up on the way.

I said, "We are not late, lady, for the play has not yet begun." Then, as she flinched back, I added, "I am pleased you are keeping so well. What business do you have with us?"

But she was not a great lady for nothing. She was a vadni, which is very high up the rank tables of Kregan nobility, and after that first surprised flinch, she flared up. Her tiny face screwed up wrathfully. Her sharp nose stuck up toward us like the beak of a swifter. Blood suffused her thin cheeks.

"I should have you whipped jikaider! Insolence—who is paying for you to lie abed in idle luxury?"

"If it is gold you want, lady, gold you may have."

She sneered at this. "And where would you two brave buckos put your hands on gold enough."

"Mod—" began Pompino. I trod on his foot and said, "We can hire out to someone else, lady. Do not forget, you discharged us, turned us off in the city, and when I fought I did not fight for you."

That had rattled her. She waited until a chattering pack of empty-headed girls fluttered past, all silks and draperies, and then she said: "No. No, Jak, you told me that. Who, then, were you fighting for?"

"Better ask the Witch of Loh, Ling-li-Lwingling."

She gave a petty gesture, annoyed. "She has left the city."

"To be truthful with you, lady, I do not know what she knows. But she hinted that she knew much—"

"Oh, that is the way of a Witch of Loh. If they do not know they will always pretend they do."

"So you summoned us here tonight. Here we are. Again—what is the business you have with us? If it is to demand we pay you back for your—"

"No, no, you great lumop! Only your last fight with Prince Mefto—it was wonderful and awful and frightening—only that—but I am champion and, indeed, I never expected it, did not dare to dream—" She pulled a scrap of lace, so that the threads snapped. "But I am champion and must play again, soon, in the Mediary Games. Will you—?"

"No."

"But—"

"I will not fight again in Death Jikaida."

"Jak—"

Pompino was breathing extraordinarily hard at my ear. He'd refused to act as a piece on the board when they played Kazz-Jikaida, Blood Jikaida, and had cogent reasons for that. The plan in which I had become embroiled had succeeded, against all expectations. I wanted nothing more of stepping out onto the blue and yellow checkered sand and of fighting at the whim of a player, fighting for my life for nothing.

"As the reigning Champion you cannot have any difficulty in finding men anxious to act as your pieces."

"True. But I want you as my Princess's Swordsman—"

"No."

A brazen gong note signaled that the play was due to begin. A few late-comers hurried past, heads down. We went toward the curtains which slaves held open for us.

"I have not finished with you, Jak!"

Through the curtains the waiting tiers of seats, the stage in its magic semicircle below, the lamps, the smell of theater, the muted hum and sway—we entered the magic world and, for those moments, could forget the world of Kregen as it was now and revel in the spiritual thoughts and the acts of passion and foolishness, of cowardice and heroism, springing from the mind of a man long dead.

This traveling company of players turned out to be top quality, and the audience sat enthralled. *Jögen* was given a splendid performance. As for the eponymous hero of the piece, Jögen himself, well, what can one say? Yes, he should have known better. He should not have trusted the woman. But human nature is human nature, and we are supposed to progress through life and learn by our mistakes. Poor Jögen! We all laughed at the right places, and the women cried— some of them, not including the lady Yasuri—at the appropriate moments. At the first interval the wide stone-flagged taverna area, softly lit by shaded lights, filled with the talk of playgoers discussing the play.

I saw Lobur the Dagger, laughing, brilliant in evening dress, talking animately to a lovely girl with dark hair, all in shimmering green, and they were oblivious to anything else.

In that group of Hamalese stood a man with a shock of dark hair much like the girl's in color, with a craggy and yet noble face which was the male counterpart to her vivid femaleness, so I guessed they were father and daughter. By this man's dress, impeccable and with a minimum of jewelry, by the deference shown him by his compatriots, and by his own superb poise and sense of being, I took him to be Prince Nedfar. He wore a rapier and main gauche, whereat my brows drew down.

A scheme that was not as foolish as it appeared at first sight occurred to me; but I pushed it away. It was audacious, and that was a merit; it was also chancy, and while I have taken some pretty long chances in my time, here and now it

seemed to me was not the time or place. I'd steal the fellow's
flier, and curse him for a Hamalese as I flew away.

In many playhouses of Kregen the slaves beat three gongs
at the end of the intervals. The first is to tell you to order
your last drink; the second is to tell you to sup up and put
your glass down; and the last is to say that you have only a
few murs to reach your seat and if you are not there in time,
then, by Beng Lomier the Blessed, patron saint of every strolling
player, the slaves will bar the curtains on you.

The first gong note clashed out over the taverna.

"A Stuvan for me," quoth Pompino.

"A light yellow, Jak," said the lady Yasuri.

I fetched the drinks. The flagged area emptied as the
people returned to their seats, anxious to be settled in time
and miss nothing, and the second gong had not struck. The
Hamalese were arguing about just who had ordered what, as
tiresome people do in bars.

The curtains over the doorless opening to the entrance
parted and four men walked in. They did not look, even at a
cursory glance, like devotees of the stage. They wore dark
clothes, dust-stained, and furry caps under which, I was
prepared to wager, they had iron skulls. Their faces were
grainy, hard, with lips thinned with purpose. Pompino looked,
and said: "Hai!" and eased himself back from the little table
at which he and Yasuri sat.

Do not forget, Pompino the Iarvin was a Khibil. What is
more important—he had been chosen by the Star Lords to be
a kregoinye and act in moments of emergency for them.

The newcomers looked around, orienting themselves. They
saw the Hamalese, who were still squabbling about the drink
order. A group of locals went out, and the place looked very
empty, and the four men turned their slate-gray eyes on us.

One said something to his companions. He was bigger than
the others, bulky with power, and his gloved hands made
quick, hard gestures. He advanced toward us.

He bowed. His words were perfectly civil; but he did not
smile as he spoke. Nor did he remove his hat, which is a
mark of respect not quite as common on Kregen as on Earth,
but which would have been perfectly proper in the circumstances.

"You are the lady Yasuri, Yasuri Lucrina, Vadni of Cremorra?"

Yasuri put her hand to her lips. "Yes . . ."

"Then I have to tell you that the king is dead, that the kingdom is overrun, that your vadvarate is gone——"

Yasuri let out a high shriek at the words. She fell back against the chair. Her face was stricken. Pompino looked at her in alarm.

The hard-faced man went on speaking, and as he spoke he moved like a scuttling tiklo of the desert.

"The king is dead, and King Ortyg the Splendid reigns in glory. He commands instant obedience, lady—and he commands your death!"

The messenger of this ill news sprang even as he spoke.

His sword cleared scabbard and, twinkling like a bar of light, slashed down at Yasuri's unprotected head.

My own thraxter was there, the two blades clashed, and thrummed with the vibration of the blow. My blade turned and his slid along and so I turned with the coming thrust and he leaped away, yelling in anger, and the point fell short.

There was no time to give him room to get set. His three comrades were rushing upon us, bared steel aflame. I leaped the table that had impeded my thrust, and crossed swords with the fellow, forcing him back, angling him away from Yasuri.

He fought viciously and well, shocked to find opposition preventing him from carrying out a mission that had seemed so easy of accomplishment. He shouted insults as he fought, and I saw the first of his bully-blade comrades hurling on, and so I was quick.

They both went down, skewered, and the third was engaged even as Pompino roared in at my side to take the fourth.

We were rather sharp with them. Pompino stepped back, his blade held up. With his left hand he smoothed his whiskers.

"What rubbish they choose to send," he said.

"They nearly did it." I bent to wipe the thraxter on the clothes of the first. "Had they just done the deed instead of parlaying around. . . ."

Yasuri put her hand on my arm. She was shaking.

"King Ortyg," she whispered. "I am lost, lost—he hates my family dreadfully. They but gloated on my misery—"

"They both went down, skewered."

"And they paid the price," Pompino said, and snicked his blade away.

"You wish to continue with Jögen?" I said as the gong sounded.

She shook her head. "No—no, I cannot—"

Then Prince Nedfar and the other Hamalese with him was there. He was smiling. He held out his hand. "Let me shake the hands of two brave men who know how to protect a lady. Cramphs like this deserve to die a thousand deaths." He bent his stare upon Yasuri. "You are well, lady?"

"Yes—yes, thank you."

He introduced himself, and the chief personages of his retinue. In that number he included his daughter, the Princess Thefi, but not, I was intrigued to notice, Lobur the Dagger.

"I am a connoisseur of swordplay. I have seldom seen two Bladesmen do their work so finely. You must visit me—"

Pompino's face began to stain red and his foxy features bristled up uglily. He was going to burst out with shatteringly rude and impolitic remarks about rasts of Hamal and stinking Hamalese—and so I stepped in quickly and said all the right things, and thanked this damned condescending prince for his kind words on our swordplay, and smirked and smiled, and so got us out of it with the promise to visit him on the following day at The Montilla's Head.

Yasuri was almost overcome.

"Now you see, Jak," Pompino whispered as we escorted her back to The Star of Laybrites "—now we can see the hand of the Star Lords clearly!"

"Oh, aye. We were sent there tonight to save Yasuri's life. And it is useless to question why the Star Lords want her hide saved. She isn't a bad old biddy; just the result of bad breeding. Let us hope we can retire gracefully now."

We saw her safely home and then went back to our inn.

"And, Jak, if you think I'm going to see that rast of a Hamalese tomorrow, then you can think again."

"I have no love for the folk of Hamal while they continue to obey mad Empress Thyllis. But they are not evil of themselves." I yawned. "Anyway, think of the chance! Now we can get into the hotel without skulking there at night. Now we can smile and act graciously, and get up on the roof, and then—"

Pompino looked up. He nodded.

"To steal their voller I will act like a craven. One must dare all things in service to the Everoinye."

I did not confide to him my feelings on that score.

Chapter Five

We Meet Drogo the Kildoi in the Jolly Vosk

"We are off to see Execution Jikaida this afternoon, Jak, Pompino. You will join us?"

Lobur the Dagger spoke cheerfully, because Kov Thrangulf stood with the group smiling and nodding. No one cared much for Kov Thrangulf; but he performed some mysterious function in Prince Nedfar's entourage. Also he was a kov, which is by way of being a terrestrial duke, and so was a man of power of himself.

"I think not, Lobur; but thank you all the same."

Lobur had not recognized me as Drax, Gray Mask—well, by Zair! had he done so I would have been mortally chagrined.

We had taken to visiting the group around the prince and we sensed that they were glad of company, being isolated in this city where, although LionardDen was neutral in the wars Hamal was waging within the Dawn Lands, there were many who hated Hamal and all things Hamalian with blind hostility. We spent time here, and joked and laughed around; but we had not had a single chance to get up on the roof and steal the voller. The airboat was kept under heavy guard, and we had not, so far, been able to get away from our new-found friends. Of course, the slightest suspicion that we were interested in the voller with the view to her purloining would bring disaster. We had to take it easy, tsleetha-tsleethi, and await our opportunity.

As for Prince Nedfar, after the debacle of the alliance with Prince Mefto, he had remained here to indulge himself in Jikaida. So he said. I began to entertain uneasy suspicions that he had ulterior motives. The treaty that was supposed to have released many powerful armies to fight against Vallia might still be concluded—with some pawn other than Prince Mefto.

This business of going to witness Execution Jikaida was a nuisance. The so-called game was ordinary Jikaida, played to the rules, and with living men and women as pieces—just as they do in Kazz-Jikaida. But these pieces were condemned criminals. The moves were made and the piece being taken would be cut down, there and then, on the spot, and the game proceed. This was not my idea of fun.

It was not Lobur's, either, as I could see, and the prince himself had made an excuse. This fat, hard-breathing, smelly Kov Thrangulf was the one panting to go. And Lobur, perforce, as a mere aide to the prince, had to acquiesce.

The oldest families of Hamal hold especial pride in their lineal descent from the ancients, and mark this by including the name ham in their own names. Thus I was, as you know, in all honor Hamun ham Farthytu in Hamal. Paline Valley and Nulty and those skirling times seemed long and long ago now; but such is the accumulation of tradition and the weight of incumbence, that I knew if I turned up at Paline Valley now I would be received as the rightful Amak. Unless, of course, a usurper had managed to arrange the bokkertu and through legal means taken the title and the estates. Then, the cramph, he'd have another fight on his hands.

Lobur the Dagger was a mere Horter of Hamal, a simple gentleman. He was in the prince's service and joyed in that. But I discovered his name. This was Lobur ham Hufadet, and his family were honored citizens of Trefimlad. He was madly, overwhelmingly, besottedly in love with the prince's daughter, the Princess Thefi. A match did not seem in their stars, by reason of their station. But on Kregen all things are possible as, by Zair, had I not shown? This fat and unpleasant Kov Thrangulf did not have the honor of placing the ham in his name. He was a kov, a powerful and wealthy man; but he did not own to the ham. Yes, you will say—a common, a conventional, situation. Agreed. From it all manner of devilments and schemes might spring. And—they did. But, as is my wont, I will hew to the path of chronology and relate to you what happened between Lobur the Dagger and the Princess Thefi and Kov Thrangulf, when what happened impinged upon this my own story. Suffice it for the moment, there in Jikaida City, I had my heart set on that voller.

Failing the voller, then I might have to walk out. Either way, I had no wish to linger in LionardDen.

Pompino said, "I trust you enjoy yourselves this afternoon. I am for the merezo where they are racing for high stakes."

As we walked off, shouting the remberees, I knew Pompino lied. He was serious, deadly serious, on a sudden.

"I have had no chance to tell you before, Jak—we are altogether too chummy with these yetches of Hamalese. But—I have had a communication from the Star Lords."

"The Gdoinye spoke to you?"

"Yes. We are quits of our work with Yasuri—"

"*We are!*"

"Aye. If that assassination attempt was all it was about, well and good. What matters now is we will not be prevented from leaving."

Whatever the situation might appear to be on the surface, I knew well enough that the Star Lords planned long and darkly into the future. What they did they did with fell purpose. Yasuri was important in ways we could not comprehend. But, we were quit of her. I joyed in that, and spared a thought for Yasuri and wondered what she would do now. But that was her business—aye, hers and the Star Lords', no doubt.

"Most of that lot from Hamal are watching Execution Jikaida," I said. I spoke lightly as we walked along in the streaming mingled lights of the Suns of Scorpio. "We are known in the hotel now. Why should we not—?"

"Capital. I am with you."

So we turned around and retraced our steps.

Well, now. . . . If the old blood thumps a little faster around the body, and the sweat starts out on the brow, and the palms grow damp and the throat dry—at memory, mere memory? We were not working for the Everoinye now, we were working for ourselves and for all the help we had ever had from the Star Lords that made not the slightest difference, or so I thought. I recall as we walked along in the suns shine that I contemplated hiring out as a caravan guard and trekking back over the Desolate Waste, as we had planned. But the idea of the voller obsessed us. The speed of a flier is phenomenal compared to a saddle animal.

The caravans continued to ply, one had only just arrived today, and the last had brought in the company of strolling players and the four stikitches who had so signally failed to earn their hire.

Pompino hitched his sword belt.

"Let us have a wet first—in honor of Dav Olmes, for example, or Konec, or—"

"Let us take a drink, anyway, you procrastinating fambly!"

I wanted to give the Hamalese time to get to the Jikaida deren, those massive central blocks where the bloody games of Jikaida were played, before we raided the hotel.

Any hostelry would do, provided it was of the better sort, and not a mere dopa den. The jade and ruby brilliance fell about us. The sweet scents of Kregen intoxicated us with life. Ah, Kregen, Kregen—well, we found a tavern and were about to enter when a man came flying through air and almost brought us both down. And, as far as I know, they don't play exactly that kind of Rugby on Kregen. The fellow hauled himself up. He was a Brokelsh, squat and hairy and gibbering with rage. He shook his fist at the tavern and then lurched off, rumbling and cursing, swearing about a Havil-forsaken Kildoi.

I chilled.

We went in. I am well aware how foolish, how superficial, it is to say, "I chilled." But, by Vox, that is exactly right. I felt the cold clamp around me. I did chill, and you may cavil all you wish at the expression. It is apt and it is right. . . .

The Kildoi was instantly visible, surrounded by a gang of roughs. They were not attacking him, but they were not friendly. Now Prince Mefto the Kazzur was a Kildoi. He had bested me in swordplay—oh, yes, I had cut off his tail hand at the last—but he had proved the superior swordsman. Kildois have four arms and a powerful tail with a hand. Korero, my comrade who carried his shields at my back in battle, was a Kildoi. They are marvels—and this specimen although sporting a beard darker than the golden blaze of Korero or Mefto, was just such a one, bronzed, powerful, superb in physique, cunning and most proficient with his five hands.

"We don't want your sort in here," shouted one of the roughs, a cloth around his neck stained greasily with sweat.

"Prince Mefto was a great man!" declared another, a runt of an Och slopping ale.

"Aye," said another. "Prince Mefto may have lost our wagers, because his side thought he would be chopped. But you can't say things about him here. He'll be back to win again—"

Sweat rag chimed in. "You'd better clear off, schtump, five hands or no, before we blatter you."

"You misunderstand me, my friends—" began the Kildoi.

"No we don't. You're asking questions about Mefto the Kazzur and we're all his friends here, and you bear him no good will."

A flung dagger streaked from the gloom of the counter. The Kildoi put up a hand and deflected the dagger. The action was instinctive and unthinking, and I recognized the superb Disciplines that gave Korero such wonderful command of his shields.

"I see you are not friendly," said the Kildoi. "So I will retire—"

A blackjack swung for his head, and he leaned and moved and the blackjack spun away, harmlessly. The very contempt of his actions, innate in their display of consummate skill, incensed these fellows. Mefto had always been a favorite, and these people did not know the full story. In the next instant summoning their courage, they leaped upon the Kildoi.

I started in to help, intrigued by all this, and, after a pause, Pompino joined me. There was a deal of shoving and banging, and swearing, and a collection of black eyes and bloody noses before the three of us burst from the door of the tavern. On a wooden bracket the inflated skin of a vosk swung in the wind, and the inn was called The Jolly Vosk.

"Whoever you are," said the Kildoi, with a jerk of the thumb of his upper right hand, "my thanks. The sign over the tavern proclaims the denizens within."

We walked off along the sidewalk, and we began to laugh. Snatches of the bizarre flying acrobatics of the fellows in there as the Kildoi threw them hither and yon recurred to us, and we laughed.

"Lahal, I am Drogo, and a Kildoi, as you see."

We made the pappattu, me as Jak and Pompino with his full name. Then Pompino burst out with: "And, Drogo, this is the same Jak who cut off the tail hand of that bastard Mefto."

Drogo stopped dead. He turned that magnificent head to study me more closely. I looked back.

His eyes carried that peculiar green-flecked grayness of

uneasy seas, of light shining through rain-slashed window
panes—the images are easy but they convey only a little of
the sense of inner strength and compulsion, of dedication and
awareness, the eyes of this Kildoi, Drogo, revealed.

Presently he took a breath. His arms hung limply at his
sides. I noticed that one end of his moustaches was shorter
than the other. His teeth were white, even, and showed top
and bottom when he smiled.

He smiled now, a bleak smile like snow on the moors.

"I am surprised you are still alive."

"That's what we all say," burbled on Pompino.

"Mefto was foolish," I said, deliberately turning along the
flagstones and walking on, forcing them to keep pace.

"Any man who faces Mefto in swordplay is foolish."

"Aye," I said, and with feeling. "Aye, by Zair!"

As is generally the case on Kregen no one pays much attention to the strange gods and spirits by whom a man
swears; it is only when they give away your country of origin
when you do not want that information revealed that they attract attention.

Pompino laughed, a little too high.

"We never did get that wet."

"I see I was the unwitting cause of your thirst—"

"No, no, horter, not so." Pompino, I felt sure, was now
uneasy, had come to a slower appreciation of smoldering pas-
sions in this man. He kept walking on, a little too swagger-
ingly, and laughing. "Oh, no—"

I said, "You were not the cause of the thirst. You merely
prevented our quenching it."

He gave me another expressionless look that, with those
eyes and that face, could never be truly expressionless. I
thought he was trying to sum me up, and running into difficulty.

"I am remiss," he said, and the note of ritual was strong in
his voice. "Let me buy you both a drink. I insist. It is all I
can do, at the least, to express my thanks."

So we went into the next inn, a jolly place where they
served a capital ale, and we hoisted stoups. We went to a
window seat and sat down just as though we were old comrades. I fretted. I was shilly-shallying over this business of the
voller.

Now, in other times I would have gone raging up to the

roof, a scarlet breechclout wrapped about me and a sword flaming in my fist, and down to the Ice Floes of Sicce for any damned Hamalese who got in the way. But, now, I was taking my time, making excuses, seizing every opportunity to prevaricate.

Many times on Kregen I have noticed that when I shilly-shally for no apparent reason, when things do not work out with the old peremptory promptness, there is usually an underlying cause. Often to have rushed on headlong would have been to rush headlong into disaster. And, Zair knows, that has happened, often and often. . . .

But the voller beckoned, and I hesitated and did not know why.

The Star Lords had discharged us from our immediate duty, the Gdoinye had so informed Pompino.

Then why hesitate?

But it was pleasant to sit in the window seat of a comfortable inn in the grateful afternoon radiance of the Suns of Scorpio, with a cool flagon of best ale on the clean-scrubbed table. . . . And, believe me, doing just that is just as important a part of life on Kregen as dashing about with flashing swords.

My thoughts had taken me away a trifle from the conversation. I heard Pompino talking and the words: ". . . a capital voller . . ." leaped out at me.

I listened. This Drogo was clearly seeking Mefto—and it was no great guess that he was seeking with no good will. He could be a bounty hunter. He could be a wronged husband. He could be a stikitche. But Pompino must have told him that Prince Mefto had returned to Shanodrin, the land the Kazzur had won for himself in blood and death. Now Drogo wished to get out of Jikaida City as fast as he could—and a caravan, besides being slow, was also not on the schedule for departure for some time.

"An airboat? Aye," said Drogo, and drank.

"It is a great chance—" Pompino was not such a fool, after all.

To have this Kildoi with us when we essayed the airboat would make success much more certain.

I pushed aside the startled inner reflection that this was not how I would have thought and acted only a few years ago.

There were wheels within wheels here, and I was canny enough by now to let the wheels run themselves for a space.

Drogo said, "If you will have me, I will join you—"

"Agreed!" said Pompino, and he sat back and quaffed his ale.

I sat back, also, but I did not drink.

Drogo did not look at me. He made rings with his flagon on the scrubbed wood.

"And you, Jak?"

"Why, Horter Drogo, is it that you Kildois always seem to have only one name?"

His smile was again like those damned ice floes of the far north.

"But we do not. We do not parade our names, that is all."

"Point taken—and, as for your joining us, why, yes, and right heartily." I put warmth into my voice. Foolish, I felt, to antagonize him for no reason.

"Then no harm is done."

What he meant by that I was not sure. I did know that the old intemperate Dray Prescot might well have challenged him to speak plain, blast his eyes.

He went on, "We are of Balintol, as you know, and we keep ourselves to ourselves. There are not many of us. All the first families know one another. The use of family names is felt to be—to be—"

"Drink up, Horter Drogo," I said, "and let me get you the other half."

That, at the time, seemed as good a way as any of ending that conversation.

Once again I promised myself I'd have a good long talk with Korero when I got back to Vallia. My comrade who carried his enormous shields at my back was a man of a mysterious people, that was for sure.

It was, naturally, left to Pompino, when I returned with the drinks, to say, "And you are chasing this rast Mefto to—"

"One of us will kill the other." Drogo took his flagon into his lower left hand. The other three hands visible clenched into fists. "I shall not face him with swords. So he may die. I devoutly hope so."

Like Korero, this Drogo did not habitually swear by gods and demons as do most folk of Kregen.

"You are no swordsman yourself?"

He glanced across at me, and his fists unclenched, and he took a pull of ale.

"Oh, yes, I own to some skill. But my masters suggested I would be better served by taking up some other weapon—"

"And?" interrupted Pompino.

Drogo made himself laugh. His teeth were white and even, and his tongue was very red.

"I manage with an axe, polearms, the bow, a knife—"

I said, "All at once, no doubt." As I spoke I heard the sour note of envy in my voice.

"When necessary."

By Vox! But I had walked into that one with my chin!

"You have met Katakis?"

Offhandedly, he answered obliquely. "The little streams run into the great river."

I nodded. "And Djangs?"

He frowned. "No—I do not know of them."

"Oh," I said. "I just wondered."

I stood up.

"If we intend to take this confounded voller, then let us be about our business."

Chapter Six

Concerning a Shortcut

Most men are not mere walking bundles of reflexes. Most men have deeper layers of thought and emotions below the superficialities of life. Among the many people a man bumps into on his way through life there must be some, a few, for whom he feels enough interest to be fascinated by those deeper levels.

And this really has little to do with friendship, which is by way of being an altogether different idea.

As we walked along in the radiance from the twin suns of Antares, I pondered the enigma of this Drogo the Kildoi.

Pompino was prattling on about Jikaida and his own honest conviction that he did not have a head for the game, and Drogo was nodding civilly and saying that, yes, he quite enjoyed the Game of Moons, if he was in the mood, and that he found Vajikry surprisingly challenging for what appeared so simple a game although the version they played in Balintol, his homeland, was markedly different from that played here in the continent of Havilfar. I wondered how he had got here and his adventures on the way. Korero never spoke of himself. Balintol is a shrouded land and a fit birthplace for the men it breeds.

Onron, the lady Yasuri's coachman, caught up with us as we passed through the colonnades surrounding the Kyro of the Gambits. His bright yellow favor glistened. We were about to cross into the Foreign Quarter, where the Blue and the Yellow held no favor one above the other.

"I've been looking for you all over, you pair of hulus," he puffed out. He was riding a freymul, the poor man's zorca, with a chocolate-colored back and streaks of yellow beneath, and Onron had ridden the animal hard. Clots of foam fluffed back from his patient mouth. Sweat stained all down his neck, matting the fine brown hairs.

"Hai, Beaky!" greeted Pompino, jovially.

"May your whiskers shrivel, you—" Onron threw the reins over the freymul's head and stood to face us. "My lady demands your presence—at once. The word she used was Bratch."

"Why should we jump for her any more?"

The Kildoi, Drogo, had disappeared into the shadows. Onron scratched his beak. He was not used to this kind of address respecting his lady.

"You had better go at once," he warned.

Pompino glanced at me, and his bright eye told me that the Star Lords had relieved him of a burden. The case appeared to me, suddenly, and I confess somewhat startlingly, as being different. A tug at his sleeve pulled him a little apart.

"The Everoinye have discharged you of the obligation to Yasuri, Pompino. The Gdoinye spoke to you. But not to me. . . ."

His foxy face took on a shrewd, calculating expression, and yet, I was grateful to see, a sympathetic look also.

"You could be right. The Gdoinye did not speak to you."

"Hurry, you famblys!" called Onron.

"Yet, the voller—"

"Drogo will turn up when Onron is gone. I shall go to the lady Yasuri and see what she requires. If you and Drogo can manage the flier, you will command the air. You can pick me up later at the inn."

"Yes." He stroked his whiskers. "Yes, Jak. You have my word as a kregoinye. I will return for you."

"Good—then we must both hurry."

He turned away at once and started off along the colonnade, his lithe form flickering in light and shade past the columns. He heard Onron's indignant yells right enough; he just ignored them. I turned to the Rapa.

"I will come, Onron—so stop your caterwauling."

He stuck his beak into the air, offended, and climbed back on the freymul. There was no question of my riding, so, perforce, I walked smartly off for the Star of Laybrites.

The thought crossed my mind that more stikitches, assassins, had come in with the caravan that had brought Drogo, and Yasuri's life was again in peril. But that did not make sense. For one thing, this King Ortyg would not know his men had failed. And, for another, had there been assassins there would have been no time for Yasuri to dispatch Onron in this fashion.

One objection to the first point could be that the new King Ortyg of Yasuri's country employed a Wizard of Loh to go into lupu and spy out for him what was happening here. That was possible. I quickened my steps, although recognizing the validity of the second point.

The Rapa coachman took off on the freymul, yelling back that he would tell the lady that I was obeying her and convey to her the news of Pompino's ingratitude and treachery. Onron shot off along the avenue among the crowds, and I took a shortcut.

There are shortcuts in life and there are shortcuts. This one took me through a poor quarter where they spent their time in tiny workshops making tawdry souvenirs of Jikaida for the visitors to pay through the nose for in the souks. And, this shortcut was a shortcut to disaster. The Watch was out, backed up by soldiers in their armor and hard black and white checkered cloaks, helmets shining.

A yelling mob rushed through the narrow alleyway, sweeping away stalls and awnings in their panic. I could see the soldiers riding them down, laying about them with the flats of their swords. Two men almost knocked me flying. I ducked into a doorway with the stink of days-old vegetables wafting out. The rout rushed past. Then—well, I suppose I should not have done what I did—but, being me, I did.

A woman carrying a baby fell onto the slimy cobbles.

The pursuing totrixes hammered their six hooves into the ground, prancing on, and the woman would be run down.

Darting out, with only the most cursory of looks, I scooped her up, baby and all, and started back for my doorway.

A totrix, rearing up, shouldered me away. I spun about, staggering, clutching the woman. A Watchman hit me over the head with his bludgeon. He was shouting, excited, frantic.

"Here's one of the rasts—" And he hit me again.

That was it, for a space.

The blackness remained, the blackness of Notor Zan, and I did not open my eyes. The place where they had thrown me stank. A dismal moaning and groaning filled the air. And, in my aching head the famous old Bells of Beng Kishi clashed and clanged. I winced. Cautiously, I opened one eye.

The place was arched with ribbed brick, slimy and malodorous, and a few smoky torches sputtered along the walls. The place was a dungeon, a chundrog, and the prison would extend about us with iron bars and stone walls and many guards.

Water dripped from that arched ceiling and splashed upon us, green and slimy, stinking. Rivulets of the water trickled down to open drains along the center. The people were crammed in. They were poor. They were tattered and half of them were starving. They moaned in long dismal monotones. And the air stifled with fear.

Gradually I pulled myself together and sorted out what had happened.

Criminals had been sought, and the Watch had scooped up a ripe bunch, and anyone who got in the way was taken up also. It is a dreadfully familiar story. The Nine Masked Guardians who ran LionardDen were fanatical about the order of the city. Many visitors stayed here, and the reputation of the city rested on reports of conditions. Who would journey to a city of thieves, or a city of revolution—even to play Death Jikaida?

There was no sign in this tangled company of the woman and her baby and I just hoped they were all right. The people looked like a field of old rags ready for the incinerators. I have said that the Star Lords never lifted a finger to help me, and although this is not strictly accurate, for they once enabled me to overhear a conversation to my advantage in the island of Faol of North Havilfar, it was precisely in the kind of situation in which I found myself now that no help could be expected from the Everoinye. I expected none.

A group of ruffians near me, all gleaming eye and broken teeth and rags, were discussing future possibilities.

"It is Death Jikaida, you may be sure."

"No—they want fighting men for that."

"We can fight—aye, and will fight, if they put spears into our hands."

"Kazz-Jikaida," said another, shaking. "Blood Jikaida. My brother was cut down in that, two seasons ago."

A man with lop ears and a broken nose, very villainous,

stilled them all as he spoke. "It will not be that." He spoke
heavily, with a wheeze. "It is Execution Jikaida—"

"No! No!" The shouts of horror were as much protestations as outbursts of terror. "Why, Nath, why?"

"They had a blood-letting yesterday, did they not? And the
great ones demand another game—I know, may they all rot
in the Ice Floes of Sicce forever and ever."

The uproar told me that these ill-used people put store by
the words of this Nath. It seemed he possessed enough of the
yrium, that mysterious force that demands from other men
respect and obedience, to command them.

Lop-eared Nath, he was called, and he looked a right vil-
lain.

We were fed a thin gruel and most of it was dilse, that
profuse plant that pretends to nourish, and fills a man's belly
for a time and then leaves him more hungry than before. We
drank abominable water. This chundrog was Spartan, a dungeon from which it would be well-nigh impossible to escape
except in death. I began to think along those lines. A feigned
death. . . .

Engaging in conversation with the nearest group, I soon
discovered that plan was a bubble-dream.

"Anyone who pretends death is stuck through with a spear,
to make sure." Lop-eared Nath appeared to relish his words.
"Listen, dom, we only get out of here one way. We go to act
as pieces in Execution Jikaida."

"But there is a chance in that. All the pieces will not be
taken, not all killed."

"Aye. A chance."

A man with a snaggle of black teeth and one eye chuckled.
He was half off his head already.

"It depends who we get to act as player."

"May Havil shine his mercy upon us," said a woman, and
she made the secret sign of Havil the Green.

We spent three days and nights in the hell-hole. At one
point a man in resplendent clothes and a blue and yellow
checkered mask over his face appeared. Lanterns illuminated
his figure as he stood upon a dais beside the lenken door. The
people babbled to a stupefied silence.

"You are all given a trial, and the evidence is against you
and you are all condemned." This man, the representative of
the Nine Masked Guardians, spoke in a booming, confident

voice. He lifted a ring-clustered hand. "The trial was fair and just, according to the laws of the republic. You are all appointed to act as pieces in Execution Jikaida—"

He got no further. The yells and shrieks, the imploring screams, all smashed and racketed to that slimed brick roof. He turned away, disgusted with the animal-like behavior of the mob beneath him, and walked out with a measured, pompous, confident tread. We were left to face our fate.

What the devil had happened to Pompino and Drogo? Had they taken the voller? What ailed Yasuri? These questions flew up in my head, and I saw them as the petty concerns they were.

On the morrow I faced Execution Jikaida, and, by Krun, that was a concern that shook a fellow right down to his boots.

Execution Jikaida may be conducted in a number of different ways, and I guessed we'd get the stickiest.

Guards shepherded us along the next afternoon—we could judge the time because the afternoon was the time for this particularly nasty form of the game—and we shuffled out, loaded with chains manacled and fettered to our hands and legs. Screams and sobs echoed about that dolorous procession.

At a wooden door we were each given a large drink of raw dopa.

I drank the dopa.

Some of the people calmed down, others slobbered, some fell fainting. The guards dealt with them all faithfully.

At last we were marched down a long stone corridor. At the far end double doors arched, and these, we guessed, led out onto the board. A Jiktar smart in his soldier's uniform, stood by the door, backed by a squad of men. His face, although grim, betrayed a feeling that in my heightened state I hardly recognized as pity.

"Take heart!" he bellowed. "Not all of you will die. It depends on the game. Some will live. Pray to your gods that you will be among the fortunate."

Lop-eared Nath shouted up, truculent, fierce. "And who is to act as our player?"

"You?"

Nath shrank back. "Not me!"

I said, "Jiktar, how can the player be harmed?"

He looked hard at me.

"You are a foreigner? Yes, I see. Then you were foolish to commit a crime in our city. The object of the game is to take the Princess, is this not so? To place her in hyrkaida? Well, then, her Pallan is the player in Execution Jikaida."

I saw it all.

The Pallan is the most powerful piece on the board, and, also, as a consequence, the piece the opposing player most wishes to dispose of.

The smells of this dismal place rose about me. The water dripped. And the people with their bellies afire with dopa moaned softly, given over to their own destruction.

"Thank you, Jiktar," I said, and shuffled off back into the amorphous mass of people.

"Wait!"

The word hit me like a leaden bullet slung by a slinger.

"Yes."

"You, dom, will be the player."

The eyes of the people about me showed white. Some started to caterwaul their fears, others cried out, some shrieked.

"But—"

"*Shastum!*" The Jiktar roared out, instantly halting the growing noise. "Silence. Move out!"

I did not move.

Into that cowed silence I said, "And who acts as player when I am slain?"

"The next in line. There is no interruption in play. Move out! *Grak!*"

It all made sense. Any fumble-wit might make the moves. The poorer the player—the more the deaths.

The double doors were thrown open. Mingled streaming light poured in, the glorious radiance of the Suns of Scorpio, illuminating a stairway of brilliance out to horror.

Chapter Seven

Execution Jikaida

We played black.

Each one of us wore a grimy black breechclout and a tattered favor marking the rank of the piece we represented—and that was all.

Almost all the black breechclouts carried rusted stains—dark and dreadful mementoes of past games.

The brilliance of the day outside smote in with pain. We walked out, for we hardly marched, and so were shepherded willy-nilly to our places on the yellow and blue sanded squares. The terraces were packed. The spectators craned forward. The rituals with their incantations and sacrifices and prayers were all passed. We marched out to a hush, a long hollow waiting silence.

Up there against the brightness of the day the ranks of Bowmen of Loh brooded down, tall and spare; but they were there on this day to perform a slightly different function from their usual task of shafting any wight foolish enough to run. Now they were insurance, in case the men in black were too slow.

One young lad—his face was so contorted with fear it took a moment to realize he was apim—when he was positioned by the marshals upon his square in the front rank, simply ran. He did not know where he was running. Head down, screaming, he fled from horror—and ran into the arms of the men in black, into the arms of horror upon horror.

What the men in black and their instruments did to the young man rooted every other piece wearing the black to the square on which he stood. Rooted him there as though he had grown into the solid ground beneath.

The trumpets blew. The banners waved. The crowd craned forward as the white pieces emerged.

So we understood what kind of Execution Jikaida we played. I stood on my square, feeling—well, feeling that I had had some ups and downs in my life upon Kregen, sudden and dizzy swoops from greatness to disaster. And I had clawed my way back, only once more to be thrust down. The situation was no novelty in that respect; but this was like to be the last time I was so cast down. This time was the casting down and out.

The white pieces were not men condemned to execution. They were soldiers, in garish fancy-dress uniforms, with white favors everywhere. They carried weapons. They were off duty, performing a part of their agreement entered into when they signed on, and earning themselves a tidy bonus apiece.

When they took a piece from the black side they would kill him, chop him—or her—down without thought. When a black piece took one of them, he would simply walk quietly off the board, most probably to sit on the substitutes bench to watch the remainder of the game.

As the Pallan I stood next to the Princess.

She stood there, drooping, pale, and I saw she was the woman I had so uselessly attempted to rescue from the trampling hooves of the totrixes. She wore a black breechclout and, because she was the Princess, a forlorn black crown of drooping feathers.

I looked again. In her arms she cradled the baby.

The bastards had even wrapped a scrap of black cloth about the baby's skeletal ribs. I felt sick.

If I lost the game, then hyrkaida would not be a mere civilized checkmate—it would be the swift and lethal swordblow finishing this woman—and her child.

"What is your name, doma?"

She jerked as though I had assaulted her. Her eyes shifted sideways. She colored. She shook her head.

"They don't mind if we talk a little, quietly."

"Yes . . . I am Liana whom men once called the Sprite."

"Lahal, Liana the Sprite. I am Jak."

"Lahal, Jak—will it be very—very terrible?"

"For some of the swods and Deldars, and some of the superior pieces, yes, it will be terrible. But you will be safe—"

"Unless you lose!"

"Yes."

Up there lolling on the terraces, ensconced on their comfortable seats, the audience stared down avidly. It seemed to me outrageous that anyone could take pleasure from all this. Although I detested Kazz-Jikaida, where the pieces fought for the squares on which they stood, at least then there was some chance. But here, just to stand and wait to be butchered! And it was useless running. The men in black and their ghastly instruments hovered.

The throng murmured with excitement. They were sick, all of them, sick to their twisted minds.

And perhaps the sickest of all was the white player.

He—or she—would have paid an enormous sum for the privilege of playing Execution Jikaida. I looked at the white throne, at the far end, and the tiny glittering figure there.

An immediate advantage was conferred by that position, the usual one that overlooked the board. From my level place it was going to be difficult to see all the board and appreciate what pieces stood on what squares.

But, then, that was all a part of the fun of the game to these sickening blood-batteners watching.

These wealthy people whose obsession with Jikaida led them to make the difficult journey here and play in Blood and Death Jikaida employed a Jikaidast to advise them in their games. A Jikaidast, a professional who played the game for a living as well as for the absorbed joy of it, would sit at their side and the moves would be seriously discussed. The massive clepsydra would drip its water, drop by drop, as the move was pondered, and a brazen gong would signal that time had run out. What normally happened then would happen here as a matter of course—just another poor devil would be chopped.

The marshals were finishing pushing and prodding the black pieces. The whites were set and ready. The chief marshal, perspiring, rosy of face, a trifle flummoxed, came up to me.

"You ready, lad?"

"Tell me, who is the player yonder? Who the Jikaidast?"

"Why bother your head over—"

"*Who?*"

He blinked and wiped the sweat away. He was in a hurry to get back to his quarters and a stoup of ale.

"Kov Loriman the Hunter. The Jikaidast is Master Scatulo."

I smiled.

The grimace must have had some effect on the marshal, for he took himself off very smartly.

Master Scatulo! Well, Bevon the Brukaj, who had been Scatulo's slave, had told me pertinent things of Scatulo's play. Here was the first ray of sunshine through the clouds.

"Jak. . . ." Liana's quavering voice brought my attention back to the immediate proceedings. "I think they begin. . . ."

"Trust in Havil the Green," I said. How incongruous that remark would have been only a few seasons ago!

"Rather in Havandua the Green Wonder."

"If you will."

Quite naturally white took first move. This was not from any similar tradition to that in the chess of our Earth; simply that we blacks were here to be chopped.

Now—many a Pallan playing for black, I gathered, had desperately sought never to put himself in a position where he might be taken. After all, the object of the game from white's point of view was to win and enhance his prestige in the league tables. Just because black's pieces were slain did not affect the play. This was real Jikaida, not Death Jikaida.

The proper rules were observed and play would have to be skilled. So a Pallan might seek to screen himself. I fancied, with a quick stab of gratitude to Bevon, that Master Scatulo might be in for a surprise.

So the game began, the call of "Rank your Deldars" rang out, and we set to.

It was very far from pretty.

The lines began to form, cunning diagonals of swods propped by Deldars, reaching out to the far drins.*

Scatulo chose the Princess's Kapt's swod's opening. I replied cautiously, opening up just one line. I zeunted—that is, vaulted over a line of pieces—fairly early so as to retain a better grip on the center. The zeunt was to enable the board

---

* It is not necessary to go into a full explanation of Jikaida to understand the course of this game. The rules and a description of Poron Jikaida were published as an Appendix to *A Sword for Kregen*, the second volume in the Jikaida Cycle of the Saga of Dray Prescot.

A.B.A.

to be clearer in my mind, as well as to place me in a good position. The first swod was taken by the whites. I could not prevent that.

The soldier with his white favors gleaming lifted his sword, the wretch with the scrap of black cloth around him threw up his arms and screamed, and the blade sliced down.

The men in red ran onto the board and carted him away.

The game proceeded.

The orders for the moves were carried by beautiful girls wearing black or white favors, and with their red-velvet-covered wands of office. Their draperies swirled. We lost more men.

Gradually I gleaned an understanding of just what Scatulo was up to. I do not pretend to be a master player; but I have some skill. And, by Zair, I needed it then!

The disadvantage of standing on the board, with the disorienting perspectives reaching out and the pieces all on a level, was greatly offset by the ability to hold the positions in my head. Blindfold Jikaida and multi-game Jikaida are capital teaching methods.

Pointless to go through the game move by move—or blow by blow. Every time white took a black piece, a man or woman died. It was necessary, it was vital, that I concentrate on the game and not allow the horror of the situation to unnerve me.

Those words to Liana the Sprite had been hollow. I did not think I had much chance of winning, and when I lost she would die.

The shaming thought drilled into my brain—suppose, just suppose, it was my Delia who stood there! Suppose it was Delia of Delphond, Delia of the Blue Mountains, who stood there, straight and supple, wearing that stained black breechclout? Or, just suppose it was my wayward daughter Dayra, who was called Ros the Claw? Or that other daughter of mine, Lela, whom I had not seen for long and long? Why should my reactions then be any different? Were they not all women, like Liana the Sprite? Was not my duty to them all?

As the game progressed and I sniffed out Scatulo's play I think some near sublime passion overcame me, so that Liana and Delia and all the beautiful and helpless women of two worlds were represented by that single shrinking form.

But why only the beautiful? Why exclude those women

who have not been favored of the gods with divine faces and forms? Were not they all women? Some women are very devils, as I know; but they are not the helpless of two worlds. And, would it be right to exclude them, just because of that?

Scatulo essayed a clever move down the right-hand side and I countered with the correct answer, as I had played with Master Hork in Vondium. The tiered stands buzzed afresh with appreciation. To the Ice Floes of Sicce with you all, I felt like shouting up at them and their smug knowingness.

Now Scatulo knew he was in a game. I think this Kov Loriman the Hunter, who had engaged Scatulo for the game, must have fancied himself and overridden the Jikaidast, for some odd moves were made from time to time. Trying to be quick I seized the opportunity of one such move and zeunted a Kapt over with a good chance of reaching the Princess in two moves.

The Kapt could not, for the moment, be taken. Scatulo moved a piece across which, although blocking his nearest Kapt, threatened on the next move but one to take my Kapt.

I looked at the situation in my head, for it was down at the far end of the board. The blue and yellows zigzagged their way across the board, the black pieces stood, apathetic, frenzied, shaking—but all standing faithfully on their ordered squares through fear of the instruments of the men in black. The white pieces were lounging there, earning a bonus. The stands were quiet, sensing a stroke.

Master Hork had discussed many famous old games with me. I remembered one in particular. In my head I looked at the situation and made the necessary move. If Scatulo did not respond with the single correct move available to him—I had him.

This, I may add, came as a surprise.

As I stood, waiting for Scatulo—or his employer—to make his move, the strangest sensation swept over me. Scatulo had seen the danger, for it had raced in with speed, and his own developing attack was abandoned. I felt—I realized that I had become engrossed in the game. This was needful—by Zair! but it was needful. It had given me this chance. The strange sensation was like coming up out of a deep cave into the light, and remembering that an outside world existed, that daylight smiled over the land, that the whole world was not confined by walls and darkness.

And this burgeoning feeling was not because we blacks might win. It was a realization that my first thought that I had been callous to become engrossed in a game where men died was not the truth. That absorption in the game, despite the blood and the screams, had been necessary. I had to believe that.

Now, facing me, was the final enormity.

Had I not realized my absorption, had I been still engrossed in the game as a contest of skills, divorced from the blood and death, there would have been no problem until the aftermath.

For, you see, my move, the winning move, demanded that the Pallan vault the line of pieces and alight at the end on the one square that would place the white Princess in hyrkaida.

That single crucial square was occupied by a black piece, who did not have the Pallan's powers and could not attack the Princess and end the game.

And a Pallan may capture a piece of his own color.

As we waited and the water dripped in the clespydra and the time passed I found I hoped, almost hoped, that Scatulo would see the danger, and make the only move that would save him.

And then, angrily, I pushed the betraying thought away.

If I did not do what had to be done, the game would go on and many more of the black pieces would die.

Many more.

For my attack had borne the hallmarks of frenzy, which was a part of the gambit which had already sacrificed a Hikdar—who was a man, shaking and trembling, cut down in blood—and to abandon it now would be worse, far worse.

The clepsydra was nearly on its time, the lenken arm of the hammer lifted to crash down resoundingly on the gong— Scatulo made his move and the lissom girl dashed off. The moment I saw the direction in which she sped, I knew the game was in my hand. Scatulo's move was good, exceeding good; but, then, so had been the move of Queen Hathshi of Murn-Chem in that long ago game against the Jikaidast Master Chuan-lui-Hong.

Without hesitation, my moment of doubt passed, I started to walk up the long line of pieces. As I went I lifted up my voice in that old foretop hailing bellow.

"Do you bare the throat?"

That was pure panache, pure exhibitionism, pure self-indulgence.

But, by the Black Chunkrah! Didn't we condemned criminals wearing the black deserve a trifle of flamboyance now—now that we had won?

And then—by Zair; but it hit me shrewdly. It rocked me back. There was I, strutting, marching up along the line of pieces, black and white mingled, simulating that vaulting move unique to Jikaida of Kregen, zeunting in to place the white Princess in hyrkaida. There I was, stupidly proud, scarcely crediting I had pulled it off, puffed up with self-pride—knowing what I had to do to win.

So I halted at the end of the line and looked on the square containing the black piece, and it was Lop-eared Nath.

He stared at me, quite clearly imagining I was zeunting over him to a good attacking position beyond.

His lop-ears, his broken nose, the hairs on his chest, the shadowed cage of his ribs, his thin arms and legs, the piece of black cloth hitched around him, his hair all wild and disarranged and jumping alive-oh, too—there he stood, this Lop-eared Nath.

I could see the way his stomach sagged and tautened as he breathed under the jut of his ribs.

He was sweating.

But, then, so were we all.

He cracked his lips open as I marched up. He was a stringy old bird, as tough as they come.

"How's it going then, dom? By the Green Entrails of Beng Teaubu! We're up the sharp end here."

"Lop-eared Nath."

I was still staring in a stricken fashion at him and the black and white pieces leading up to him were all staring at me. The soldiers in their fancy white favors and stupidly garish holiday uniforms were interested. The black pieces looked sick with fear.

"Go on, then, dom—get onto the square!"

I shook my head. It was an effort.

In only heartbeats the move must be declared, for I had started off without the usual declamation and I was fearful I would be penalized.

"You being the Pallan and all, and up here right near the

Princess—that has to be good, don't it?" He shivered and looked around warily. "Are we going to win? I don't care if we win or lose, so long's I come out alive—course, I feel sorry for Liana and her baby and all. But a fellow's got to live—and I have a quarter to run—"

"D'you play Jikaida, Nath?"

"Me? No—the Game of Moons. What're you waiting for?"

A buzzing and a murmuring began in the tiers and the marshals began to stir themselves.

"A Pallan, Lop-eared Nath, may capture a piece of his own color—not the Princess, not the Aeilssa, of course."

"Yeah? You'd better get onto your square, dom, else those bastards in black'll have your guts out with their pinchers."

"Lop-eared Nath—you are on my square."

He didn't understand, not at first.

"Can't be—I'm on it, aren't I?"

"Yes. But I am acting the Pallan."

Then he saw.

"You wouldn't—me! You bastard! You're not one of us—you're a damned foreigner! By the Slimy Eyeball of Beng Teaubu! If I was in the quarter—"

"A lot of other people will die, Nath, if you live, here—and there is nothing to say you will not die anyway."

The marshals approached ready to sort out what this little contretemps might be, and the men in black hefted their instruments with a sharp and pungent professional interest.

The world is made up of people like Lop-eared Nath—oh, not in his profession or appearance or interests or way of speech—but in his inherent inwardness. Or so it is comforting to believe. He saw it. He saw the whole picture, and his part in it. I thought, for a stupid instant, that he would leap on me.

A drop of sweat dripped off the end of his nose. He squinted up in the streaming mingled radiance of Zim and Genodras, and I knew he was partaking of the sunshine for the last time.

"Yeh, I slit the old fool's throat, and took his money—and I spent it, too. So I suppose it all adds up in the end. . . . And—I'm glad for Liana. Use to call her the Sprite, afore her man ran off."

Suddenly, Lop-eared Nath lifted up his arms and laughed.

"Ended up here, most like. But I'm glad for her, and the baby—now, stranger—tell them to get on with it."

So it was done, and Lop-eared Nath paid his dues, and I called "Hyrkaida" and whites conceded and it was over.

Slaves ran out with rakes and buckets of fresh sand, blue and yellow, to cover the bloodstains. The next game would start after an interval for refreshments.

We condemned marched back into the cells.

Liana the Sprite, holding her baby carefully, contrived to walk at my side.

So we went back into the place of imprisonment, leaving the place of horror. I was under the impression that we would be called out again; but Liana said, "No, Jak. We won—thanks to Havandua the Green Wonder. We will be spared. We will not be driven out to another Execution Jikaida." Her thin face turned to me, and she looked relaxed and at ease, the terror gone.

"Oh, no, they are harsh but just. We will not be killed. They will sell us as slaves."

Chapter Eight

Hunch, Nodgen and I Are Auctioned Off

Hunch, the Tryfant slave who with Nodgen the Brokelsh and me cared for our master's animals, was a very devil for roast chicken. Now he came flying back over the prostrate forms of the exhausted slaves in the retinue, stepping on out-flung arms and legs, thumping on narrow stomachs, almost tripping, yet miraculously keeping his balance, the roast chicken clasped fiercely in his fist.

"Come back here! By Llunyush the Juice! I'll have you!"

Fat Ringo, the master's chief cook, pursued Hunch with a carving knife in one hand and a meat cleaver in the other. Fat Ringo was uttering the most blood-curdling threats as he ran, fat and purple and perspiring.

The first moon of the night, She of the Veils, was just lift-ing over the flat grazing land to the east and lighting in gold and rose the faces of the mountains ahead. The night blazed with the stars of Kregen. Nodgen pulled his tattered rags out of the way of the hunt. His chains clanked. I rolled over and sat up and, seeing what was toward, gave a groan and started to jostle a calsany or two in the way.

Everybody on Kregen knows what calsanys do when they are upset or frightened. Hunch saw that swaying movement. He darted for the herd, shoving the animals this way and that, hurtling past with a quickly whispered, "My thanks, Jak!"

The calsanys started up.

Everywhere on the ground the slaves rolled over and sat up and a chorus of protestations and curses began—then the slaves were hauling their tattered rags around themselves and moving off as fast as they could.

"I'll fritter your tripes and season with garlic and serve 'em up, you hulu!" shrieked Fat Ringo.

He danced around, purple, gasping, shaking the knife and the cleaver. But he made no attempt to push in among the calsanys.

With another groan—for I had been beaten mercilessly twice the day before—I lifted my aching bones and shuffled off out of the way.

The iron chains festooning my emaciated body hampered my movements. I dragged along like a half-crushed beetle. But no one was going to sleep near a bunch of calsanys in that condition.

This whole ludicrous scene was hilarious in a kind of skull and crossbones way. Once Hunch was off by himself he'd wolf the chicken down and scatter the bones, and then no one could say, for sure, that a chicken had ever existed. Fat Ringo knew that. He backed off from the calsanys, shaking his kitchen implements and foaming.

"I'll have you—so help me Llunyush the Juice!—I'll have you!"

Hunch was too sly to answer. He was beyond the calsanys and no doubt was well started on the first leg. He wouldn't save any for me, and I did not fault him for that. The evidence had to be annihilated utterly—as Hunch would say.

The slaves were rolling up again and cursing rasts who disturbed their sleep. Sleep, to a slave, is the most precious of balms. Fat Ringo shook his cleaver, and breathed deeply, and started back to his fire. He was an apim—almost all superior cooks are apim—and when he saw me he aimed a kick at my backside as he lumbered past.

"I know who it was!" he brayed.

I rolled away and found a comfortable depression in the ground and hauled my rags about me. "Yeah? Well, try to prove it then." And I closed my eyes and sought sleep.

On the morrow the caravan would start off again early and march most of the day, with a suitable pause for refreshment. In our case that would be a heel of bread and an onion, if we were lucky. In the evening we would each receive our bowl of porridge and four palines—three if Fat Ringo was in a bad mood. Our lord and master would sit grandly in his tent, with all the appurtenances of gracious living brought with him on the expedition—folding table and chairs, folding washstand, chests and storage jars filled with the goodies that made his rich life the richer. Fat Ringo's choicest delicacies would be brought on golden platters to the great man.

Strom Phrutius was his name, a damned strom from one of the mingled kingdoms of the Dawn Lands, immensely wealthy and yet only a strom, which is equivalent to an Earthly count, and covetously desirous of making himself a kov—or, at the least, a vad. I guessed the old buzzard would make himself a king if he had half a chance.

So that was why he was on the expedition.

He'd bought me and a gaggle of slaves to make his journey comfortable, and so here I was. Four separate attempts at escape I'd made, and four separate times I'd been caught and dragged back by the heels. They had been desperate, frenzied, chaotic bursts of ill planning and stupid execution. I'd reverted, in many ways, to the Dray Prescot who had first been brought to Kregen. But the lash and the chains had made me realize that I must retain my hold on the deeper—if only by a hairsbreadth deeper—realization that there are other ways of gaining one's end than by thumping a few skulls.

The caravan consisted of a vast quantity of animals, many wagons and coaches, lines of folk trudging on foot, and our aim was to be through the passes of the mountains before the snow choked them. Once over that massif, we would be fair set for our goal. Well, the goal of the masters, not of the slaves. Their goal was food and sleep.

Being chained up and confined to the animals with Strom Phrutius, I was totally unaware of the names and quality of the other great ones who undertook this expedition. Every now and then a gaily attired party would ride past, their zorcas pretty and cavorting in the suns' light, their every action indicating the joy of the hunt and of life.

I'd go back to the curry comb, and ponder—had Pompino and Drogo seized the airboat and were they safe? Was Yasuri still alive? And—was Vallia still afloat?

All that had to wait—all that was part of another life. I was slave. I ministered to the animals. I was slave.

Day by day as we marched the mountains neared. We trudged across the high pass before the snow trapped us. On we went over a barren land where men thirsted. The dust powdered us and the grit beneath our feet lacerated our flesh.

Hunch was not fettered. Many of the slaves were not chained. Nodgen the Brokelsh, surly, marched in nik-fetters.

I was chained.

Me they regarded as a wild leem, a monstrous beast of savagery and malice.

And I worked. The animals looked sleek and cared for and I knew every one in the remuda, every one who hauled a cart. The six krahniks who pulled Strom Phrutius's coach were strong, dedicated animals, and I knew each one, and called it by its name.

And my chains remained, and I was slave.

Five-handed Eos Bakchi, the Vallian spirit of good luck, had turned away from me. Equally, his counterpart in Havilfar, Himindur the Three-eyed, had closed each and every eyeball against me.

Those mountains were a relatively small and local grouping and the passes led onto a land that, while it was not true desert, was, all the same, highly unpleasant to travelers short of water and food. We were supplied with ample quantities of both. By the time we reached streams and fields of green grass and pretty stands of trees we had traveled a goodly distance and we had passed no habitations, seen no people, had appeared to travel through an empty land.

A slave, unless he particularly cares, does not see much of the way or know a great deal of what is going on. In order to save my skin I had buckled down to the task of caring for the animals. One calculation—the distance we had traveled—was either easy to make or impossible, depending on whose estimates of speeds, progress made and time spent the slaves accepted.

We measured time by the passage of the suns, by the water dole and by the time of sleeping. If I say the desert was not real desert and we had plenty of water, and yet say also that men thirsted—these statements are not incompatible.

Everyone, including the animals, drank before us slaves.

So that when we reached the first stream, tinkling away between crumbly banks under letha trees, we slaves broke in ragged stumbling runs, tripped by our chains, out mouths furnaces of fire, fell full length to gulp the water. Oh, yes, we were whipped back by the slave masters. But we drank, by Krun!

Hunch licked his lips. "That cramph Fat Ringo taunted me, said we are to be sold off in the city. Us expendables."

"An expensive way of utilizing manpower—"

"No. Phrutius needed insurance across the mountains and desert. If I wasn't so scared. . . ." He was a Tryfant, and you know I am neutral concerning them. But he was usually a cheerful sort, not much over four foot six tall, and with a lopsided expression that conveyed all the guile of a six-year old scenting ice cream in the offing. "I escaped once—and when I was caught—" He did not go on. There was no need to go. He told me he came from the little kovnate of Covinglee in the Dawn Lands and his father had been a brass founder but had fallen on evil times. "He was overly fond of playing Vajikry and spent all his time and money on the game. We were turned out penniless and I ended up slave."

Next to Jikaida, the supreme board game of Kregen, stand Jikalla and Vajikry. Hunch had turned to the Game of Moons out of desperate resentment.

The next day when a city came into sight along a straight ride between trees we knew our fate loomed close. We all wore dirty gray breechclouts, were filthy and covered with sores and wounds, and our hair swirled like bargain-priced Medusae. We were refuse of humanity.

"Perhaps here is where we make a run for it, Hunch."

"As Tryflor is my witness! My legs are too tired to run, dom."

The city, whose name none of us knew, possessed a number of fine bagnios, all stone walls and iron bars and whipping posts, and in one of these we were quartered for the night. We were given no food or water and we all had a whipping, gratis and for nothing. Guards in jerkins of leather and brass patrolled with barbed spears, their whiskered faces sullen, and the watch fires burned in the towers.

Toward morning we were roused by kicks and blows and we shuffled out to stand in dazed lines. Fires burned in open hearths. We were all male slaves of many races. We waited as patient slaves always wait, forcing themselves to be incurious about what is going on for fear of the knowledge and the horror it will bring too early, before the horror arrives. Buckets of water were produced and we were instructed to get to work sluicing the water over ourselves and cleaning the muck off. Guards in jerkins produced sharp knives.

Some of us started to yell, then, the horror here; but—

"Quiet down, you onkers! Quiet!" The slave masters bellowed. They shoved and pushed keeping us in line; they did not hit us with their whips or bludgeons.

And the sharp knives were used to slice off great handfuls of our hair, to trim our beards, to make us look less like fearsome monsters of the jungle.

Then we ate. We ate mergem—which is one of the marvels of Kregen, being a leguminous plant which, dried, will last for years and may then be reconstituted and is fortifying and nourishing—and it was mixed with milk and not water, and spiced with orange honey. We ate to stupefaction.

Our bodies were smeared with oil. Some of us were corked. Our sores were treated and many were painted over, although that practice should not fool even a purblind slave buyer.

Then we were herded out to be auctioned off.

If I do not go into the business it is because I find it degrading—degrading to the sellers and the buyers, not to the slaves. In this they stand apart as mere things, and this does not demean them but removes them from the orbit of creatures who buy and sell slaves.

The slave block built of dusty brick rose head high over the wide courtyard where trees drooped in the heat. Men and women filled this space, most with attendants to minister to their wants. The auctioneers took it turn by turn to shout the wares and display the good points of the merchandise before they sloped off to slake their thirsts. We waited in line. We were all numbered and the personal ownership of Strom Phrutius was attested on the chip of painted wood we carried. Lose that, slave, and you have an ear off!

Other groups with their chips of wood bearing their owners' titles waited in line.

Hunch said, "We are not all here."

"No. The masters are bound to keep some slaves—those they had before they bought us. You told me, we were bought for the journey. Expendable. How many of us died on the way?"

"A lot, by Tryflor, a lot!"

Those slaves who had survived Execution Jikaida with me formed a small grouping of our own. But we would all be sold off.

Looking back at the pathetic and brutal scene, I suppose I should not wonder that there was trouble.

After all, although I was slave, I was also Dray Prescot.

And he, as you know, is an onker of onkers, thick skulled as a vosk.

Nodgen, surly and red-eyed, Hunch, apprehensive, and I stood together. We had struck up a companionship in our sufferings.

To speed sales up we were being sold in lots. The auctioneer waiting for us, rivulets of sweat running over his fat cheeks, the brilliance of his clothes stained with dust, bellowed out: "Grak! Grak! You bunch of useless rasts."

He snatched Hunch's wood chip and read off the details.

"Zorcahandlers. Experts at the management of animals. What am I bid for this prime purchase of skilled men?" He lifted Hunch's arm and half-turned him. "Not a mark on him, in his prime—" He looked at me. "C'mere, slave!" He grabbed.

The slave handlers started to run onto the auction block from the sides. People in the cleared area began to yell. The auctioneer lay on the dusty ground with a bloody nose. I looked about, dazed—it had been quick, by Vox!

What would have happened then is anybody's guess. I do not think they would have killed me straight away. Rather, they would have netted me, chained me up, and then wreaked their vengeance.

A voice, a penetrating, bull voice smashed from the crowd. "Hold!"

A man stepped front and center. I saw him clearly and yet he meant nothing. He wore black clothes and he did not sweat. His weapons glittered. He stood, tall, straight-backed, dominating. He bellowed again, and he made a bid. It was a good bid. The auctioneer, holding his streaming nose, scuttled back to the block and, business as ever sustaining him, started to raise the price by those famous auctioneers' tricks.

He took two bids off the wall before the tall fellow in black shouted menacingly, and then he knocked us down to him.

I will not tell you the price. The gold was paid. The man in the black armor took up the end of the chain binding us.

When he had dragged our little coffle out of the press and got us beyond the wall into a kyro where animals lolloped along and the trees drooped and the white-painted walls glowed in the lights of the suns, he halted us.

He frowned. The black bar of his eyebrows met over his nose.

"If you," he said to me, "or any of you, try to treat me or my people as you served that fat auctioneer—" He drew his sword. It glittered. "Your heads will be off so fast you'll still be licking your lips when they hit the ground!"

Chapter Nine

Into the Humped Land

"Better for us if we were still owned by that rast Phrutius," said Hunch, and he shivered. The other slaves in the tiny mud-walled compound agreed, with many and varicolored oaths.

Our new master in his black armor was Tarkshur—known as Tarkshur the Lash.

His face lowered in pride and power, a fierce face with a gape-jawed mouth over snaggly teeth, with wide-spaced eyes that gazed in contempt upon the world, narrow and cold, with thick black hair carefully oiled and curled over a low brow. His nostrils flared that contempt. He was accustomed to command. And as he spoke to us so his long whiplike tail flicked back and forth over one shoulder or the other, and to the tip of that sinuous tail was strapped six inches of daggered steel.

This stinking little compound with its crumbling mud walls wouldn't hold an agile man for long. But our chains had been fastened to stout wooden posts driven deep into the earth. We were effectively hobbled. Escape was just not on—at least, not for the moment.

When you are slave to a Kataki slavemaster, escape is usually not on—not forever, for most folk. Katakis—they are loathed and detested by those unfortunates who fall into their clutches.

A little Och, a small representative of that race of diffs who usually stand six inches shorter than a Tryfant, was clearly ill. He had been corked. His face screwed up with inward pain, and his thick dun-colored hair was gray rather than black at the tips. His master, the Kataki Tarkshur the

Lash gave the Och a cursory glance and then jerked his tail at the overseer of his small group of retainers.

This man, another Kataki, stepped in and with a single thrust dispatched the little Och.

The body was dragged away.

Tarkshur surveyed us.

"We are going on an expedition where you will earn your keep. Any man who fails will die. There will be much bread and mergem for you, and palines if you—" Katakis rarely smile. They do know how to, for I have seen that phenomenon. He finished, "But then, if you fail you know your reward."

When he had gone we were too tired and dispirited to discuss his words. But Nodgen, a Brokelsh with some spirit left, growled out, "Expedition? By the Resplendent Bridzikelsh! I'd like to have his throat between my fists."

"Aye," said Hunch. "And his tail slicing around to rip out your guts."

"Katakis!" spat the Brokelsh, and he shivered up all his coarse bristle of hair. "I hate 'em!"

Over the next few days animals were brought into the small encampment set up just outside the city walls. The Kataki had flown here with his private retinue of just six mercenaries and was preparing his expedition. His voller had been placed in the city-maintained park, with others, and was to all intents and purposes to us slaves as far off as though it were on the Maiden with the Many Smiles. He had much gold, and he spent it procuring supplies. He came, so the slaves whispered, from Klardimoin, and where away that was no one had the slightest idea.

Hunch and I were given the task of caring for the beasts. There were other encampments outside the city walls and it was clear they all prepared themselves as we were doing. The city, all white walls and rounded domes and shadowed kyros within the blaze of the suns, was Astrashum, and we learned here and there that it was the city from which men ventured into the Humped Land.

When I learned this I instantly thought of Pompino and his dreams of wealth and magic, and much was made clear to me.

It seemed that, willy-nilly, I was to be taken into the mysterious land of Moderdrin, the Land of the Fifth Note. What might befall me there, I thought, could hardly be worse than what was happening now. . . .

Well, illusions beget illusions.

The expedition as a whole was well-planned and the animals and slaves formed a long winding procession as we set off. We slaves had simply been given our orders that morning and off we went without any fanfare. What the great ones had been doing in the matter of eve-of-departure parties was best summed up by the way they kept to their coaches as the long procession wended through the cultivated land to the wastes beyond.

And then I stared.

Each chief member of the expedition moved surrounded by his or her people, so that we formed separate clumps like beads on a string. There, visible as the long lines turned to parallel a river before the last ford, I saw a preysany walking sedately along, with a loaded calsany following, and a little Och walking beside the pack animal. And, flopping about on the preysany's back, a figure in a respectable although shabby dark-blue gown, besprinkled with arcane symbols in silver thread, a figure with a massive lopsided turban garlanded with strings of pearls and diamonds—all of them phoney, I knew—a figure of a man with red Lohvian hair, and with a short sword girded to his plump middle.

"Deb-Lu-Quienyin!" I said, aloud, astonished.

He was a Wizard of Loh who had lost his powers and, fallen on hard times, had journeyed to Jikaida City to recoup both his fortunes and his wizardry. Why should he, of all people, hazard the expedition on which we now entered?

His little Och slave was Ionno the Ladle, walking now on two legs, now on four as he brought his two middle appendages into action to help him keep up. Once I had treated Ochs as fearsome monsters; now they had lessened in frightfulness as other and more hideous monsters of Kregen had been encountered.

And a little Och crone had once ministered to me in the foul clutches of the Phokaym.

"You know him?"

"Aye, Hunch. He is—" I hesitated. I had been about to say he was a Wizard of Loh. But all men share the awe of those famous sorcerers, and so, knowing Deb-Lu-Quienyin was touchy on the subject of his lost powers although carrying it off very well, I said, "He traveled with me to Jikaida City."

"There is that rast Phrutius," said Hunch, nodding to another part of the caravan.

"Aye," I said, looking carefully as we turned again to ford the river. "And there is a bunch of Hamalese—and I am not mistaken." The carriages and wagons and saddle animals splashed across and I saw, quite clearly, the upright form of Prince Nedfar, with his close retinue, crossing over. With him rode Lobur the Dagger and the Prince's daughter, Princess Thefi.

"Sink me!" I burst out. "If I can but get to speak with any of them—"

But the chance was not offered. Katakis are man managers. We slaves were chained close.

The caravan continued and the way became hard and the land thin and attenuated. We still ate well, as Tarkshur had promised. He wanted us fit and strong, and it was easy to surmise that the reasons for that would not make pleasant hearing.

The days and nights passed over, as they must do, and we worked on our chains with bits of rock. But stone takes a long long time to wear away iron, and the Katakis were up to the tricks of chained slaves.

We plodded on and, I own, I was intrigued. The ample food sustained us. There was the opportunity to think of other things than merely the best way to find something to eat. The city of Astrashum, it seemed to me, catered for expeditions out into the Humped Lands. Perhaps the inhabitants knew better than to go themselves? Perhaps some had gone, and never returned?

Gold and magic, was it, awaiting us out here?

In the streaming mingled lights of Antares as we trudged on over that hostile land where the ground cracked in the heat and noisome vapors gushed forth, and in the roseate radiance of the seven moons of Kregen as they passed in procession night by night among the stars, there was opportunity for me to observe the other components of the expedition. I could not call any of them friends, in the real sense, although the old Wizard of Loh and I had warmed, one to the other, in our days in another caravan.

One night I crawled in my chains, carrying them silently,

and hit a Kataki guard over the head, and dumped his unconscious body outside the ring of chain slaves. But that was as far as I reached, for the Jiktar of the retinue, Galid the Krevarr, chose that moment to rumble a deep-throated question in the shadows and then to stroll across, annoyed that the guard had not replied.

With Jiktar Galid came the ominous form of Tarkshur.

Now, I paused. Again and again I ponder—did I do right?

There was a slender chance. I could have dealt with these two, I believe. My chains would rip their throats out before their tail-blades ripped mine. But the noise would be unavoidable, and the others would come running, and other guards would join in. Slave owners band together when slaves break out.

And—those miserable wights with whom I passed the days would all suffer—that was as true as Zim and Genodras rise each morning.

So I melted back into the shadows, and lay among the coffle, and we were all asleep when the commotion began. In the end, because the Katakis found it impossible to believe we cowed slaves could have performed that deed, the mischief was put down to a light-fingered rogue from an adjoining camp, and we escaped punishment.

I breathed easier.

Hunch said, "Would that I had hit the rast. He would not have got up again."

I said nothing. The sentiments he expressed were valiant enough. But he was a Tryfant and the rest of the slaves were cowed to near-imbecility. All, that is, excepting the Brokelsh, Nodgen.

Just supposing I had won free. Would Deb-Lu-Quienyin have helped me? Could he help? There was no point in approaching Phrutius. And the Hamalese—I was just an acquaintance, and, to be honest, they might not even recognize or remember me. And any debt, such as it was, outstanding from Lobur the Dagger was owed to Drax, Gray Mask—dare I own to being one and the same?

The other components of the expedition gradually became known, more or less. A Sorcerer of the Cult of Almuensis traveled in style, and everyone said the milk-white zorcas were enchanted beasts. Certainly, they were fine animals with their well-groomed close-coupled bodies and tall spindly legs.

Each one's single spiral horn gleamed with polish and gold. They were almost as splendid animals as those found on the plains of the Blue Mountains. Whether or not they were real zorcas or animals of illusion no one knew or cared to find out.

This sorcerer traveled in a majestic palanquin borne by garnished krahniks, a swaying structure fabricated from silks of peach and orange and lemon, pastel colors soothing in all ordinary seeming, and yet eerily eye-watering.

His retinue of hired guards contained a dozen stout-bodied Chuliks, indomitable, fierce, inhuman, and their tusks were banded in gold.

These Chuliks were probably real—although they might well be apparitions, like the milk-white zorcas they rode. I wondered what Quienyin would have to say about this Sorcerer of the Cult of Almuensis, and his bodyguard.

There was a flying man from down south by the Shrouded Sea. His expedition was in nowise as magnificent as some of the others, and he and his friends spent most of the day winging freely ahead of the expedition. They proved of great use in spying out the way and of seeking water holes and routes that were the best way to go through the wilderness.

To an observer who was not a slave we must have made a splendid spectacle. The barbaric trappings of the warriors and the colors of the carriages and palanquins, the high-stepping saddle animals, the flying men, the glint and glitter of armor and weapons, the flicker of spoked wheels, the trailing waft of multicolored scarves—all must have presented a blaze of brilliance under the Suns of Scorpio.

Heads thrust forward, choking dry dust from the trample of hooves and the churning of wheels, we slaves in our chains blundered on. There was no high and heady sense of excitement for us.

We passed a night beside a dry gulley and the next day, early, we started on the last stretch across the badlands.

Truth to tell, all that mattered little to me. I was now determined that, with the aid of Nodgen the Brokelsh and, I hoped, of Hunch the Tryfant, I would break free the moment we hit decent water and trees to give us a chance. We'd smash our way out, and to the Ice Floes of Sicce anyone who tried to stop us.

As I had said, making my ludicrous attempt on the airboat, that was the theory.

This was the day when, toiling on and trying to make ourselves believe we could, indeed, see trees ahead through the haze, we became aware of riders pacing our progress.

Men in the long column pointed, and heads craned to look.

Off along the low ridges paralleling our course the riders swung along easily. They rode swarths, those fearsome saddle dinosaurs with four legs and snouting wedge-shaped heads, and their lances all raked into the sky, like skeletal fingers threatening our lives.

Stumbling along in my chains I tried to estimate the numbers of riders. The vakkas lined along in single file, and their looming presence, ominous and brooding, struck a chill into us all.

There must have been upwards of five hundred of them.

Occasional winks of glitter smote back from armor or weapons; but the general impression was one of dark menace, somber and foreboding, biding the time to strike.

Then someone raised a shout: "Trees! There are trees—and a river!" And we all struggled to look eagerly ahead, and when we thought once more to gaze upon those dark lines of swarth-mounted warriors—they had vanished, every one.

"I was a mercenary, once," said Nodgen. "Almost got to be a real paktun, and to wear the silver pakmort at my throat." He shook his bullet-bristle head. "Never did like fighting swarthmen. Big and clumsy; but strong. Knock you over in a twinkling, by Belzid's Belly."

Those long lines of iron riders reminded me in their frieze-like ghostly effect of some of the famous passages from *Ulbereth the Dark Reiver*. Whatever they portended, no one in the caravan could pretend it did not bode ill for us.

"A paktun?" Hunch was interested as we hurried on for the shelter of the trees. "Get into any big battles?"

"Aye, one or two."

To the best of my knowledge, Nodgen had been a cutpurse running with Lop-eared Nath's gang in his quarter of LionardDen. But, then, when a man has upward of two hundred years of life, as Kregans have, he may do many things, many things. . . .

We were drawing near the trees and work lay ahead.

"Go on, then, Nodgen. Tell us!" Hunch was eager.

"Nothing in it—all a lot of yelling and dust and sweating and running—"

"Running? You lost?"

Nodgen's bristles quivered. The Brokelsh are recognized as an uncouth race of diffs, with deplorable manners. He made an unfavorable comment in lurid language concerning the ancestry and level of military intelligence of the general in question.

Then we were in among the first trees and instead of breaking ranks to make camp, Galid the Krevarr strode up with his whip going like a fiddler's elbow, urging us on. We stumbled on through the trees and down a long loamy slope where flowers blossomed most beautifully—although, at the moment, they meant very little to us slaves.

We burst out on the far side of the belt of trees and a most remarkable vista broke upon our eyes. Even the slaves cried out in wonder. On we were urged, down the slope. Before us spread a wide expanse extending as far as we could see under clear skies, with only the merest wisps of cloudlets.

That wide and extensive sunken plain was covered in rounded hills like tells. Hundreds of them reared from the ground as far as the eye could see. Their humps broke upward in serried ranks, in confused patterns, in haphazard clumpings. None was nearer than a dwabur or so to its neighbor. They varied in size, both as to height and extent, but each was crowned with a fantastic jumble of turreted towers, with fairy-tale battlements and spidery spires from which the mingled radiance of Antares struck sparks of fire.

Now every one of us could see why this place was called the Humped Land.

Our expedition hurried on. All this talk of gold lying about waiting to be picked up had given me the impression I would find mine workings, tailings glittering under the suns. But if these were mine workings then they were totally unlike any mine engineering I had seen on two worlds.

Any thought that by this headlong rush we had escaped the riders who had so ominously scouted us vanished as the long lines of swarthmen appeared over on both flanks, trotting out from the trees, pacing us.

Prince Nedfar and his group galloped past, their zorcas splendid, and following them rode a group of men mounted

on swarths. They were led by a fierce, tall, upright man who
lashed his scaly-swarth with vicious strokes of his crop. These
were the purply-green scaled swarths of this part of Kregen.
The jutmen of the caravan made threatening gestures. But
any fool could see we were heavily outnumbered. The caravan struggled on and those dark powerful lines of riders
herded us.

The swarthmen of the caravan returned, evidently attempting to protect the flanks. But no attack was made. In the
period that followed before the suns sank it was made perfectly plain to us that we were being herded, were being
shepherded into a predetermined course between the monu-
mental mounds.

As we passed the nearest pile vegetation and trees growing
on the miniature mountain were clearly visible, with streams
falling in cataracts, and winding paths leading up to the walls
and towers at the summit.

The suns declined. One hump—for to call these impressive
mounds humps does not belittle their awesome character—
one hump, then, lay directly before us, and to this particular
one and no other it was clear the ominous riders were direct-
ing us. When we were within running distance the riders,
with no warning and acting with consummate skill, lanced
their swarths upon us.

Arrows curved against the darkling air. One or two slaves
screamed and fell as the shafts pierced them.

In a straggling, bolting, panicking mob, we fled for the
stone gateway at the foot of the mount.

There were ugly scenes as the carriages jammed trying to
force their way through the stone gateway. But the riders cur-
vetted away, and loosed as they went, Parthian shots that fell
among us. Men screamed. Animals whinnied and neighed
and shrieked. The dust smoked up, glinting in the slanting
rays of the suns.

Tarkshur lashed his zorca alongside us, swearing foully, his
black armor a blot of darkness against the last of the light.

"Wait, wait—let these craven fools press on. There is
time."

He was a damned Kataki; but he was right in this. The
swarths melted back into the creeping shadows. They had
done what was clearly expected of them. Gradually the caravan crowded in through the gate and when we followed on

last we saw the carts and coaches and beasts of burden all crammed into a wide area, bounded by high stone walls, with a dominating gateway at the far end. The gates were closed. The uproar continued.

I looked at Hunch and Nodgen and we three crept into a corner by the outer gate, out of the way of all those dangerous hooves and claws. A number of slaves were not so fortunate—or not so smartly craven—and were trampled to death.

Just what the hell would have happened then nobody could say. Over the inner portals a light bloomed, a pale corpsegreen lych-light. Against it the shape of a woman showed, her hair a halo of translucent silver, her face in shadow. She lifted her arms and a voice, magnified artificially, echoed over the expedition.

"Listen to me, travelers, and be apprised."

The silence dropped as a stone drops down a well.

"Do you all enter here of your own free will?"

No single person took up the shout. A chorus spurted up at once, men and women shrieking in their fear. "Yes! Yes!"

Even as the affirmative uproar went on, I fancied that Prince Nedfar, and Lobur the Dagger, for two, would not be shouting thus.

But the clamor continued.

"Let there be no mistake. You enter here to escape the riders who await you outside with steel and fire. It is of your own free will and on your own ibs. Let it be so written."

"Yes, yes, yes!" the mob shrieked.

"By the Triple Tails of Targ the Untouchable!" Tarkshur lashed his zorca to still the animal. His lowering face filled with fury. "This is a nonsense! It is all a trick!"

The nearest people turned to look at him. They saw his imperious manner, his impatient gestures, they saw all the alive dominance of him in his black armor. He pointed at the open gate through which we had all crowded to safety.

"There is no danger. The swarthriders are gone! Roko," he bellowed at one of his Kataki mercenaries, "ride out and show these cowardly fools."

Obediently the Kataki, Roko, turned his zorca and rode back out through the opening. Now many faces turned in the last of the light to watch. Tarkshur spurred across.

Practically no time passed.

Roko's zorca sprang back through the opening. His head was up and his spiral horn was broken.

Roko sat, clamped into the saddle, his tail wrapped around the zorca's body like a second girth. Through Roko's neck above the gilt rim of his iron corselet a long barbed arrow stuck wickedly. Flaming rags wrapped about the arrow burned up into his predatory Kataki face.

The silver-haired woman's voice keened out, chillingly.

"In fire and steel will you all die outside this Moder."

"Take us in! Take us in!" The screams pitched up into frenzy. Men were beating at the closed far doors.

"Of your own free will?"

I was looking at Tarkshur the Lash. He looked sullen, vicious, crafty. There was no fear there. He shouted with the rest.

"Yes, yes! Of our own free will!"

The shrieking mob clamored to be allowed in—of their own free will. The suns sank, shafting ruby and emerald fires in brilliant dying sparkles against an inscription deeply incised in the rock above the gateway. The woman lowered her arms.

Slowly, the gates opened.

Chapter Ten

Down the Moder

"I, for one," declared Nodgen, spitting, "say I do not enter this place of my own free will."

"Nor me," said Hunch.

We were moving forward with the rabble all jostling and pushing to get through the inner door before the swarthriders roared in to shaft the laggards. It seemed important to me to say aloud that I, too, did not enter here of my own free will.

I said it.

We shuffled along, as always caring for the draught animals and beasts of burden in our care. Beyond the arched gateway stretched a wide area, shadowed with dappled trees and vines, with stone-flagged squares upon the ground, and the hint of stone-built stalls at either side. Here we halted, looking about, seeing yet another gate in the far wall.

We were simply slaves and so at intemperately bellowed orders fruitfully interlarded with that vile word "Grak!" we set about making camp, caring for the animals, preparing food for our masters. These great ones went a way apart and conferred together. There were nine expeditions in the greater expedition, nine supreme great ones to talk, on to the other as they pleased.

Nine is the sacred and magical number on Kregen.

Among the superb establishments of these masterful folk with their remudas of zorcas and totrixes and swarths, their fine coaches, their wagons and strings of pack animals, their multitude of slaves, it amused me greatly that old Deb-Lu-Quienyin with his preysany to ride, his pack calsany and his little Och slave, must be accepted on terms equal to one of the nine principals.

Against the high glitter of the stars the overreaching mass

of the hill lifted above us. The Moder appeared to be moving
against the star-filled night, to lean and be ready to fall upon
us. The slaves did not often look up.

The hushed conference of the nine masters broke up. Tarkshur came strutting back to our camp and bellowed for Galid
the Krevarr, the Jiktar of his five remaining paktuns. At least,
I assumed they were mercenaries, although they might well
be his retainers from his estates in unknown Klardimoin.

What Tarkshur had to say was revealed to the slaves after
we had all eaten. The meal was good—very good.

Then we were paraded for the master.

He came walking down toward us, and the Maiden with
the Many Smiles shone down into the stone-walled area and
illuminated the scene with her fuzzy pinkish light.

He halted before the first in line, a shambling Rapa with a
bent beak. To him, Tarkshur dealt a savage buffet in the
midriff. The slave collapsed, puking. Tarkshur snorted his
contempt and walked on to the next. This was Nodgen. Tarkshur struck him forcefully in the guts, and Nodgen grunted
and reeled, and remained upright.

"Him," said Tarkshur.

Galid and the other Katakis shepherded Nodgen the Brokelsh to one side.

Along the rank Tarkshur went, striking each man. He
chose nine who resisted his blow. Nine slaves, in their tattered old gray slave breechclouts, stood to one side. I was one
of the nine.

"Now get your heads down. Sleep. Rest. In the morning—
we go up!"

And, in the morning—we went up.

Each superior master with his retainers had chosen nine
slaves—excepting the old Wizard of Loh, of course. Up the
stony path we trailed, toiling up as the suns brightened.

Below us the panorama of the Humped Land spread out,
hundreds of Moders rising like boils from the sunken plain.

Each slave was burdened with a piled-up mass of impedi-
menta. I carried an enormous coil of rope, a few picks and
shovels, twisted torches, and a sack of food. Also, around my
shoulders on a leathern strap dangled half a dozen water
bottles. It was a puffing old climb up, I can tell you.

We were venturing into a—place—of gold and magic and
it occurred to me to wonder who would return alive.

Occasionally I caught a glimpse of Deb-Lu-Quienyin struggling on. He used a massive staff to assist him. Also, he had four new slaves and I guessed he had borrowed these from one of the other expeditions and my guess—proved right—was that they came with the compliments of Prince Nedfar.

Much vegetation obscured our view but at last we came out to a cleared area at the top and saw a square-cut gateway leading into the base of the tower-pinnacled building crowning the Moder. The gates were of bronze-bound lenk and they were closed.

It was daylight, with the twin suns shining; yet the light that grew in a niche above the gate shone forth brightly. Against the glow a woman's figure showed—a woman with translucent golden hair. Her voice was deeper, mellower than her sister's who guarded the lower portal.

"You are welcome, travelers. Do you desire ingress?"

The shouts of "aye" deafened.

"Of your own free will?"

"Aye!" and "Aye!"

"Then enter, and fare you well."

The gates opened. We passed through. The moment the last person entered the hall beyond the gates, lit by torches, the gates slammed. Their closing rang a heavy and ominous clang as of prison bars upon our hearing.

I, for one, knew we wouldn't get out as easily as we had entered.

The devil of being a slave, inter alia, is that you just don't know what is going on.

The hall in which we stood was coated thickly with dust. Many footprints showed in the dust—and while most of them pointed toward the double doors at the opposite side, four or five sets angled off to the corners—and without moving from where we stood we could see the dark and rusty stains on the stone floor at the abruptly terminated ends of the footprints.

At the side of the door an inscription was incised.

Useless for me to attempt to render it into an Earthly language. The problem lay in the language itself, a kind of punning play on words. The nine superior masters conferred, and now I could get a closer look at them all. Already I had met four of them. The flying man clashed his wings in frustration, trying to work out the riddle. The Sorcerer of the Cult of Almuensis gave a sarcastic and knowing chuckle, and expounded the riddle in a breath. The other three of the nine I did not know. One was a woman. One was the tall and upright swarth rider I had seen attempting to guard our flanks. The last was an enigma, being swathed in an enveloping cloak of emerald and ruby checks, diamonds of artful color that dazzled the eyes.

"You have the right of it, San Yagno," said Prince Nedfar. At this the sorcerer preened. He looked both ludicrous in his fussy and over-elaborate clothes, and decidedly impressive to those of a superstitious mind. He had powers, that was sooth; what those powers might be I fancied would be tested very soon.

"Speak up, then, and do not keep us waiting," growled Tarkshur.

The sorcerer gathered himself, lifted his amulet of power he kept hung on a golden chain about his neck, and said, "The answer is there is no answer this side of the deepest of Cottmer's Caverns."

His words echoed to silence, and the doors opened of themselves.

We pushed through, the masters first, their retinues next, and we slaves last. For the slaves this order of precedence had suddenly become highly significant.

The next chamber, lighted by torches, contained two doors.

The obvious question was—which?

From our breakfast I had filched a helping of mergem mixed with fat and bread and orange honey, rolled into a doughy ball. Now I took a piece of this from where it snugged between me and my breechclout, rolled it around my fingers for a time, then popped it into my mouth and began to chew. Let the great ones get on with solving their riddles of the right door. That was their business—not mine.

A heated debate went on. In the end they solved whatever puzzle it was and they chose to take the left-hand door.

I didn't say, "You'll be sorry!" in a singsong voice, for I didn't know if they were right or wrong; but it would have been nice to understand a little more of what the hell was going on. We picked up our gear and trailed off through the left-hand doorway.

Shouts warned us, otherwise, we would have fallen.

A steep stairway slanted down. The walls glistened with moisture and mica drops. The stairs were worn. So somebody had chosen the left-hand door and gone down here before. We descended. I began to suspect that the whole hill, the entire structure of the Moder, was honeycombed with a maze of corridors and tunnels and stairways and slopes up or down, a bewildering ants nest of a place.

At the bottom three doors confronted us. I had enjoyed my piece of mergem and felt I might take an interest in whatever the puzzle might be. There was no puzzle. Each door was opened to reveal a long corridor beyond. The three corridors ran parallel.

"The left-hand one again?" said Prince Nedfar.

"I always prefer to stick to the right," said this tall swarth-rider. He was full and fleshy, with a veined face, and his armor was trim and compact, surprising in so worldly a lord. He carried a small arsenal of weapons, in the true Kregan way, and his people were all well-equipped.

"An eminently sensible system," said Nedfar, and from where I was standing in the shuffling, goggling throng of slaves, his easy air of irony struck me as highly refreshing.

The woman said something, and then the man who wanted to go right snapped out, "I shall go alone, then—"

The way he offered no special marks of deference to the prince was immediately explained as the mysterious figure in the red and green checkered cloak spoke up.

"Best not to split up too soon, kov. There is a long way to go yet."

"If the prize is at the end—I shall go," said this kov.

Well, with seventy-five slaves all milling about and shouldering their burdens, I was pushed aside. The retinues of the great ones closed up, further obscuring my view. When it was all sorted out we went traipsing along the center corridor.

There were quite clearly other decisions that were made by the important people up front. We slaves tailed along in a long procession that wound through corridors and crossed chambers and penetrated the shadows, one after the other when the way was narrow, pushing on in a gaggle across the wider spaces. We went through open doorways following the one ahead and so had to make no heart-searching decisions. We halted at times, and then were called on, and so we knew that some one or other of the clever folk up front had solved another puzzle.

A tough-looking Fristle eased up alongside of me as we

passed through a corridor wide enough for two. His cat face showed bruise marks, and he had lost fur beside his ear.

"I hope the master falls down a hole," he said, companionably.

He was not one of Tarkshur's slaves.

"Who is your master?"

"Why, that Fristle-hating Kov Loriman—Kov Loriman the Hunter, they call him. And he hunts anything that moves."

He had to be the armored swarth-rider, and he had to be the Kov Loriman the Hunter against whom I had played Execution Jikaida. A few questions elicited these facts. Loriman was renowned for hunting; it was his craze. He had visited the island of Faol many times—only, not recently. Now he was on this expedition because he had heard rumors of gold and magic and gigantic monsters, and he was anxious to test himself and his swordarm against the most horrific monsters imaginable.

"Well, dom," I said to the Fristle. "You don't have to go far on Kregen to find yourself a horrific monster."

"I agree, dom. But these ones of Moderdrin are special."

We were just passing an open door in the corridor as he spoke, and we both looked into the room beyond.

The charred body of a slave lay in the doorway, headless, and his blood still smoked.

"See?"

Chapter Eleven

Prince Tyfar

Well, I mean—where on two worlds these day can you expect to stroll along and pick up gold just lying about without something getting in the way? And—magic as well?

So there were monsters.

Hunch gave me a queasy look.

Nodgen rumbled that, by Belzid's Belly, he wished he had his spear with him.

Hitching up the coil of rope, which had an infuriating habit of slipping, I said, "I'd as lief have these chains off. They do not make for easy expeditioning."

"Galid the Krevarr has the key."

On we went until our way was halted by a press of slaves crowding back in the center of a wide and shadowed hall. Tall black drapes hung at intervals around the walls, and cressets lit the place fitfully. A monstrous stone idol reared up facing us, bloated, swag-bellied, fiery-eyed, and blocking the way ahead.

Four tables arranged in the form of a cross stood near the center of the hall, and a chain hung suspended from shadows in the roof. Each table was covered with a series of squares, and each square was marked with a symbol. In addition, the squares were colored in diagonals, slanting lines of red, green and black. The slaves formed a jostling circle about the tables as the leaders contemplated the nature of this problem.

"Judging by what has gone before," observed Prince Nedfar, "it would seem that we are to select a combination of these squares, depress them, and then pull the chain."

"Ah, but," said the fellow in the red and green checkered cloak. "If the combination is not the right one—what will pulling the chain bring?"

We slaves shivered at this.

"What do you suggest, Tyr Ungovich?" The woman spoke and I looked at her, able to see her more clearly than before. She wore a long white gown that looked incongruously out of place in these surroundings, and her yellow hair, which fell just short of her shoulders, was confined by a jeweled band. Her feet were clad in slippers. I shook my head at that. Her face—she had a high, clear face with a perfect skin of a dusky rose color, and with a sprinkling of freckles across the bridge of her nose I imagined must cause her acute embarrassment—quite needlessly. The habitual authority she held was delightfully softened by a natural charm. I could still think that, and she a slave owner and me a slave.

At her back stood two Pachaks, clearly twins, and their faces bore the hard, dedicated, no-nonsense looks of hyr-paktuns who have given their honor in the nikobi code of allegiance into good hands. At their throats the golden glitter of the pakzhan proclaimed that they were hyr-paktuns, and conscious of the high dignity within the mercenary fraternity that position conferred upon them.

"My lady?" said this Tyr Ungovich, and he did not lift the hood of his checkered cloak to speak.

"It is to you we owe our safe arrival here," said the flying man. He rustled his wings. "Your guidance has been invaluable, Tyr Ungovich—"

Yagno, the sorcerer, pushed himself forward. "The answer appears a simple progression of symbols—the alphabet reversed, or twinned—"

"Or tripled, or squared, perhaps?" The voice of Ungovich, cold and mocking from his hood, congealed in the dusty air.

Old Deb-Lu-Quienyin stood with the others and said nothing.

"Well, we must get on!" Loriman the Hunter spoke pettishly. "If there is gold here, then it keeps itself to itself. Have a slave pull the chain, anyway—"

"Yes," said Ungovich. "Why not do that?"

The backward movement among the slaves resembled the rustling withdrawal of a wave as it slips back down a shingly beach.

Kov Loriman beckoned. "You—yetch—here."

The slave to whom he pointed was one of his own, as, of course, he would have to be. The fellow shrank back. He was a Gon, and his hair was beginning to bristle out in short white spears. Loriman shouted, and one of his guards, a Rapa, stalked across and hauled the Gon out. The fellow was shaking with terror.

"Haul, slave!" said Loriman in that icy, unimpassioned voice of the man who has ordered slaves about unthinkingly since he could toddle.

Seeing there was nothing for it, the Gon took the chain in both fists. The chain was of bronze and the links were as thick as thumbs, as wide as saucers.

"Haul with a will," said Loriman, and stepped back a pace.

The Gon stretched up. His wire brush bristle of white hair glinted. He hauled.

Instantly, with an eerie shriek, the chain transformed itself into a long bronze shape of horror. Like a python it wrapped folds about the Gon, squeezed.

His eyes popped. He shrieked. And, over the shrieks, the sounds of his rib cage breaking in and crushing all within in a squelching red jelly drove everyone back in the grip of supernatural horror.

"By Sasco!" Loriman fought his panic, overcame it, gave vent to his anger.

The others reacted in their various ways. Watching, I saw this Kyr Ungovich standing, unmoved.

The lady put a laced cloth to her mouth.

Prince Nedfar said, "No more. We read the riddle."

The bronze chain dangling from the shadows became once more a bronze chain. Slaves dragged the crushed corpse into a corner. Another mark was chalked up against this great Kov Loriman the Hunter.

They tried series of patterns, pushing various symbols and trying the chain. They lost more slaves. Not all were crushed by the serpent chain. Some vanished through a trapdoor that opened with a gush of vile smoke. Others charred and then burned as the chain glowed with inner fires.

Every slave prayed that his master would not attempt to read the riddle, and having done so, pick on him to prove him right—or wrong.

A young man, just about to enter the prime of life, standing with Prince Nedfar and Princess Thefi chewed his lower lip. I had taken scant notice of him, foolishly, as I learned. He wore simple armor, and carried as well as a rapier and

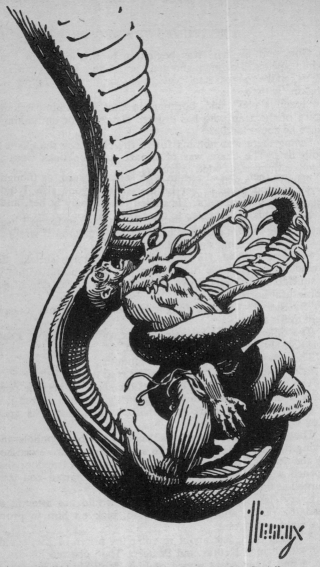

"Like a python it wrapped about the Gon."

main gauche and a thraxter slung around him. Also, and this I did remark, swinging from his belt hung a single-bladed, spike-headed, short-hafted axe. When he moved toward the cross of the four tables, and spoke up, I took notice of him.

His features were regular and pleasing, with dark hair and frank bold eyes which he kept veiled, as I saw, and he moved as it were diffidently, as though always hiding his light.

"Father," he said, "let me try."

Prince Nedfar gestured to the four tables.

"The riddle is yours, my son."

Princess Thefi looked at him with some concern, as though she understood more of her brother than anyone else. I did not think they were twins. He smiled reassuringly at her, and moved with his hesitant step to the tables, and looked down.

He spoke up as though he had pondered what he would say during the preceding tragedies.

"There are lines of red, green and black. No one has marked them before. The symbols have taken all attention." He looked up and gestured to the walls. "See the long black drapes, separated? Then, I think, this is the answer." And he stabbed his hand down a long row of the black squares.

"Perhaps—" said the sorcerer, almost sneering.

The others waited. Prince Nedfar motioned to a slave and this wight moved reluctantly forward. He shook uncontrollably.

"Wait!" The Young prince stepped toward the chain. Before anyone could stop him he seized the links in his two fists, reached up and hauled down with a will.

"No!" Princess Thefi shrieked. "Ty! No!"

She leaped forward, her arms outstretched.

The chain rattled down from the shadows, a mere bronze chain, clinking and clanking into a puddle of bronze links on the stone floor.

And the monstrous idol moved.

Groaning, spitting dust from its edges, it revolved.

Beyond lay a round opening, black as the cloak of Notor Zan.

"By Havil, boy!" said Nedfar. His face expressed anger and anguish. He shook his head as though to clear away phantoms.

Lobur the Dagger leaped forward. He clapped the young

prince—this Ty—on the shoulder in a familiar gesture of friendship.

"Bravo, Ty! Well done! It is a Jikai—prince, my prince, a veritable Jikai!"

The shouts broke out then, of acclamation and, from us slaves, of heartfelt relief. Very soon we picked up our bundles and burdens and followed the great ones into the tunnel with flaring torches to light our going.

When the tunnel opened out into a proper stone corridor once more and we faced five doors, each of a different size, and so halted to tackle the next problem, I made it my business to edge alongside one of the slaves I knew to be the property of the Hamalese.

This slave was a Khibil, and his proud foxy face was woefully fallen away from its normal expression of hauteur, such as I was used to seeing on Pompino's face. I struck up the aimless kind of conversation that seemed fitting to these surroundings, and at my more pointed questions the Khibil grew a little more animated.

"The young prince? Prince Tyfar? Aye, he is a fair one, hard but fair. He don't have us striped unless the crime was very bad. And he stops unjust punishments, for fun, like—you know."

I nodded. Indeed, I did know. But this Hamalese Prince Tyfar was not all sweetness and light. Oh, no! He was, I was told, regarded as a bit of a ninny and, because of that, the slaves whispered, was the black sheep of the prince's family. He liked to take himself off and disappear—and not adventuring, either, as a prince should. He was often dragged out of libraries, as a youngster, kicking and screaming, and forced to go to the practice arenas for play at sterner games.

I mentioned the axe.

"Aye," said the Khibil, as the leaders wrangled over which one of the five doors to chance first. They had lost a number of slaves and were growing cautious with their supplies of human trapfodder. "I heard it said—from a big Fristle fifi who was employed by the nursemaids—that in spite of them, Prince Tyfar had himself taught the axe from axe-masters. He is very good, so they say."

I thought, idly, it might be interesting to see how he aquitted himself against an axeman—and I thought of Inch of Ng'groga—by Zair! If Inch and Seg and Balass and Oby and

Korero and some other of my choice comrades were here now! We'd make a fine old rumpus of this pestiferous maze of corridors, though, wouldn't we? And then I realized I had been saying that a lot just lately, if only my friends were here. They were not. I was on my own. And I was slave.

The Khibil told me Prince Tyfar had arrived in Jikaida City in his little single-place voller only a day or so before Prince Nedfar, his father, left on the expedition. "And," went on the Khibil. "Some rasts stole our voller. Yes! Thieved our voller from the roof, right under our noses."

By Krun! But that was good news!

I could guess that Pompino, at least, had hung about waiting for me to show up. Drogo would have fretted to be gone. So, in the end, they had left—and I in the slave chundrog awaiting Execution Jikaida.

Thought of my comrades, many of whom I had not seen for far too long, made me realize that I had numbered Korero the Shield, with an irrational but instinctive grasp upon reality, instead of Turko the Shield. Ah—where was my old Khamster comrade now?

The sobering reflection struck me shrewdly that Turko did not know of the creation of the Emperor's Sword Watch. By Krun! But I could guess what his ironic comment would be!

A movement from up front heralded our onward progress and that one of the five doors had been selected. On we went and, taking the middle door, pressed forward along a wide stone-flagged corridor. One side consisted of firecrystal, that Kregan substance, almost stone, that being fireproof and transparent admits of the light from fires beyond to illuminate the darkest corners of a subterranean world. The light was bright.

The opposite wall was punctuated at regular intervals by the rectangular outlines of doors. Each door we passed was thrown open and cursory glances inside revealed bronze-bound chests broken open, bales ripped apart, costly silks and fabrics scattered about, overturned and shattered amphorae.

Also, among this debris of frantic searches lay the bodies of men. Most were hideously ripped apart, just like the bales. Not all were slaves—I saw a Rapa sprawled with his iron armor crushed in and at his throat the golden glitter of the pakzhan.

"Monsters!" whispered the Khibil. He did not look happy.

But, then, who would in this diabolical maze within the Moder, without armor and arms, chained in slavery?

And then an even more sobering thought trotted up to chill the blood. In here, in the Moder with its denizens of monsters—would even arms and armor be of any use?

Hunch was casting nervous glances about, and shivering. But Nodgen the Brokelsh had no doubts.

"By Belzid's Belly! I wish I had my spear!"

We slaves were all jostling along the corridor, and a sullen-looking Brokelsh humped with a monstrous pile of bundles on his shoulders cursed at Nodgen.

"By Belzid is it, Brokkerim? Well, by Bakkar, you do not know how well off you are! Your Kataki has not lost any of his slaves! This great rast Loriman has lost four of us already."

"Peace, dom," said Nodgen. "We all fly the same fluttrell here."

The Brokelsh swore a resounding curse and struggled on. I was aware that just because men belong to the same race does not mean they are immediately and instinctively comrades in adversity. This is a sad thought.

"Anyway," said Hunch, with a shake of his shoulders. "He is right."

"So far," said Nodgen, and poor Hunch shook again.

And, in that moment, it seemed Hunch's worse fears were to be realized. For Tarkshur the Lash lumbered his ferocious way through the press of slaves, yelling for his idle, layabout bunch of lumops. A lumop, as you know, is an insulting way of calling a fellow a useless oaf. Now we were to prove ourselves for our Kataki master.

The room Tarkshur had elected to enter frowned upon us as we crowded up. His paktuns stood ready with drawn swords. We looked inside.

The other slaves passed along the fire-lit corridor, and the sudden spurts of action ahead were signaled by screams and the clash of weapons.

"You!" said Tarkshur, pointing at a Fristle whose cat-whiskers quivered up in anticipatory fear. "Inside!"

There was no hope in all of Kregen for that Fristle. He had to enter the room. He did so. He went in slowly, his eyes swiveling about, his body hunched over, cringing at the expected horror about to befall him.

He reached the center of the room and stood, unharmed.

Tarkshur was no fool. His baleful eyes surveyed us and saw me. "You—inside!" So, in I went, to stand beside the Fristle. Presently, one by one, we all stood within the chamber.

The walls were draped in red silk. A dais stood at the far end and on the dais lifted a golden chalice. At each side two golden candlesticks lifted their four candles, the flames burning tall and straight, unwaveringly. The air smelled of musk.

"The chalice is of gold," said Galid the Krevarr. "But it will be heavy to carry."

We all knew the Jiktar of Tarkshur's bodyguard was not thinking of the pains of the slaves, but of the speed of the party. But—gold is gold, to the eternal damnation of many a choice spirit.

"The chalice *and* the candlesticks." Tarkshur made no bones about it. "Gold is what we have come for, and gold is what I mean to heave. *Take it!*"

Two slaves, prodded by swords, reluctantly approached the chalice. It possessed a lid carved in the semblance of a trophy of arms, crowned by a helmet of the Podian pattern, plumed and visored, and around the chalice itself glittered scenes of war. The two slaves took each a handle and lifted. The chalice did not move.

"Don't lift it!" screamed Hunch—and the decorated lid rose, lifted of its own accord, and a wisp of blue smoke emerged.

We all staggered back. In a bunch we turned for the door ignoring the massive bellows of command from Tarkshur. The door through which we had walked was gone—all four walls were uniformly clothed in scarlet silk.

"Out, out!" shrieked the slaves.

The blue mist wavered and grew. Sickly, we stared upon the gruesome sight as the smoke thickened into the semblance of a human skeleton. The skeleton was apim and in its bony fists it gripped a sword and shield, all fashioned from the blue smoke. Those blue-smoke bony jaws opened. The thing spoke.

The words were harsh and croaked out like rusty nails drawn from sodden wood. We stood, petrified, and listened. The Kregish words were full of inner meanings; but a doggerel translation will give the flavor of what the ghastly apparition spoke.

One of One and you are done.
One of Two will make you rue.
One of Three your lack you see.
One of Four will give you more.

Tarkshur laughed, suddenly, that grisly laugh of the Kataki that heralds no joy. "Give me more!" he shouted.

Nothing happened.

"But, notor, how?" said Galid.

The Katakis looked about, swishing their tails on which the strapped steel glittered. Tärkshur pushed his helmet up. Then, wise in the way of the men a slave master handles, he swung his ugly face on us. "Well, slaves?"

The answer was quite obvious; but I was in no mood to point the way for this rast Tarkshur to get more. So I said nothing. In the end a grim-faced Fristle, who had beforetimes received surreptitious favors from Galid, put his bundle down and advanced to the dais. He half-turned to face Tarkshur.

"Master—I think—the candlesticks—"

"Of course." Tarkshur swaggered forward. "It is clear."

Hunch took a great risk. He spoke out without being given permission to speak.

"Master—may I speak? More, yes. But—more of what?"

"What?"

Tarkshur was not puzzled. He even, in his good humor, did not lay his lash across Hunch's back. "More gold, you onker."

I said, "I think not. More tricks, or more monsters."

Tarkshur's tail lifted and quivered. He stared at me. Oh, I do not think he bothered to look at my face, even then. Katakis are man-managers and they treat men like objects. "Come you here."

Slowly, I walked across the room and stood before him.

"You will be flogged. Jikaider. You are slave."

"Yes, master."

I could feel the chains dragging on my legs, the weight of the bundle on my shoulders. The air smelled of musk. The slaves at my back were breathing with open mouths, their sounds made a dolorous mewling in the silk-robed room.

Tarkshur gestured to Hunch, Nodgen and the Fristle. They moved up and we four slaves positioned ourselves before the candlesticks.

"Now, slaves, pull the candlesticks. Pull all four together."

Galid the Krevarr and two of the Katakis moved up to supervise our work. Tarkshur stood by me.

"Pull!"

Nodgen, Hunch and the Fristle pulled.

I did not pull.

The screech of metal on metal as the candlesticks raked forward was followed immediately by the bellow of rage from Tarkshur and drowned instantly in the clash of stone and in the shrieks of terror as the floor fell away. We eight plunged into stygian darkness.

Chapter Twelve

The Illusion of a Krozair Longsword

We struck an unseen floor in a tumbled mass. Those damned steel tail-blades of the Katakis could do someone a nasty mischief now and I rolled up into a ball and shielded myself as much as possible with the bundles and the rope.

"Help! Help! Help!" Hunch was crying.

"By the Trip-Tails—" was followed by the scrunching wetness of a hard object squashing into a mouth.

"Belzid—"

We squirmed there in the darkness and sorted ourselves out. Tarkshur was raving. Galid was bellowing to his two men.

The musky smell increased as a tiny warm wind blew about us.

"Where is the slave? Where is he? I'll have his tripes out! I'll fry his eyeballs!" Tarkshur was frothing.

Dragging myself off and feeling ahead at every step, I eased away from the noise. The chains clanked and I cursed.

Then a long narrow slit of light abruptly sprang into existence high in the darkness. It stretched out of sight in one direction, and ended in blackness by my head. The perspective indicated that slot of light stretched a long way down a corridor. The slit widened. The light grew. Presently we saw that bronze shutters were lowering from a wall of fire-crystal. All too soon I was revealed in the light.

The Katakis sprang up and swished their tail-blades, looking at Tarkshur. But only two rose, Galid and another. The remaining Kataki lay where he had fallen and his tail-blade thrust hard through his own throat.

At his side, twisted in death, lay the Fristle. His cat-like head twisted down at an unnatural angle.

Hunch was yelling and trying to run, and falling, and squirming about.

"Silence!" bellowed Tarkshur. He looked at me. He began to walk. He began to strut. He was going to slay me, of a certainty. You can often tell by the way a Kataki holds his tail—just so.

Galid the Krevarr yelled.

"Notor! Look! By Takroti, notor—look!"

We all swiveled.

The opposite wall shone in the light. The opposite wall led into a paradise.

For as far as we could see down the corridor the light reflected back from a profusion of precious objects, of luxuries, of the delights of the senses and of the flesh, a jostling multitude of everything a man might crave and long for. Useless to attempt to catalog that outpouring of sumptuousness. We just stared, open-mouthed.

Tarkshur forgot all about killing me—and that, by Krun, means for any Kataki only the greatest of interests in life had supervened. Katakis love killing. It is an irony and one of their burdens that, being slave masters, to indulge their pastime means to destroy their profits along with the merchandise.

At about the same time we noticed an oddity about that display of wealth and luxury. Although the wall stretched away for as far as we could see, most of it was walled by fire-crystal. There were just eight openings. Eight openings for us eight who had fallen here. And, even as we looked, so fire-crystal shutters slid down over two of the openings, shutting up the display beyond.

A beautiful Fristle fifi surrounded by the richest food and the most ornamental of treasure chests, clearly the lack of the Fristle whose neck was broken, was thus shut up.

I will not speak of what the dead Kataki had lacked, and what was gradually walled off from us. What his comrade had lacked, likewise, I will not speak of—but that opening was clear. With a mad yell of lascivious exhilaration, the Kataki paktun leaped past the fire-crystal. In seconds he had vanished from our sight.

"Stand, Galid!" commanded Tarkshur.

Galid the Krevarr quivered.

"There is plenty of time. We have only to take our fill and

make our way back. The others will assemble the key." Tarkshur swung on us three slaves. "You will not be slain—you
will carry the treasure out—when we are ready."

Hunch and Nodgen stood, shaking. Hunch's fear had gone.
Nodgen was still getting over the smash on the head that had
dizzied him. Two of the openings showed piled up treasure,
and the other things of the good life that would delight an
honest Tryfant or Brokelsh. Tarkshur saw. He sneered.

"Do not think—" he began.

A demoniac scream bounced in vibrating echoes from the
walls. A shape, a shape from nightmare, bounded along the
corridor toward us.

With a leap, we three slaves came to life and dodged out
of the way. Let the two armed men tackle this monster. . . .

It looked like a prickly pear, bristled with brown spines,
with ten tentacular arms slashing about, each tipped with a
poisonous sting. It bounced. It hissed. It gave off a stink like
the sewers on Saturday night.

With a snap Tarkshur hurled his helmet down and closed
his shield across. Galid did likewise. They faced the monster
and they fought. They were both good fighting men. And, at
that, the monster was not so very fierce, not so very frightening, after all. A poor bouncing stinging bristle ball. For a
naked slave, unarmed, the monster might well have spelled
doom. Against two tough and agile Katakis, armed and accoutered, the monster was slashed into a dozen segments in
no time, its tentacular arms splaying out pathetically. From
their tips oozed a yellowish fluid. Neither Kataki saw any
value in that liquid.

One moment Hunch was at my side, trembling, saying, "I
do not like this place at all—I am frightened clear through."
When I turned to answer him, he was gone.

"He has the right idea, our Hunch," said Nodgen.

With that he raced across the corridor and threw himself
into the opening of the fire-crystal wall. Beyond him lay a
Brokelsh paradise. I did not doubt that Hunch was already
well into his Tryfant paradise.

The two Katakis were stepping back from the dismem-
bered monster. The smell became worse as the fluids seeped.

Tarkshur saw that I stood alone.

"Rast! Where are—" Then he realized, and sharply turned
to Galid. "Stay, Jiktar! We carry the treasure *out*!"

"Yes, notor—but—"

I stepped away from the wall. I dropped the bundle from my shoulders and I turned to stare into the opening that would reveal my lack.

"Slave!" Tarkshur was yelling, and I heard his voice from a long distance. He gave his orders to Galid. "Chain the cramph fast so that he cannot escape."

But I looked into the opening, and saw. . . .

No. What I saw really centered on the object that stood just inside the opening. Farther back misty shapes swam out of my vision. Around this precious object lay a rapier and main gauche, a drexer, the cut and thrust sword we had developed in Valka, a short-hafted clansman's axe. Also there lay a folded length of scarlet cloth, of good quality, and a broad and supple lesten hide belt, with a dulled silver buckle. And, in a worn sheath a seaman's knife. Leaning against the side wall stood a tall Lohvian longbow and a quiver of arrows, each one fletched with the feathers of the zim-korf of Valka. There was, also, a jeweled shortsword like those deadly shortswords that are used with such skill by my clansmen in the melee. All these objects surrounded the central object. At this I gazed.

"Slave!" bellowed Galid's voice, from some dimension outside reality. "Hold still, you rast, while I hobble you with your own damned chains."

The object within the opening held all my attention now.

It was one of mine.

It had to be. There was the nick—it had to be!—the tiniest of nicks where I had beaten down Rog Grota, a famous Ghittawrer of Genod, in that old swifter battle on the Eye of the World. And here! It was here!

I felt a hand on my neck, forcing me down, and another hand dragging at my chains.

Slowly I returned to this other dimension from that realm of reality that had for a few heartbeats claimed me. This was the reality, this frightful expedition down into a Moder, with monsters and magic, and a foul Kataki seeking to chain me fast.

And, for the first time in a long long time, I remembered I was Dray Prescot, Lord of Strombor, Krozair of Zy.

I hit Galid. He went flying back and the look on his face

was so expressive of stunned astonishment that I nearly laughed.

"Rast!" shrieked Tarkshur, and his ichor-slimed sword raked for my guts.

The chains lopped his sword down and my left hand gripped onto his tail as the bladed steel sliced for my throat. For a space we glared, eye to eye.

"You will surely die, you rast, you—"

"I have chopped off many a Kataki tail, Tarkshur the Kleesh. Be very sure, yours will not be the last."

He gobbled with fury; he struggled; but he could not move that deadly bladed tail. His shield was clamped between our bodies, trapping his left arm. His right arm was forced out and down as the chains bore remorselessly on his sword.

In his eyes I saw a flickering shadow.

Without thought I swung. We pivoted as though we were that very weathervane I had so recently been, blown hither and yon by every vagrant breeze. Galid just hauled his blow back in time, swinging his thraxter away down the side. I kicked him where it would do the most good, and shifted my grip on Tarkshur, and so wedging his sword down in the coil of chain, got a grip on his neck above the corselet rim.

I choked—only a little, enough to let him know what was happening.

"You are a Kataki," I said. "I have no great love for Katakis. I have met one and one only who had any inkling at all of what humanity means. You are not that one."

His lowering, low-browed, fierce Kataki face was slowly turning a rich plum color. His eyes started out, bulging with fury. He had no fear of me, a mere slave, who had for a moment caught him up with chains. I choked him again and he tried to butt me and I slashed at the bridge of his nose, an upward blow that rocked his head back. He glared up and over my shoulder and a fresh look, an expression of strangled surprise flashed into that ugly face.

I threw him away.

He had not hit the floor before I had leaped after him and to the side.

The damned chains tangled me up and I pitched forward.

There was, for the moment, no danger from the Katakis.

The thing that moaned down upon us breathed a more deadly menace.

White and leprous sheets and folds of some insubstantial gossamer, like swirls of smoke, like sheerest curtains in a breeze, wafted and writhed along the corridor. An aura of blue sparks sizzled and spat. It was forcefully borne in on me that a sword would be worse than useless against this monster.

Tarkshur had not lost his senses. I did not see Galid.

The Kataki slave master flung up his hand. He still gripped his ichor-smeared sword; but he did not use it. On the middle finger of his hand glistened a ring—I had noticed it as a mere foolishness of Kataki vanity—and now, as the writhing leprous-white monster approached, the ring sparked in reply.

Long flashes of blue fire sped from the stone in the ring. The stone glowed with life. The fires met and fought with the blue sparks. Gyrating and twirling in the air, the monster lashed and shrieked and so, gradually, sank fluttering nearer and nearer to the floor. As it sank so its struggles weakened.

Tarkshur was panting, and I saw the way he kept looking at the ring and then at the monster—and never at me. I understood that the power in the ring was being drawn off in proportion to the monster's own strength.

Whatever sorcery was here in play, the power of the stone in the ring proved victorious. The leprous-white monster sank, fluttering weakly, beat at the ground and then slowly dissipated into wisps of vanishing white. A few little glittering stones scattered across the flags were all that remained.

The Kataki wiped his lips with his sword hand, and then looked at me.

"I have saved your life, you ungrateful yetch—and now, for the indignity you have inflicted, I will take it."

"Where is Galid the Krevarr?"

Tarkshur lowered his head and looked about. The Jiktar of his bodyguard was nowhere to be seen.

"You Katakis are a miserable bunch, contemptible cramphs. He is no doubt enjoying himself now at the expense of some poor devil's misery."

"You—" Tarkshur breathed deeply and his flaring nostrils in his damned Kataki face broadened. "I shall enjoy carving you."

The farce had gone on long enough.

"You, Tarkshur, will either go away now with your life, or you will die—here and now. The choice is yours."

He just didn't believe this. I felt—well, it is difficult to say, now, exactly what I felt. Imagine lying in a grave with a granite block on your chest pressing the air from your lungs. Then imagine you have summoned the strength to push the granite block away. You sit up in the grave. You put your hands on the sides. You heave yourself up. And, suddenly, the glory of the suns shines down. Yes, well, that expresses a tithe of the way I felt. . . .

Something in my face must have warned him. Suddenly, he took me seriously.

"You are chained, slave. You will not be quick. I shall surely win."

"Do not try, Kataki."

But, even then, he was not afraid. And, although I do not like Katakis as a rule, there was much to be said for this evil specimen of that degenerate race. He moved across, and his helmet was down and his shield was up and his thraxter pointed.

"What, slave, can you do?" The sword gestured. "Your chains will not take me twice."

I did not answer.

I took up the Krozair longsword into my fists, and I own, I own with pride, my hands trembled as I took up that superb brand. But do not mistake me. It had not been the longsword that had caused me to rise from a long sleep. And, I half think, it was not that I was a Krozair of Zy, and had called my membership of that Mystic and Martial Order to mind that spurred me. Perhaps it was a mingling. Perhaps it was that I had, with surprise, realized that I, Dray Prescot, Lord of Strombor and Krozair of Zy, did have a responsibility to myself, that to deny my nature too long was to stunt my own growth.

So I faced this Tarkshur the Lash and in my fists the Krozair blade gleamed splendidly. I held the sword with that cunning two-handed grip, the fists spaced exactly, so that enormous leverage and tremendous speed are obtained with precision.

Tarkshur sneered.

"That lump of iron! A mere bar! You are a fool!"

"I shall not tell you again, Tarkshur. Why I do not wish to slay you passes my comprehension. But you may take your life, and depart—"

He sprang.

The fight was brief.

It was as though an explosion of released passion broke all along my muscles, driving my fists into the weaving pattern of destruction that finished with a smashed shield, a shattered thraxter, a sliced helmet—and Tarkshur the Kataki running screaming along the corridor, spilling blood as he ran.

I had kept faith with myself. I had not slain him.

The blood was a pure accident. The fellow had tried to fight for just that amount of time too long, and one of the last blows intended to shred the other side of his helmet had cropped an ear.

And, the strange thing was, he kept his tail.

Two things occurred to me.

One was that I was still chained and Galid the Krevarr had the key. But there would be an answer to that. The other was that the Whip-tail would know me again.

How interesting that, as slave, I had not thought to call Katakis by their slang name, Whip-tail!

Aloud, I said, "There is a thing I lack. The key to unlock these chains."

I looked into the opening of the fire-crystal wall. The key was there all right, a clumsy thing of iron. As I retrieved it, it occurred to me to wonder if this was the very same key that Galid had had in his possession, or was it a simulacrum. Was the Krozair longsword that old weapon of mine with which I had gone a-roving as a Krozair over the inner sea? The chains were unlocked and I threw them from me. Whatever the answer might be, the key worked, the longsword was real.

I was alone in the Moder with its magics and its monsters.

Well, by Zair! And didn't that suit me best?

Yes and no, I told myself. There is nothing to equal the fine free feeling of adventuring alone, and there is nothing to equal the sharing of adventures with a gallant company of good friends and doughty blade comrades.

So I took out that length of scarlet cloth and discarding the gray slave breechclout I wrapped the scarlet about me and pulled the end up and tucked it in and secured all with the broad and supple lesten hide belt. I pulled the belt in tightly and the dulled silver buckle snicked home sweetly.

Never having cared much for straps over my chest I secured the weaponry to belts around my waist, different belts each to its own weapon or pair of weapons. Equally, I do recognize the value of shoulder straps from time to time, and will use them when the necessity arises. As, now, I slung the water bottles back on. I will not tolerate dangling ends of scarves and belts and fol-de-rols. A fighting man must be trim. A ravishingly exotic dangling scarf can be grabbed by your enemy to reel you in like a fish, to be gaffed—through the guts.

Of that wonderful Kregan arsenal displayed I selected the rapier and main-gauche. Also I took the drexer, for that sword holds a place of especial affection, seeing that it is a superior refinement on the Havilfarese thraxter and the Vallian clanxer, and with elements of the Savanti sword—those we could contrive—embodied.

As to why there was not a Savanti sword among those articles I lacked—I thought about this, and came to the conclusion that whatever of sorcery and magic ran this Moder, it, he or she did not have the power to set against that of the Savanti nal Aphrasöe. This is not surprising. Those mortal but superhuman men and women of the Swinging City would go through this place as a plough goes through rich loam.

My old seaman's knife went over my right hip. When I handled it I own I gulped. I felt the awe. This was the knife I had first acquired on Kregen, seasons upon seasons ago. Could it be real? Or was it a mere semblance, fool's gold, made of dreams and moonshine?

The clansmen's shortsword I left. The drexer would serve in that weapon's office. There was a Ghittawrer longsword, also, one I had owned when I had been with Gafard, the Sea Zhantil, the King's Striker; this I did not touch. I took the Lohvian longbow and the quiver. Then I looked at the bundle I had carried as a slave, and the remnants of the two monsters slain in this magic-filled corridor.

Now it would be disingenuous of me to suggest that I took the magical properties of the Moder over seriously. In long conversations with the wise men of Valka, and various Wizards of Loh I had known, the uses and abuses of magic had afforded lively debates. Wizards of Loh have real and formidable powers, as I well knew. There are many kinds of sorcerer on Kregen, and I usually steered clear of too close an entanglement with any of them. This place reeked of magic and illusion and it was vital to take everything that happened at face value, as though it were real.

An illusion of a monster biting your head off can kill you as headless as a real one.

At the same time, an illusion is harmless if you understand the nature of the hallucination.

That remained to be discovered in this den of iniquity.

Picking up the bag of food and the coil of rope I set myself, and thought to look into the Tryfant and Brokelsh paradises. I hollered out: "Hunch!" "Nodgen!" a long time. No answers being received, and not caring to enter, decided me.

So, alone, wearing the brave old scarlet, armed with my pretty arsenal of weapons, off I set.

By Zair! But didn't doing just that bring back the hosts of memories!

Those sparkles of glitter left when the leprous-white monster had vanished drew my attention again. Our discussions of magic at home in Esser Rarioch had often dwelled on the phenomenon of power being contained within reciprocal power. I thought of the blue sparks from the stone in Tarkshur's ring. I picked up the scattered stones. Maybe, they would serve.

And that yellow liquid dripping from the poison stings of the bouncing bristle ball. . . .

Lacking a suitable container, I stated that fact, and picked up a handy little vial from within my own opening in the fire-crystal wall. Whatever power was operating here would, I judged, not provide anyone with something they did not lack. But the parameters were wide. So, with a vial of poison ichor as well as the stones, I marched off along the corridor seeking a way out.

As I marched along in the brave old scarlet a refrain of that favorite drinking song of the swods kept going around and around in my skull. "Sogandar the Upright and the Sylvie," that notorious song is called, and the refrain goes, "No idea at all, at all, no idea at all. . . ." And as the swods sing they fairly bust their guts laughing at the incongruous notions their lewd imaginations provide.

Well, the song fitted me, now.

I had no idea what I was getting into, no idea at all, at all, no idea at all . . .

Chapter Thirteen

How an Undead Chulik Kept Vigil

Just as Tarkshur's Kataki expedition had become separated from the main body, so other expeditions had gone their own ways. There were a few monsters I met, prowling about—for loose monsters seemed to prowl about the corridors the deeper we went—and there were two or three lively encounters before I was able to clear them away from the path.

I did not enter any of the rooms which lay invitingly open along the route, for I was attempting to find my way out.

Shouts ahead of me along a corridor fitfully illuminated by torches indicated I had come up with a part, at the least, of the expedition which had entered with me. Perhaps. Perhaps this place was crawling with travelers lost and desperate to find their way out.

A thing shaped like a chavonth stalked ahead. It was moving away from me and seemed unaware of my presence. Its low slung head snouted away from me; but I knew what it looked like well enough. Chavonths are feral six-legged hunting cats, and this one's head would be a mask of ferocious cunning, blazing eyes, and splinter-sharp teeth. Normal chavonths are covered in a hide patterned in fur hexagonals of blue, gray and black. This one looked dusty. . . .

From a side door where he had evidently been looting, for his arms were filled with gold goblets and bracelets and strings of gems, a man sprang out. He was a Rapa. He saw the chavonth even as the big cat leaped.

The Rapa was quick. He evaded the first lithe spring. But his leg was struck by a sweep of the chavonth's front paw.

I blinked.

Instead of that Rapa leg being ripped by sharp talons, the

limb was abruptly coated in dust. Then I saw the horror, as the Rapa screamed shrilly in shocked fear.

His leg was not covered in dust. His leg *was* dust.

He collapsed and the dust-chavonth sprang on him.

Instantly, Rapa, gold, gems, all were mere heaps of dust.

The dust-chavonth heard me then, and swiveled his head, snarling.

He leaped.

The steel with which an honest man defends himself against mortal perils would be unavailing here.

I turned to run, dodging across the corridor in jagged leaps. Dusty padding followed me in bounds.

The image of that Rapa collapsing and turning to dust hung before my eyes. And I saw . . . If memory did not play tricks. . . .

Turning, I swung the Krozair brand up and with a quick prayer slashed at his hate-filled mask.

The cold steel bit.

Instantly, the dust-chavonth shrieked a high shrilling vibration of agony. He changed. The dust vanished. I was facing a real chavonth, and under those hexagons of black, gray and blue his hearts beat savagely.

But a real chavonth, savage and powerful though he might be, is not the same adversary as a dust-chavonth.

The longsword slashed and hacked and the chavonth limped away, yeowling, leaving a trail of blood spots, vanished into the gloom beyond the reach of the torches.

Men shouted down and I shouted back. They came up bearing torches and I saw the twin Pachaks. They looked as fierce as the chavonth.

"You are unharmed, notor?"

"Aye. The beast has gone."

"It was a dust-chavonth—you are lucky—"

"I saw that a poor Rapa it slew and turned to dust lost his life and his gold and gems—but his sword remained true to itself."

"A chance, notor."

They called me notor, Havilfarese for lord, without thought. Truly, I had changed from the beaten and chained slave who had entered here. I did not think anyone would recognize me.

We did not touch the heap of dust as we passed. Somehow,

I did not think it would ward off a dust-chavonth. It might in all probability turn all who touched it to dust.

The lady these twin hyr-paktuns served still wore her white gown. But it was streaked with grime and was torn. Her slippers were gone. She wore a pair of white fur boots. Her rose-red face and her yellow hair looked still out of place here.

"Llahal, notor. You are most welcome—I have not seen you before?"

"Llahal, lady. I am Jak—no, that is sooth." Then I thought to convince them I had come into the Moder with another party. "You are an expedition new to these places?"

"Yes. I am Ariane nal Amklana."

She said Ariane nal Amklana. Amklana was a proud and beautiful city in Hyrklana, and because she used the word "nal" for "of" I knew she was the chief lady of that city.

"Llahal, my lady. Shall we join forces?"

The two Pachaks nodded as she turned to them. They had seen the little affray with the dust chavonth.

"The notor will be a useful addition," said one.

"Useful," agreed his twin.

"Is there anyone else with you?" I said.

"Longweill, a flying man. He is farther up the corridor."

I nodded. So these two had become separated from the others. The lady Ariane looked in nowise afraid, rather, she stared on every new thing with the rapt absorption of a child, delighted at the splendors, terrified by the horrors. I felt I could come to like her, given time.

"We must try to find our way back to the others," she explained to me as we walked on up the corridor. "I am going into no more rooms of horror. I did not come here for gold."

I forebore to ask why she had come. Again the feeling struck me that only the most dire of reasons could have forced her to come at all, given that she must have understood far more of the dangers than ever we slaves had.

Longweill, the flying man, made the pappattu in a spatter of Llahals, and then, together and with a crowd of retainers and slaves, we continued this nightmare journey.

A mere catalog of the monsters we encountered and the dangers we passed would, I feel, weary. Suffice it that as we penetrated farther into the Moder and discovered more of the maze of corridors and rooms and chambers, and riddled riddles, and fought monsters, we battled against the forces of sorcery and of death.

The flying man, Longweill, was a Thief.

He made no bones about it. There are thieves and Thieves. After all, those ruffianly Blue Mountain Boys who owe allegiance to Delia of the Blue Mountains are as bonny a bunch of reivers as you will find on Kregen.

"By Diproo the Nimble-fingered!" he said, as we gazed up at the blank ending of the corridor we had been traversing. "Now how do we get through here?"

As a Thief he was first-class, I daresay. But I had up to now not been impressed by his powers of survival in a place like this. He took good care of his own skin, and his slaves were loaded with loot. Like us all, now he wanted out.

And getting out was far more difficult than getting in.

The sensation was distinctly odd, considering what had gone before, when I was consulted as to our best course.

"If we cannot go straight on, then we must of necessity go up or down."

So we looked for a trapdoor, in floor or ceiling.

When one of the Pachaks, the indomitable twin called Logu Fre-Da, curling his tail-hand high over his head, pointing, indicated a trapdoor in the ceiling we all crowded over.

Logu Fre-Da's twin, Modo Fre-Da, looked up and shook his head. His straw-yellow hair swirled. He lifted his upper left hand and made a gesture of negation.

"We have been trending down, to escape at the bottom of this pestiferous ants nest, have we not, brother?"

"You are right, brother." Logu Fre-Da turned to his lady. "Lady—we must search for another opening."

Longweill pushed through. His wings clashed together and then parted and blew our hair streaming in the downdraught as he flew up to take a closer look at the trapdoor. "No," he called down. "Who is to say there is any way out? This whole business stinks of traps, and I am expert in those. Up is the way out, the way we came in."

"By Papachak the All Powerful," quoth Modo. "He could be right, brother."

"I do not think so, brother."

"Hai, tikshim!" called down the flying man. "Remember your place among us notors."

Now tikshim, which equates with "my man"—only in an

even more condescending and insulting way—is intensely annoying to whomever it is addressed. Logu Fre-Da turned away sharply from under the trapdoor in the ceiling. Modo went with him, and they began to speak in fierce whispers, one to the other.

Longweill, the flying man, pushed the trapdoor up.

He should not have done so—of course.

The jelly-like substance that poured out in a glutinous blob enveloped him. Only his wings protruded through the transparent mass. We saw him. The blob of gluey substance fell to the floor. Longweill was consumed. The blob sucked him into its substance. His wings fell and rustled slackly on the floor.

We all crowded back.

The blob started to roll after us.

Glistening brown and umber streaks writhed within the blob as it rolled, and the oily texture of the mass picked up dust and the scattered detritus of the floor. This rubbish was ingested as the blob rolled, infolding and slipping away, to be left as a trail on the floor where the blob had passed. The blob glistened.

Well, man kept back the darkness and the creatures of darkness with his ally, fire—a chancy and often untrustworthy ally, admitted by all—and the rolling glistening blob looked oily to me.

Snatching a torch from the hand of a faltering Gon I turned and hurled the blazing brand at the rolling glistening blob.

It was oily.

It burned.

Waiting, I wondered what fresh deviltry would spew forth from this monster, as we had seen other monsters rise from their destroyed predecessors.

Smoke, in this den of deviltry, was always a menace. . . .

The smoke from the burning glister-blob rose in a black and pungent cloud. It writhed up, coiling and twisting, and in the brilliance of the flames beneath we stood back, shielding our faces, fearfully watching and waiting for the smoke to assume a more awful form.

In a black flat ribbon the smoke poured toward us, writhing some five feet off the ground. Many of the slaves started to run in deadly earnest. Steel, against insubstantial smoke,

would avail us nothing. About five paces from us—and the
two Pachaks stood with me together with a numim whose
lion-face bore an iron-hearted resolve—the smoke abruptly
switched sideways as though caught by a powerful wind. We
could hear no wind. Yet the smoke thrust a long tongue
against the side of the corridor wall, and split into many
probing fingers, streaming, and so passed it seemed through
the wall and was gone.

Naghan the Doorn, the numim, said, "A grating." He
crossed to the wall and called for torches. In the glow we
looked. The grating was there, right enough, man height and
wide enough for even my broad shoulders; but the bars confined holes no larger than bean shoots. No amount of peering
in the flung light of the torches revealed what lay beyond.

The conference was brief. Picks and sledgehammers were
produced and the slaves went at the grating with a smash.

"Poor Longweill," said the lady Ariane. "He was so hot-
tempered. He would never listen."

"You knew him before?"

"Oh, no. We met when Tyr Ungovich organized the expedition. In Astrashum. Expeditions from all over Havilfar are
constantly arriving and departing." She laughed, more ner-
vously than I liked. "Departing from the city to come here, I
mean."

"Aye."

"And we must find the others. Prince Nedfar has already
two parts of the key." This statement made her pause, and
color stained up into those rosy cheeks. She turned her eyes
on me, gray-green eyes, fathomless. "Notor Jak—do you
have any part of the key?"

"No, my lady. Not a single part."

"Oh!" she said, and bit her lip.

The picks and sledges were smashing away the stone
grating.

It occurred to me to say, "And you, my lady. Do you?"

"Why, no—more's the pity. We must find the nine parts of
the key before we can unlock the door at the exit and so win
free from this terrible place."

"With," I pointed out, "or without what we came for."

She searched my face, seriously, and the tip of her tongue
crept out to lick her lips until she remembered, and instead

of licking her lips, said briskly: "Oh, but I must have what I came for. It is vital."

Still I forebore to question her. That was her business. Mine was getting out of here with a whole skin—as I then thought.

The lion-man, Naghan the Doorn, shouted across, "The way is open, my lady."

"Very good, Naghan. I will follow."

And, at that, what was revealed beyond the smashed-open grating was not particularly promising. But everyone in the Moder, I am sure, felt the desire to push on. To retrace our steps would be failure and would lead to disaster.

Narrow steps led downward, wide enough for one person at a time. The walls and roof were stained with moisture and far far away, echoing with a hollowness of enfolding distance, the sound of dripping water reached up.

The steps were slippery. Men fell, and others fell with them; but there was always one stout fellow to hold and to give the others a chance to pick themselves up each time. So we penetrated down.

"We are going from one zone to another, that is certain," said Modo Fre-Da. He half turned his head to speak to me as I followed him. The two Pachaks and the numim surrounded the lady, and my help was relegated to the rear. That suited me.

"Zone?"

"Aye—" Then there was a slipping at our backs, and we had to brace ourselves to hold the mass of men pressing down.

My thoughtless question was thus forgotten. But, all the same, it was relatively easy to guess what Modo meant by a zone. Other considerations weighed on our minds as we came out onto a graveled floor and cast the light of the torches into a vast and hollow space, filled with the sound of running water, to see what fresh terrors confronted us.

Now there are torches and there are torches on Kregen. If you can get hold of the wood of certain of the trees, and use pitch and wax prepared in certain ways, you may build yourself a torch that is a king among torches, or you may wind up with a piece of burning wood that casts its light no more than half a dozen paces. The wizards and sorcerers have means of creating lights, magical lanterns, you might call them, that cast a mellow radiance for a considerable distance. Yagno would have one of those for sure—I wondered if old Quienyin also had one in his meager belongings.

Our torches were reasonably bright, varying in quality, and shed their lights over some seventeen or eighteen paces. Light-colored objects and movement could be picked out beyond that.

So we saw the glinting shimmering waterfall erratically revealed. We walked closer over the gravel.

The water fell from somewhere out of sight, curving to fall into a stone-faced pool in which a stone island supported a shrine. In the shrine the marble idol leered at us. I, for one, was having nothing whatsoever to do with his ruby eyeballs.

"Spread out," ordered the lady Ariane. "And see what there is to see."

We found ourselves in a cavern rather than a stone-faced corridor or hall. The water ran out an arched opening at the far end bordered by a stone-flagged path. Near a jut of rock that stretched into the stream lay the figure of a man clad in full armor, his arm outstretched. His mailed glove almost touched a small balass box, bound with gold, sitting on the ledge of rock. The water did not touch man or box.

"That box looks interesting," quoth the lady.

"Mayhap, my lady," offered Naghan the numim, "it contains the part of the key to be found in this zone."

"That we will not discover until—"

"Let me," said Logu Fre-Da, and he moved forward. He stretched out his tail-hand.

My attention had been occupied by the dead man. The armor was of the kind favored in Loh, a fashion I knew although not at that time having visited Walfarg in Loh, that mysterious continent of walled gardens and veiled women. The old Empire of Walfarg, that men called the Empire of Loh, had long since crumbled and only traces of a proud past were to be discerned in once-subject nations. This man had traveled far from the west, over the ocean to reach his end here. He was a Chulik, and his savage upthrust tusks were gilded. His skin appeared mummified, a pebbly green in configuration and color. In his left hand he gripped a weapon with a wooden haft some six feet long, and whose head of

blue steel shaped like a holly leaf was by two inches short of
a foot.

That cunning holly-leaf shape, with the nine sharp spikes
each side set alternately forward and backward, and the
lowest pair extended downward into hooks, told me the
weapon was the feared strangdja of Chem.

Logu was a hyr-paktun, a man of immense experience in
warfare and battle. He seized up the balass box in his tail
hand and, even as that tail swished up and threw the box to
his brother, his thraxter was out and just parrying in time the
savage blow from the strangdja.

The dead man came to life the instant the box was moved.

He sprang up, ferocious, his Chulik-yellow face restored to
its natural color, his tusks thrusting aggressively. He simply
charged maniacally straight for Modo, who held the box,
swinging the deadly strangdja in lethal arcs.

A single blow from that holly-leaf-blade might easily sun-
der through the Pachak's shield, a second rip his head clean
off.

"He seeks to slay the man who holds the box!" yelled
Naghan. The lion-man's own halberd slashed at the Chulik as
the Undead passed, and was caught on the strangdja. For a
single instant the two staved weapons clung and clashed, and
then with a supple quarter-staff trick, the halberd was flung
off. Naghan staggered back, raging with anger, to fling himself on again.

"Throw the box!" called Ariane in her clear voice.

The box arched up, and was caught by Logu, who waited
until the Chulik advanced, madly, insensately, and then the
box sailed over to me. I caught it and prepared to use the
Krozair blade one-handed.

Stories of the Undead circulate as freely on Kregen as on
Earth—more freely, seeing that they exist there. They are often called Kaotim, for kao is one of the many words for
death, and they are to be avoided. Whether or not this example could be slain by steel I did not know, although suspect-
ing he might well be, seeing that he had resumed his living
appearance when recalled to life.

"Throw the box, Jak!" called Ariane.

I threw it—to her.

"You rast!" screeched Naghan at me, and fairly flung himself forward. But the Krozair brand flamed before him. The

superb Krozair longsword is not to be bested by a polearm no
matter how redoubtable its reputation or deadly its execution.

So the Chulik Kaotim sought to get past me, aiming a
blow at Ariane, and I chopped him. Could one feel sorry for
slaying a man who was already dead?

When the Kaotim's second leg was chopped he had to fall,
for the Undead had been hopping and fighting on one. He hit
the stone coping to the stream, and struggled to rise, and his
stumps of legs bathed in the water and no blood gushed from
their severed ends.

Finally, Naghan, with a cry of: "In the name of Numi-
Hyrjiv the Golden Splendor!" brought his halberd down. The
Kaotim's Chulik head rolled. No blood splashed. The gilt
tusks shone in the light of the torches. The armored body lay
still.

For a moment there existed a silence in which the roar of
the waterfall sounded thin and distant.

I said, "If the key part is so important, as, indeed it is, it
would not have been entrusted to so feeble a charge." I
turned away. "Whatever is in the box—it will not be the
key."

I do not know who opened the box.

All they found was a coil of hair, and a blue silk ribbon,
and a tiny pearl and silver brooch.

The lady Ariane said, "Put the things back in the box.
Place it back on the ledge from whence it came."

This was done.

We stood back.

The Chulik head rolled. The legs walked. As Osiris was
joined together so that nameless Chulik adventurer resumed
his full stature, legs and head once more attached to his
body. Painfully, he crawled to the stone ledge and stretched
out his hand toward the box—and so once more died.

His yellow skin marbled over and granulated to that
death-green color. He remained, fast locked in the undying
flesh, his ib forever barred from the Ice Floes of Sicce and
the sunny uplands beyond.

Chapter Fourteen

Kov Loriman Mentions the Hunting Sword

The torches threw grotesque arabesques of light and shadow on the ripple-reflecting roof of the tunnel. The stream ran wide and deep at our side. We pressed on along the stone path and we took it in turns to lead, for we encountered many of the more ordinary water monsters of Kregen. Always, the two Pachaks and the numim clustered close to their lady. There were in her retinue other powerful fighting men, and between them and me we kept the way ahead clear.

"Water runs downhill," said a Brukaj, his bulldog face savage as he drew back from slashing a lizard-form back into the water from which it had writhed, hissing. "So, at least we go in the right direction."

"May your Bruk-en-im smile on us, and prove you right," I said. "For, by Makki-Grodno's disgusting diseased tripes! I am much in need of fresh air and the sight of the suns."

After a time in which more scaly horrors were slashed and smashed back into the water, it was my turn to yield the point position. Pressing back to the very water's edge, I scanned the dark, swiftly-running stream as the people passed along.

A soft voice as Ariane passed said: "I think you fight well, Jak. You are a paktun, I think."

"Of a kind, lady." I did not turn my head. The Pachaks and the numim passed along and I stepped back from the edge to bring up the rear.

Light blossomed ahead, glowing orange and lurid through the darkness. I was still in rear as we debouched into a cavern vaster than any we had yet encountered. Here the water ran into a lake that stretched out of sight, beyond the fire-crystal walls streaming their angry orange light, past the weird

"We encountered many of the water-monsters."

structures that broke the surface of the water with promises of diabolism.

"Well, by all the Ibs of the Lily City!" said Ariane. "We will not meddle with *them*!"

Fastened by rusty chains and rusty rings at the stone-faced jetty lay seven ships, sunken, their superstructures alone rising above the waters. They were carved and decorated grotesquely. Many skeletons were chained to the oars. In the clear water hundreds of darting shapes sped dizzyingly. They were not fish. Their jaws gaped with needle-teeth, and their eyes blazed. We drew back from the edge with a shudder.

The gravel expanse began where the stone ended, and then more stone flags started again, some twenty paces farther on.

No one offered to step upon the gravel.

Tarkshur, Strom Phrutius, Kov Loriman and, even, Prince Nedfar, would simply have told a slave to attempt to cross. I looked at the lady Ariane nal Amklana and wondered what she would do.

"Naghan!" She spoke briskly. "Tell some of the slaves to break a piece away from the nearest boat. Throw it on the gravel."

"Quidang, my lady!"*

No slaves fell in the water as a piece of the rotten wood, the gilding peeling, was broken off. It was thrown out onto the gravel. It sank out of sight, slowly but inevitably, and a nauseating stench puffed up in black bubbles around it.

"We cannot cross there, then!"

"And we do not go back—"

"We cannot swim—"

"The boats!"

But each piece of wood we tried sank, for the stuff was heavy as lead, and rotten, and putrid with decay.

"Examine the wall for a secret door," commanded the lady.

As the slaves and retainers complied, she turned to me and bent a quizzical gaze on my harsh features.

"You say you are a paktun of a kind, Jak. And you are Jak, merely Jak and nothing else?"

Now the paktuns had called me notor, lord, without

---

* Quidang—equates with "Very Good, your orders will be carried out at once." Similar to "Aye, aye, sir."   A.B.A.

thought, and no man who is not a slave upon Kregen goes about the world with only one name. Unless he has something to hide. And anyone with an ounce of sense in his skull will invent a suitable name. I would not say I was Jak the Drang, for in Havilfar no less than Hamal, that name would be linked with the Emperor of Vallia. So, without a smile, but as graciously as I could, I said, "If it please you, my lady, I am sometimes called Jak the Sturr."

Now sturr means a fellow who is mostly silent, and a trifle boorish, and, not to put too fine a point upon it, not particularly favored by the gods in handsomeness. I picked the name out of the air, for, by Krun! I was building up a pretty head of boorish anger and resentment at the tricks and traps of this Moder. By Makki-Grodno's leprous left earlobe! Yes!

She laughed, a tinkle of silver in that gloomy torch-lit cavern.

"Then you are misnamed, I declare, by Huvon the Lightning."

I did not smile. Huvon is a popular deity in Hyrklana, and I was not going to pretend to this woman that I came from that island. If she asked where I hailed from. . . .

"And, Jak the Unsturr—where in Kregen are you from?"

"Djanduin, my lady."

"Djanduin! But you are not a Djang!"

"No. But I have my home there. The Djangs and I get along."

"Yes." She wrinkled up her nose, considering. "Yes. I think you and they would—Obdjang and Dwadjang both."

What, I wondered, as shouts rang out along the rocky wall, would she say if I told her I was the King of Djanduin? For a start she would not believe me. And who would blame her?

We walked over the wall and Naghan the Doorn indicated an opening in the wall. I would have preferred to have found a boat and gone gliding down the stream to the outside world. But as no craft were available we were in for another confounded corridor. Anyway, there were probably more waterfalls, and things with jaws that were not fish, and all kinds of blood-sucking leechs and lampreys and Opaz-alone knew what down the river. . . .

The room into which we pressed at the end of the corridor presented us with another puzzle. I let them get on with it.

Whatever it was Ariane had come here for, the scent was growing cold as far as I was concerned. Yet every step we took could bring a horrible death, and therefore this Moder had to be taken seriously, very seriously indeed, by Vox!

The room was some hundred paces wide and broad with a fire-crystal roof from which light poured. We had entered by a square-cut opening which was the right-hand one of three. Across the room towered a throne draped in somber purple. The throne itself was fashioned from gold, and surrounded by a frieze of human skulls. Bones and skulls formed the decorations around the walls. On the throne sat the wizened body of an old woman. She had, we all judged, died of chivrel, that wasting disease that makes of Kregans old folk before their time.

Her robes were magnificent, cloth of gold and silver, studded with gems and laced with gold wire. Her skeletal fingers were smothered in jeweled rings. Her crown blazed.

A series of nine white-marble steps led up to the throne. Each side and tethered by iron links crouched two leems, motionless, their yellow eyes in their fierce wedge-shaped heads fastened upon us. The fangs were exposed.

On the third step up to the throne lay the armored body of a Kataki. He had been a famous warrior, one judged, a slave master, powerful, in his prime. Now he moldered away and he had not been dead for as long as most of the Undead in this fearsome place. The silence hung as an intense weight upon us.

"He is not, I judge, a Kaotim," observed Ariane. She was remarkably composed. "He was an adventurer, who failed the test."

We all nodded solemnly.

On seven tables spread with white linen down the left hand side of the chamber a feast lay spread out. The viands looked succulent, the wines superb. Not one of us was foolish enough to touch a scrap of food or a drop of drink.

Going as near as I felt sensible to the dead Kataki I saw that his face was black and his eye sockets were empty.

A small spindly-legged table to the right of the lowest step contained on its mosaic surface a golden handbell.

The lady Ariane paused before this little table, and looked down. She mused within her own thoughts before she said lightly, "To ring or not to ring?"

"To touch, or not to touch—anything," I said.

"True, Jak the Unsturr."

Mulishly, I said, "It is Jak the Sturr, my lady."

She frowned. "I do not choose to be crossed."

Well, it was a petty matter and not worth arguing about. Not here, where a ghastly death might leap upon us at any moment.

Faintly at first, and then growing steadily louder, the sounds of voices; the shuffle of feet and the clink of weapons sounded at our backs. We looked around as the noises strengthened.

"From the center door," said Naghan. "Best, my lady, we keep out of sight."

Silently, all of us, slaves fearful and retainers not much happier, we crowded behind the seven tables and crouched down. It was a jostle and we were cramped; but the fighting men positioned themselves ready to leap out if the occasion warranted.

The noises spurted into the chamber and then a voice broke out, hard, high and yet lighthearted.

"Thank Havil! There is real light ahead. Courage, my friend."

"Courage?" came a wheezing voice. "It is more a pair of strong legs, like yours, I am in dire need of at this moment."

Out into the light from the central opening stepped Deb-Lu-Quienyin and, with him and leading a small bunch of warriors and slaves, came Prince Tyfar. They stared about, much as we had done when we first entered.

The lady Ariane stood up, and smoothed her white gown.

"Lahal, prince!"

The shock was profound. Ariane laughed mischievously.

I frowned. She had risked an arrow through that pretty head of hers—the warriors with Prince Tyfar lowered their bows reluctantly. The prince smiled and walked forward, his hands outstretched.

"My lady Ariane! Lahal and Lahal. What a pleasant sight in this infernal prison!"

We all stood up from where we had hidden behind the tables and we all felt foolish, I daresay. After a space for mutual greetings, our stories were told. Very similar they were, too. As Ariane and the flying man had been separated, so the Wizard of Loh and the young prince of Hamal had been cut off from the main party by a falling block of stone. Now, together, we studied our present predicament.

Deb-Lu-Quienyin walked across to peer at the dead Kataki, and I observed how these people, like ours, had learned to do nothing foolish until everything that could be worked out had been worked out. He saw me. His face expressed surprise; but no great surprise, no shock. He smiled his old smile.

"Why, Lahal, Jak. How nice to see you again—you have had success, I trust?"

I greeted him in turn and then Ariane broke in to say, "So you two know each other? How nice!"

Prince Tyfar and I made the pappattu, and he gave me a hard look. "A lone adventurer, down here?"

"There are few people with you, prince."

"Yes, true—your party?"

I pointed up, down, and around. "Havil alone knows."

"You are welcome to join our party—"

I looked at him. He was a fine, sprightly, well-set-up young man, and the axe that dangled at his belt looked freshly cleaned. He was a prince of Hamal.

I said, "And you are at liberty to join me."

His eyebrows went up. His right hand dropped betrayingly toward his axe. Then his face creased. He threw his head back. He laughed. "By Krun! You are a jokester—and that is good, down here."

"If you two have finished?" Ariane looked cross. This was man's business and she felt a little left out—or so I judged the situation. "How do we go on?" She motioned to the three doors. "The left-hand one?"

Quienyin sighed. "That will probably take us back again where we do not wish to go. And the way is hard."

In the pause that followed we all heard the noises from the third door. There was about them a familiar ring.

Quienyin nodded. "We have all been working our way through these places and have, by different routes, converged on this chamber. That, I judge, is the rest of the party."

We all agreed and did not shelter behind the tables.

The Wizard of Loh was both right and wrong. When the newcomers walked out into the chamber we saw that they were the people belonging to Kov Lorimer the Hunter. He strode ahead, swinging his sword about, enraged, looking for quarry. He had only two slaves and many of his fighting men carried bundles of loot.

The pappattu was made and he gave me a queasy look for which I did not blame him. After all, I could easily be a monster waiting the opportunity to rend him into pieces. But Quienyin's word sufficed.

"These passages writhe like a boloth's guts," Lorimer said, and his full fleshy face exhibited passion. "When do we get to the real treasure house? By Spikatur Hunting Sword! I need to get my hands on—" He checked himself and then blustered on—"Gold and gems! Aye, by Sasco! That is what I came for and that is what I will have!"

So, I said to myself, this fine fleshy bucko was down the Moder for something other than gold or gems. . . .

While the slaves and retainers wandered about the chamber seeking to read its riddles, I got hold of Quienyin and steered him to the center where we might talk. From our fascinating conversations under the stars as we rested in that caravan in which we traveled to Jikaida City, I knew him to be a pleasant old buffer—for a Wizard of Loh!—who felt the loss of his sorcerous powers most keenly. Yet I had sensed in him a groping for comradeship passing strange in a thaumaturge and not to be simply explained away merely because he had lost his arts of sorcery.

"Spikatur Hunting Sword," he said and puffed out his cheeks. "The kov let slip more—well, little enough is known of that secret order—"

"I heard rumors it was a new religion out of Pandahem—"

"You see? Stories, rumors, nothing known for certain. Whatever the truth, its members are Dedicated to Hunting. That, at least, is sure." He pushed at his turban. "And it is the least—nothing vital is known."

"I am most happy to see you alive and well, San. You seek your powers here—"

The intelligent inquisitiveness he had exhibited over this matter of Kov Loriman's secret allegiances shriveled at my words. He rode the tragedy extremely well, and showed a brave and proud face to the world. He was a Wizard of Loh. Instant obedience from ordinary mortals had been habitual to him. Sucking up, to find no easier way of saying it, from simple men who feared him had been his lot in life. But this loss had changed him greatly. He was troubled. He and I had come to an understanding out there on the Desolate Waste.

"Thank you, Jak. But, I crave your indulgence, do not tell these people I am a Wizard of Loh." His old eyes shifted to peer suspiciously at a massive Chulik, one of Lorimer's bully boys, who prowled past bashing his spear against the floor. "I have told them I am a Magician of the humbler sort, whose tricks are mere sleight of hand. I do not think it would go well if they knew—"

"Rest assured. And so you have a secret. Do not we all?"

"Had I my powers, young man, I Would Read Your Secret!"

He spoke in capital letters, our San Deb-Lu-Quienyin.

He pulled his shortsword around. That betrayed him, if folk knew he was a Wizard of Loh.

"We have descended many levels within the zones. I think we are on the fifth zone now. What I seek lies on the lowest zone of all, the ninth zone. San Orien advised me."

"And is there truly a way out?"

"Yes. If you have the nine parts of the key. They fit together to unlock the outer door. But without the nine parts you will never leave."

"I hear Prince Nedfar has two."

"He had three when we were parted. His son, Prince Tyfar, has one. We must ask that boor Lorimer—"

"Cautious, San, how you speak of him!"

"Aye, young man, You are Indubitably Right."

"And what of this famous sorcerer, San Yagno? Is he real?"

"He has powers. Great powers. But—he is not a Wizard of Loh, by the Seven Arcades, no!"

"And the creature—apim or diff—within the swathing red and green checkered cloak, this Tyr Ungovich?"

Quienyin looked troubled, and scratched up under his massy turban. A wisp of red hair fell; but not all men from Loh have red hair, and not all men with red hair are Wizards of Loh.

"He is an enigma. Without my powers I cannot riddle him."

"He it was, I believe, who arranged your expedition?"

"That is so."

The others were still searching around and finding nothing of use. And—no one had been messily killed, either.

"Now, San, these keys—or parts of the key. How are they recognized?"

He did look surprised now. "How is it that you venture in here and do not know that, Jak?"

I stared at him. "A secret for a secret, San?"

"Ah!"

"I came here with your expedition as a slave. I won free—from that heap of foulness, Tarkshur the Lash—"

The look that passed across the Wizard of Loh's face was not so much unreadable as amazing. I saw compassion there, and sympathy, a lively indignation.

"You are fortunate, my friend, to be alive and whole."

"So now you understand my dilemma. I must pass myself off as one of the notors—"

Now he smiled, a creasing of his face that charmed. He was no fool.

"Oh, but, Jak. On the Desolate Waste, when we played Jikaida with Pompino and Bevon—why, I knew then you were more than a paktun, more than a hyr-paktun—a notor?" He shook his head. "I shall retain a *few* powers."

"Well, for the sweet sake of Opaz—"

"Ah!" Again he smiled. "This dreadful place, to a normal man, is addling your wits, Jak. You are a prince, at the least. But, I will Keep my Own Counsel, as You will Keep Yours. We are, each of us, In the Other's Hands."

"Agreed. If we chance upon Tarkshur—"

"Then we bluff. I observed the slaves, looking at each establishment, all eight of them. Ionno the Ladle is with the main party. I did not recognize you—"

"You would not expect to see a man you knew, as slave, surely? Especially here?"

"Every man may be slave."

Before I could make some mundane acquiescent reply, Loriman walked past, ostentatiously poking at the floor the Chulik had already sounded. "Some of us," said this Loriman the Hunter, "are seeking ways of egress instead of chattering." He walked on and gave us a mean look. He would have said more, but I called across in as cheery a voice as I could muster, "We confer on a plan."

He bridled at my lack of proper respect for his exalted rank of kov, and I heard Quienyin's wheezy chuckle.

"Give us a moment more—kov."

When he had gone on with his useless floor-prodding, the Wizard of Loh said, "You do have a plan?"

"Tell me how you recognize the parts of the key."

"Each zone carries its own notification, its symbol. The three topmost ones are bronze, silver and gold, for they are the petty baubles men struggle for, and kill."

"Yes."

"The next three are named for gems. Diamond, Emerald, Ruby."

"That follows. We are in the Emerald zone now. And the lowest three?"

"Gramarye, Necromancy and—and the ninth I will not, for the moment, say."

"As it pleases you. But—what you seek lies there?"

"Yes."

"Emerald," I said. "Nothing as simple as that emerald and gold crown that poor old lady on the throne wears?"

"It might be her crown." Together, side by side, we walked across and halted before the marble steps. The dead Kataki slumbered; the four leems did not move.

The lady Ariane joined us. "You have something?"

"My lady," said Quienyin in his most bluffly gallant way, a veritable performance for a haughty Wizard of Loh. "My fine friend, Jak here, wonders if the crown . . . ?"

"Maybe. How to reach it? No man is going up those steps. Oh," she said, cross, "if only silly Longweill had not got himself killed!"

Prince Tyfar stomped across, his right fist curled around his axe haft. "There is no way out that I can find!"

He saw the direction of our quizzical looks.

"The queen's crown?"

"There *is* emerald in it . . ."

"And pointed out Quienyin, "bones and skulls, also."

"Well," said Tyfar, "my heart is not in it, but we will have to send someone up there."

The group of retainers and slaves who had clustered to find out what was going on suddenly became, as it were, mere wisps of smoke, vanishing into the far corners to prod and pry industriously at the solid walls.

I said, "If we attach a line to an arrow—"

"Capital!" declared Tyfar. "And I have the very man for us. He is renowned in Ruathytu as a bowman."

At Tyfar's imperious shout a bear of a man lumbered across. He was apim; but massively built and with a shock of dark hair. He wore a leather jerkin, brass-studded, and his bow was a composite reflex bow of some pull. I was quite content to let him shoot, for I judged the range demanded a flatter trajectory weapon—although I fancied Seg would argue that one.

Kov Loriman objected. He stomped up with a Fristle in tow who was holding a composite reflex bow which, although it looked much the same as the one the man from Ruathytu carried, was by its construction and the curves the product of a different philosophy. Both were good, both would do the job. They were just different tools and both equally efficient.

A wrangle ensued as to which bowman would shoot.

I did not—as you might expect—intemperately loose myself. A piece of fine thread had first to be attached to the arrow. This was done—to both shafts. Kov and prince glared at each other.

Ariane tinkled her laugh. "Let me choose—"

"This is touching honor and is not to be settled at a woman's whim," growled Loriman. "Lady."

Tyfar's face went white. But Ariane turned her brilliant eyes upon him. She checked her own words. What she was going to say, what she would have brought to the quarrel, I do not know. I do know that Prince Tyfar was set to knock the boorish kov into Kingdom Come.

Deb-Lu-Quienyin said: "Let us twirl a shaft."

Rumbling, we all agreed this was the answer and the arrow was tossed. It came down cock-feather down, and Kov Loriman, who had chosen that—unusually—smirked.

About to pass some casual comment that it was a pity all the Hamalese crossbowmen were with Prince Nedfar, I checked, almost choking. By Krun! I wasn't supposed to know anything about this expedition!

They gave me an odd look as I choked and I turned the movement into a shake of the head and a sneeze. "This dust," I said. "It gets right up my hooter, by Djan!"

The two bowmen were Professionals, no doubt of that. Loriman's Fristle drew to cheek and let fly. Now maybe it was merely the weight of the line upon the shaft, light as it was, or maybe there really did come a sudden and fierce gust of wind. Whatever caused the phenomenon—the archer missed. The shaft went skittering off a skull, caroming, and struck the ebon wall at the rear of the throne.

A blaze of crimson light devoured the arrow.

When we hauled in the line the end was charred black.

That did not encourage any of us.

Prince Tyfar's champion from Ruathytu shot next and exactly the same thing happened.

Three times each they shot, adjusting their deflection for that unpredictable wind. Six shafts burned.

"By Sasco the Wonder!" stormed Loriman. "I'll have you jikaidered! You hire yourself as a bowman and you cannot shoot as straight as a five-year old coy!"

Prince Tyfar raised his eyebrows at his bear of a man.

"My prince—there is a wind. It cannot be judged."

Loriman swung on me, his thick face flushed. "A fine idea you had!"

I said: "If a sorcerer were here he might well say the wind was an illusion."

"The arrows are blown out of true, ninny!"

Prince Tyfar's gasp was perfectly audible to us all. I ignored both that and Kov Loriman's insult. Anyway, what could he do in the way of insult and indignity to me, who had played him at Execution Jikaida?

"Then if the wind is real," I said, still in an even unimpassioned voice. "There must be holes, funnels, something from which the wind blows."

They all craned their necks to peer up into the shadows fringing the throne.

Loriman was completely unaware of his insulting behavior.

"I do not see any! Lights, you rasts, bring lights!"

Torches were brought and their light smoked up into the shadows of the throne, and a cloud of bats swooped out, redeyed, squeaking, to fly madly away around the walls. We watched them narrowly. But they appeared harmless, and perched themselves upside down on tall crannies of rock.

I said, "And, if I am right, as it seems I am, seeing some force prevents us from toppling the crown down—what happens when we do bring it down?"

"We will meet that when it comes." Prince Tyfar spoke

firmly. "And I am now convinced the part to the key is there."

"In that case," I said, "prince, call up a slinger."

"Of course, Notor Jak. Of course!"

Quickly a slinger was hauled out, a tough-bodied Brokelsh whose coarse body bristle was armored on his left side and mother naked on his right. The line was attached to one of his leaden bullets. He looked at the crown, and shrugged his shoulders, and winked his eyes, and licked his lips.

"Give me room, doms," he said, in that brokelsh way.

He swung and let fly.

The slingshot arched. The wind blew—we all knew that supernatural wind blew. The bullet flew true. He was a good slinger, that uncouth Brokelsh.

The line tightened as the leaden bullet swung about with a clatter against the crown. Prince Tyfar was among the first who took a grip and hauled.

The crown tilted. Sparks of green fire shot from it, irradiating the chamber in an eerie green glow.

"Oh, no!" cried the lady Ariane.

But the crown tilted, toppled, fell.

It crashed down onto the steps, bouncing, shedding shards of green light. It struck the Kataki corpse and rebounded high, spinning, refulgent with a glitter of gold and gems.

When it struck the bottom step a long, wailing moaning began vibrating throughout the chamber.

And the steps revolved, the throne and the drapes and the wizened crone vanished out of our sight and from the revealed black hell hole a horde of ravenous shapes from nightmare leaped full on us.

Chapter Fifteen

Of a Descent Through Monsters

The horrors skittered and hopped and flew upon us. They were hairy, squamous, warty-hided. They ran on four legs or six legs, their tales were scaled and barbed. Their eyes were red or yellow and they blazed maniacally with hate, or were smoldering green and glared with crazed venom. A whole heaping stinking gargoyle menagerie of monsters fell upon us—and not one was larger than a terrestrial cat.

We slashed away at them beating them off, seeing men fall shrieking with long orange fangs fastened through corded throats. The uproar, the stench, the sheer horror of it all beat frenziedly upon us.

Exactly how many different types of monster there were I do not know. Certainly among the hundreds that poured screeching from that hell hole there were at least twenty different sorts. And all of them, every single one, was bent upon our destruction.

The slaves did not last long.

Near naked, unarmored, weaponless, the slaves were stripped of flesh in a twinkling, and it seemed their macabre skeletons still ran, the bony jaws clacking in fear.

I saw Quienyin striking bravely about him with his short-sword, surrounded by a cloud of fluttering horrors. It was a case of wading through clutching scratching teeth and talons to reach him and assist in beating away the mind-congealing host.

"Fliktitors, Jak!" The Wizard of Loh panted as he struck. "That is what they are, Fliktitors."

The drexer in my right fist slashed and hewed. The main gauche carved a bloody path—as the saying is—and yet that was as near as you would come to the truth of the saying.

For the horrors formed a tightly packed host and each blow struck them down so that I did, in truth, carve a way through them.

Prince Tyfar battled with superb fury and cunning, and his axe hissed as it clove through spiny back and leathery wing.

The two Pachaks and the numim closed up around their lady and fought as only Pachaks and numims can fight.

The outpouring of scaled horrors ceased. The warty-hided ones ran on their six legs and were crushed. The hairy ones clawed up with curved talons and were cut down.

But men were cut down also.

When, in the end—in the long bloody end—we had finished the last mewling one, the Brokelsh slinger planting a heavy and uncouth boot upon its black and squirming neck, we stood back, panting, and surveyed the carnage.

No slaves survived.

Kov Loriman was berserk with rage, and went about slashing with his sword at the putrid corpses of the Fliktitors.

The Lady Ariane's white gown shook with her panting, and it was stained and splattered with blood, red and green.

We all felt, we survivors, that we would rest and refresh ourselves before we essayed any further the mystery and terror of this haunted place.

Loud were the voices raised in argument, loud were the quarrels between diff and apim, between men of the same race, between warrior and retainer. But we all knew, every one of us, that we must stick together.

Loriman stalked over to me, livid. "So your idea was a fine idea, ninny! This is what you have brought us to!"

I picked up the tumbled crown. It was ice cold.

"Look in this, kov, and see what there is to be seen."

The leaders crowded around as Loriman snatched the crown and shook it. An oddly shaped piece of bronze tumbled out.

"Ah!" said Tyfar.

"The key!" exclaimed Ariane. "The part from the fifth zone!"

Loriman grunted and picked it up, started to stuff it away under his armor.

I said, "I think, kov, I will take care of that."

"You rast! I am a kov—I shall—"

"You will hand that over, or, kov or no kov, you will . . ."

And then I caught myself. I breathed in deeply and slowly. Vosk-skulled onker of onkers, Dray Prescot! Quienyin stepped forward. The inflection in his voice took our attention.

"Perhaps, as she is so well guarded, the lady Ariane . . . ?"

"I would offer to carry the part of the key," said Prince Tyfar. "But will gladly yield the honor to the lady."

Loriman was outvoted. I looked curiously at Tyfar. A bright, bonny prince, the slaves had said. But a bit of a ninny, also. . . . The axe was pure compensation. He tended to glow a bit around the edges when confronted with women. And he regarded carrying the damned bit of key as some kind of honor. Well, given romantic notions and frames of reference, of course it was. But down here in this Moder with Monsters and Magic were, if you thought about it, fine times for chivalry and honor.

Everyone was glad of the food and rest. A round umbrella-shaped object, translucently white and shining, drifted in through the center door. It was some three feet in diameter and from its center a long thin tendril drooped twelve to fifteen feet, for it was rising and falling, and occasionally flicking about. Quienyin called out, "Don't touch the feeler!"

By this time down here no one touched anything if they hadn't given it all the tests they could think of—which made progress slow. This round umbrella was quick. From that slow drifting floating it exploded into action the instant its dangling tendril touched living organic substance.

That feeler locked around the neck of a Brokelsh who was not quick enough.

We expected, given the horror of this place, that the unfortunate man would be reeled in like a fish at the end of a line. Instead the round translucent horror reeled itself in, swooping down, positioning itself exactly above the man's head. I was irresistibly reminded of the cone of a flick-flick as the translucent circle closed over the man's head. It drew itself in like a hood over his head, tightly, tightly—his staring features were clearly outlined in the translucent material.

"It is a Suffocating Hood!" shouted Quienyin.

"Cut it off!" commanded Ariane.

Loriman lifted his sword.

"You will cut the man, also." Quienyin looked sick.

The Brokelsh was running in crazy circles, as though controlled, and his chest jerked spasmodically. He collapsed quickly enough, suffocated, and we could see the blueness of his face through the translucent material of the Suffocating Hood.

"Has anyone an atra with the symbol for air?" demanded the Wizard of Loh. "Hurry!"

Everyone—except me—began searching desperately through the amulets they wore around their necks or hidden upon their persons. Most folk of Kregen—not all—carry an atra or two to ward off various kinds of evil. A Fristle let out a yell. With remarkable speed, Quienyin had the atra in his hand, with a quick jerk breaking the leather thong around the Fristle's neck. The cat-man jumped. Quienyin started to force the atra up inside the tiniest of wrinkles in the lower edge of the Suffocating Hood as we gripped the shivering, dying Brokelsh. The atra was a simple, clumsily cast chunk of silver in the shape of a nine-sided figure, with the symbols for Fur, Lightning, Air and Milk, engraved on its dull surface.

After what seemed a long time, the Brokelsh breathed again, his blueness seeped away—but the horrific Suffocating Hood remained clamped around his head.

"How do we remove that ghastly thing?" whispered Ariane.

"Why waste time?" demanded Loriman. "He is only a Brokelsh." He strode across, lifting his sword. "Let me—"

"Loriman! Kov!" said Ariane, shocked. "No—"

But the Hunting Kov got the tip of his sword up the same fold were the atra had been forced. Perhaps it was the passage of air, perhaps it was the right thing to do, perhaps it was just luck. He started to twist his sword and cut into the thin material of the Suffocating Hood. He cut, also, the face of the Brokelsh. I did not think that man would mind.

The Hood, suddenly, like an umbrella opened violently against a rainstorm, swelled out, and skimmed away aloft, trailing its tendril. Loriman gave a vicious slash at the dangling line; but missed. I wondered if a sword would cut the line at all.

"Let us push on," growled Loriman.

Fortified wine was pressed on the Brokelsh. He looked shattered. But he was lucky still to be alive. Of course, maybe quiet suffocation would be preferable to what awaited him in the lower zones of this Moder. . . .

Our order of march was reorganized and we plunged with uplifted torches into that black hell hole beyond the throne.

The moment the last mercenary pushed through the whole throne construction revolved. We saw the purple drapes, the throne, the frieze of skulls and bones, the four leems, all turning back to face once more into the chamber. I wondered if a new crown would appear on the dead queen's head.

At my side, his face crimson in the torchlights, Quienyin whispered, "Those leems—had we rung the bell. . . ."

"Probably," I said. And we all hurried on into the darkness.

The way led down. Nitre glittered on the walls, and our lights reflected back from obscene carvings which appeared to writhe and cavort. I observed the way Tyfar, highly embarrassed, kept trying to engage the lady Ariane in animated conversation and her quick bird-like looks of fascination past his glowing face at those highly personal carvings. Well, one day, the youngster would learn about women. . . . We marched on down the long slope and it was at length clear that we must have penetrated down into the next zone within the Moder.

The hall we entered was a single blazing mass of ruby walls.

The walls were studded with rubies.

Some of those hard-bitten paktuns started in at once with their daggers. No lightnings flashed, no thunders rolled, no monsters leaped upon us as the first stone broke free.

The mercenary, he was one of Loriman's powerful Chuliks, reached out with a cupped palm as the ruby popped out from the wall. The deep crimson gem fell onto his palm, fell through his palm, burned a seared black hole through flesh and bone and sinew. The Chulik let out a shout—and, knowing Chuliks, I was not at all surprised that the yell was almost all of anger and outrage and only a trifle of pain.

"The Glowing Stones!" Quienyin pulled an apim back as the next stone bounced free. It struck the floor and exploded in a shower of sparks, red and brilliant even in the massy ruby light of that devilish room.

Very cautiously we looked for the opening, and found a trapdoor in the floor which, when opened by prising blades, revealed a hollow white radiance beneath. Tyfar said, "By

Krun! White is better than red!" And he dropped down, his sword pointed before him.

Yes, well, he was a brave young man. Foolhardy, perhaps.

When we all stood on the floor at the foot of the flight of stairs down—and not before—the floor tilted. Helplessly, we were all tumbled away down a long slippery slope, the reek of thick oil in our nostrils. Down and down we shot, slipping and sliding. Above our heads the white light dwindled and was gone.

The slope down which we skidded gradually eased out and became horizontal, like a chute, and deposited us, jumbled up and swearing, in a confused mass on a normal stone floor. Fire-crystal walls shed a yellow light. We picked ourselves up. Not a drop of oil stained our garments or armor. We looked about.

In the opposite wall stood just two doors, one rounded and one pointed, both shut, and between them leaned an iron-bound skeleton of an anthromorph, grinning and grotesque.

Otherwise, the chamber was bare.

"Which?" said someone, and he spoke for us all.

"I," observed Kov Loriman, "prefer to choose the right."

That was the pointed arched doorway.

For the rest of us that confirmed our decision to choose the round-headed doorway.

Of such petty stuff are great decisions made.

I did not speak aloud; but I said to myself, "Of Roman or Gothic, either will do for me . . ."

The corridor beyond looked perfectly normal. Not one of us believed it was.

But—we were wrong. A simple plain straightforward stone corridor, well-lit, led on for some way within the Moder, gently inclining down. The walls were unremarkable. At length, and with something of a relief, we came to a small chamber into which we could not all press, so perforce a bunch of warriors remained outside.

In the room, within a glass case set upon a silver and balass table, we found an object upon which we gazed with great speculation. It was a key. It was fashioned from silver. It was an ordinary key.

"Not, I think," said Ariane, "one of the parts of the Key—"

"That, lady, is obvious!" snorted Kov Loriman.

"In that case, kov," pointed out Tyfar, "there should be no difficulty for you to smash the glass and take the key. Surely?"

But Loriman was a Hunter and was not to be snared like that.

"Before I tell one of my paktuns to take the key, we will look more thoroughly."

That made sense, and so we searched the chamber.

We found nothing else and Loriman told one of his men to break the glass. The Chulik polished up his tusks with a wetted thumb and started forward, and Tyfar said, "Kov! I mean you no disrespect. We are all in this together and must accept the needle. Let my slinger smash the glass while we wait outside. . . ."

The Chulik paktun—he was a hyr-paktun—turned about at once and marched toward the door. The rest of us followed suit. Only Loriman was left in the room. He gave a disgusted snort and followed us out. Tyfar's Brokelsh slinger went through his ritual of shrugging his shoulders, winking his eyes and licking his lips. He slung.

Barkindrar, his name was, a fine slinger. From Hyrzibar's Finger. Down in the southeast of Havilfar.

The glass vanished in a welter of smashings. It tinkled to the stone floor.

A long rope-like object snapped up from the base of the shattered case and lashed, looping, around the empty space where any man must stand who had smashed the case with a sword. The diamond-backed rope, like a serpent, hissed as it coiled and lashed and, finding nothing there, collapsed limply. It hung down like a disused bell rope.

"By Krun!"

The Chulik who had been given the duty shouldered forward and hooked the key out with his dagger. The golden pakzhan glittered at his throat. The key lifted and he held it on the tip of the dagger, the point through one of the loops in the handle. He held it out to Kov Loriman, his employer.

We all tensed.

Loriman, with a coarse laugh, took from a pouch a wooden box, of a sort men use to carry cham which they chew all day, and the Chulik obediently dropped the key into the box. Loriman snapped the lid shut.

We relaxed. If Loriman had vanished in a puff of smoke

we would have been sorry. He was a powerful force to have with us, and I, for one, would have wished his end to be of a more obviously useful kind.

So we went traipsing on up the corridor and left that room far in the rear. The corridor curved gently to the right, and this, I felt, must please the Hunting Kov.

Ariane and Tyfar were deep in conversation.

Quienyin and I walked side by side.

"We must make a proper camp and rest soon, Jak. I am weary and, I fear, My Limbs are Not what They Were."

"I agree. The lady Ariane bears up wonderfully well."

I told the Wizard of Loh something of what had befallen me in the Moder, and then said, "And the openings offered what men lacked. If we could find a way back there, surely, you would find what you lack—is this not so?"

He shook his head. "All is Not What it Seems. I think you will find the equipment you have will vanish when you leave this place."

"I had the thought myself. But it is real now, and serves. Some of the treasures these avaricious men have collected are real, others are mere fool's gold. And the magical items which the more cunning among us seek share the Same Propensities."

"We are, I suggest, in the Gramarye zone?"

"We may have descended through two zones and be in the Necromantic zone. I learned what San Orien had to tell me; but each Moder is different. Some are abandoned. We know why we are in this one. . . ."

He told me that San Orien, the resident Wizard of Loh in Jikaida City, had advised him as far as he could. The secrets of the Moders were kept as far as possible from the poorer folk, and this explained no doubt the mystery of Nathjairn the Rovard and his slit throat. Other cities to the south also sent expeditions. "On the six upper zones of the Moder are seven hundred and twenty-nine different types of monster." He glanced up at me. "Which, as you will readily perceive, young man, is Nine Times Nine Times Nine."

"Oh, readily."

"The yellow poison you stoppered in your vial must be some form of protection to your skin—the Fliktitors did not scratch or bite you at all—or did you put that down to your superb swordsmanship?"

Deb-Lu-Quienyin had seen me fight Mefto the Kazzur.

I felt suitably chastened.

"And you suggest that the sparkling stones from the Leprous Sheet can be used as Tarkshur used the stone in his ring?"

"One was able to purchase little magics against some of the monsters, but their value is dubious. Yagno did a trade, as did that mysterious Ungovich. Your stones I think would be effective against another Leprous Sheet. Against any of the more Fearsome Monsters Down Here. . . ." He shook his head.

Cure-all magics were a fool's dream, anyone but a fool knew. But men might draw a little comfort from exchanging gold for magic charms.

The corridor branched and branched again and ranked doorways opened on either hand. Here Loriman demonstrated that some of his gold had not been wasted.

The inclination to look into every room we passed had still not been mastered. Quienyin and I were content merely to look; others prodded and pried in the search for treasure and magic. It would not be altogether fruitful and might weary to catalog continuously all the rooms and chambers and monsters and horrors; but Loriman's gold saved him at least twice on this level.

A warrior marched up from the shadows of a room with fluted columns of red and yellow ocher and drapes of purple and gold—very tasteful to those with that taste. The warrior wore purple armor, and carried a purple shield whereon was described a golden zygodont—all fangs and claws and membraneous wings and barbed tail. His sword looked useful, yet that cunning blade, too, was fashioned from purple metal. The visor of his helmet was closed.

Loriman bristled up at once. He swelled. The veins in his nose throbbed.

"Any man who wants a fight can have one! I am a hunter—and I hunt anything that moves!" And with a yell he threw himself into the onguard position ready to smash down onto the warrior in his closed purple armor.

Quienyin shouted, "Kov! Caution! He is no man, he is a monster! A Hollow Carapace!"

Loriman heard, luckily for him, and he jerked back. The purple-accoutered warrior strode on.

"We had best run," said Quienyin, looking about.

"A Hollow Carapace! Like a fighting man!" boomed Loriman, and his voice echoed eerily in the chamber. "Aye! I have somewhat for that monster! The tricky rast!"

From his pouch he drew forth—after snicking his sword away—a narrow box such as stylors use for their pens. From this he took forth a little animal like a pencil with squat wings. At its pointed head, which spiraled sharply, glinted moisture.

Quienyin looked pleased.

"An Acid-Head Gimlet! Charming—"

"I paid gold for this," said Loriman. "If it does not work as I was promised—"

A Chulik—he was a hyr-paktun—abruptly screeched, high in his corded throat, and leaped upon the purple warrior. His sword lifted and blurred. The Hollow Carapace shifted the purple shield to deflect the blow; but the Chulik knew all about shields and swerved his blow away beautifully to hack past the side of the shield and into the purple cuirass beyond. At least, that savage and skilled blow would have hacked into a normal cuirass unless it was of superb quality.

The sword bounced. The Chulik staggered back. "By Hlo-Hli!" he shrieked. His sword was a mere mass of molten metal, dripping, and when he dropped it it shredded away his glove and the flayed skin of his palm beneath.

"Not the shield, kov," cautioned Quienyin as the Hollow Carapace advanced, sword and shield ready.

"I know, I know," snapped Loriman. He lifted the little winged animal, the Acid-Head Gimlet. It was a dart of blue and green and brown, almost like a dragonfly. The moisture at its gimlet-shaped head glittered. Loriman launched it. It flew, its wings buzzing like ripsaws, skimmed across the space between to bury its head in the visored helmet. It rotated.

Three heartbeats—three and a half, at the most—passed before the Hollow Carapace reacted. By then it was too late. From the hole drilled by the gimlet head and bitten by the acid puffed a foul odor. Whatever caused that was invisible and was, I think, not material. For the Hollow Carapace was—hollow.

It collapsed.

It fell in on itself as a vessel exhausted of air collapses under the ambient pressure.

Bits and pieces of the armor bounced on the stone floor. We tensed anew, for we were well-accustomed to the ghastly phenomenon of fresh monsters rising from the remains of the old. The golden zygodont sprang into bestial life from the shield, sprang hissing out to charge full on us. The men fell back.

"The sword!" yelled Quienyin, dancing around beside us.

The purple sword skittered among the detritus of the Hollow Carapace. Fittingly, it was Loriman who dived for the sword, got it into his fist, swung at the golden zygodont. The blade sheared through a foreleg and Loriman swung again and the next stroke half-severed the serpent-neck. The third blow decapitated the zygodont. Everyone breathed out—shakily.

"Now thank all your gods it did not resume its true size!" said Quienyin.

I went across to the Chulik hyr-paktun who was gripping his right wrist, his hand stiffly extended. As I went so the pieces of purple armor puffed into purple smoke and dissipated.

"Drop the sword, kov!"

Loriman dropped it—just in time. He would have lost his hand—at the least.

I took out the stoppered vial of yellow poison from the Bristle Ball and pressed it against that grisly flayed palm. "Hold still, Chulik!"

He went rigid with shock, and then looked down. I took the vial away. The skin of his hand was whole again, yellow and unmarked.

The hyr-paktun stared at me with his dark slit eyes.

"You have my thanks, apim—"

"We all fly the same fluttrell here."

The golden zygodont had disappeared. Dust hung in the air. We pushed on, warily. Many rooms, many chambers, many wonderful things. . . .

And, also, many ghostly apparitions, were-creatures, ghouls from the diseased imaginings of madmen, vampires with red-dripping fangs, specters, wraiths, banshees. . . .

We walked through a long corridor fitfully illuminated by orange torches in the yellow-brown fingers of skeletons ranged against the black walls. The oppressive atmosphere crushed down. We spoke in quiet voices—even Kov Loriman. Tyfar and Ariane walked together.

"I believe we approach something of quality," said Quienyin.

Between each skeleton stood a table carved in the form of an impossible monster. On the tables rested objects of unimaginable use mingled with treasure, arms and armor, food and drink, valuables.

Now Chuliks fear very little on Kregen and their imaginations are limited. One massive warrior, straining his armor, gazed upon an artifact that would keep him in luxury for the rest of his life. It was a single enormous yellow gem, subtly carved into the likeness of a Chulik head. It fascinated him, and, clearly, he felt himself to be the most fortunate of Chuliks to be nearest. He picked it up. I can guess he could not stop himself from picking up that magnificent gem.

He cupped it in his fist and it did not burn, he did not disappear in smoke, he was unharmed.

The skeleton at his side stretched out its empty hand, still gripping the torch in the other, and fastened those bony fingers about the Chulik's wrist.

Men yelled and stumbled away. The torches threw dizzying orange lights and shadows between writhed. The Chulik pulled his hand back sharply. He could not break that skeletal grip.

"Here, Chekumte—" said a compatriot.

"Hurry," said Chekumte. "It grips hard."

The second Chulik brought his sword down in a sweeping cunning blow against the yellowed wrist bones of that skeletal arm. The sword did not shear through. The bones sheared through the sword. The point fell onto the floor with a mocking clang.

"By Hlo-Hli!" yelled Chekumte. "Bring a blade! Strike hard!"

We sheared through four swords before I thought that, in all decency, I should try the Krozair brand.

Quienyin saw my movement as I made to unsheathe the longsword.

He shook his head. "I fear not, Notor Jak. That is a form of the Snatchban. The rope at the cabinet of the silver key was another. I believe they are also found in whip forms, li-

ana forms, tentacle forms. Mortal steel will not cut them. We
do not have the blade that will."

Loriman glared along the corridor. "We must push on."

The Chulik Chekumte struggled against the bony fingers.
The pakmort shone a silver glint at his throat and his pakai
of many rings shook. He was a paktun from Loh. "Do not
leave me, comrades! I am a man, a mortal man!"

He was a Yellow Tusker, almost as lacking in humanity as
a Whip-Tail. Loriman gestured to his Chulik comrade. "Do
what you have to."

"Yes, yes, by Likshu the Treacherous!" cried Chekumte.
He writhed again, his yellow skin sheened with the sweat of
terror. "*Do it*!"

Prince Tyfar drew Ariane away, bending his head to her,
gently.

The Chulik brand slashed down.

Chekumte from Loh staggered back, his severed wrist
spouting Chulik blood.

I thought of Duhrra of the Days. . . .

My vial of yellow poison sealed the wound but did not
restore the hand. Chekumte held his stump aloft. "See,
doms!" he cried. "Now you may call me Chekumte the
Obhanded!"

"No," said his comrade. "Better Chekumte the Sko-
handed."*

The skeleton moved again. It lifted its mottled brown fingers gripping the freshly severed fleshy hand, the thick blood
dripping. Its hideous jaws opened. Blood spattered. The
jagged teeth crunched down. The skeleton's jaws closed with
a snap. The hand vanished—forever.

We shuddered and pressed on down that skeleton-guarded
corridor.

Through apparitions, through fire, through poison, we
battled our way on and we realized we were—we must
be!—approaching a crisis. The horrors multiplied, shrieking
and clawing—and then, suddenly, fell away. In a hushed ex-
pectant silence we passed through an ebon portal. Somber
drapes opened with the fetid odor of death.

A series of dusty anterooms which we treated with the ut-

---

* Ob—one. Sko—left. Mon—right.   —A.B.A.

most caution led us at length into a macabre chamber of considerable extent.

This wide and lofty hall extended about us bathed in yellow light. Quienyin perked up. We had passed through horrors and now although the threat of terrors to come existed here, plainly, we felt we had gained an important objective.

"Ah!" he said, pleased. "We must be in the penultimate hall to what San Orien called the heart and reason for being of the Moders."

The ceiling bulged low in some places, festooned with carvings of a grotesque and repulsive character. Bats swooped about high, and peered down with red eyes. A faint incense stink hung on the air and slicked flat and unpleasant on the tongue. Sounds echoed.

The opening through which we had entered remained in being and did not close on us. Directly ahead at the far end of the hall the wall rose, tiered into many shelves. In each side wall openings almost as high as the ceiling led onto short passageways. Every wall was honeycombed with slots of stone. They jutted into the hall here and there forming oddly angled aisles. Above the main doorway and inscribed deeply into the marble an inscription glittered with gold.

THE HALL OF SPECTERS

"San Orien knew of the Nine Halls surrounding the mausoleum," said Quienyin. He was peering every which way, quivering with attention, seeming to shed years from his age. "This is the Hall of Specters. There is a confusing complex of halls and corridors cradled here. And the whole place is a single vast mausoleum."

Dead bodies lay everywhere.

The walls were honeycombed with the dead.

Mummified as though in life, mere heaps of dusty rag, skeletons, masses of dried corruption, the bodies lay silently upon their biers of stone. Relaxed in the sleep of eternity, the corpses lay in rank on rank, niche on niche, tomb on tomb.

In every direction nothing but corpses.

But—were they dead?

Chapter Sixteen

In the Hall of Specters

Uneasily, we stared about. The lady Ariane said, flatly, that she could not go on any farther. So we made a camp in a corner where two walls joined at not quite a right angle and where the serried ranks of crypts were empty of corpses. It was a case of cold tack until some foraging Chuliks returned with smashed coffins. These burned with an eerie blue light; but on them were cooked up a meal and brewed Kregan tea.

Just then a Specter of Mutual Loathing walked in.

He looked just like a young and lissome youth, naked, long of hair, smooth of skin. He was smiling in friendly fashion.

"Leave him alone!" called the Wizard of Loh.

But one of the Chulik mercenaries—he was not a hyr-paktun—could not resist. With a grunt of contempt and loathing he slashed his thraxter at the smiling youth. Everything down here that was not a known friend was a monster.

The sword struck against the youth's side. He went on smiling that wide zany smile.

The Chulik yelped and went smashing backwards.

"Jak!" shouted Quienyin. "Face the youth and strike yourself!"

For a single heartbeat I did not understand what he meant—and then I saw. I whipped out the drexer and gave myself a resounding blow over the head, swinging the blade fiercely. I felt nothing. But the Specter of Mutual Loathing lost his smile. He staggered back. And purple blood sprouted from a deep wound in his head. With a wailing cry of despair he ran away, ran off, shrieking and shedding spots of purple blood that smoked as they spattered the floor.

"By Huvon!" whispered Ariane.

"A devil's trick!" shouted Loriman.

"You are to be congratulated, Notor Jak," said Tyfar.

I sheathed the unbloodied sword. "Rather, prince, thank Quienyin, here, who saw through the devil's trick."

The Chulik paktun came forward. His kax was deeply marked by the blow he had struck at the Specter of Mutual Loathing.

"By Likshu the Treacherous!" he panted. "I struck only with sufficient force to slice a naked man—had I struck full force . . ." His powerful fingers traced the ugly mark in his cuirass.

"He was but a simple monster," said Quienyin. "He must have prowled down here and lost himself."

"You do not reassure us, Master Quienyin." Tyfar drew his eyebrows down. Then he gave a small gesture with a hand that seemed to imply that what Krun brought, Krun brought. "But we are much dependent on your wisdom."

"There are much worse monsters here?" demanded Ariane.

Tyfar gave Quienyin no time to answer. "If there are," he said firmly, smiling at Ariane, "then we will meet them, aye, and best them, too!"

We set sentries and took turns to sleep. We lords—and I relished in a distant muffled way the irony of being numbered among the notors—each took a watch, acting as Guard-Hiks.*

The Hall of Specters formed one arm of a nine-armed complex of chambers, and each of these halls possessed its own resounding and macabre name. At the center, so Quienyin informed us, lay the mystery of this zone. There, we anticipated, also, we would find the eighth part of the key to get us out of here.

His quota of sleep being short, Quienyin joined me as I stood my watch. We talked quietly. He told me that San Orien's explanation for the existence of the Moders seemed reasonable and to be given a due meed of credulity. Originally the mounds—low then and simple—were used as places of burial. The habit of the living to bury costly treasures with the dead brought the inevitable train of grave-robbers. So the structures grew more complex and the traps more hideous.

---

* Hik. Abbreviation for Hikdar, roughly equivalent to a captain, a company commander . . . Its use here is correct Kregish.   —A.B.A.

The Undead stirred at disturbances. Illusion prevailed, for the Moders were controlled by a people who, although sadly shrunken in numbers in these latter days, retained awesome powers.

"There is more to it than that," I said.

"Assuredly. The Moder-lords—to give them a euphemistic title—discovered much about their own natures as they watched the dying struggles of would-be robbers. They discovered that not only did they enjoy the intellectual stimulation of providing ever more elaborate puzzles and traps, they found also, and to their undisguised joy, that they could feed from fear."

I nodded. "Other people have discovered that—think of the rasts who infest the Jikhorkdun and squeal at the blood in the arena. Or," I added darkly, "think of Kazz-Jikaida. . . ."

"No, no, young man. The Moder-lords feed directly from the psyches of the frightened."

"That is possible?"

His comical turban slipped and he pushed it back; but the gesture was not the usual irritated push. "I Must Confess that many a famous Wizard of Loh shares that dark desire."

He looked not at all proud of that.

He went on after a space in which I let him gather his thoughts: "San Orien believed there was but one Moder-lord to each dark labyrinth, sitting in his battlemented towers on high and giggling and chuckling to himself as he ran the poor demented creatures below."

"They all came here of their own free will."

"You wound sorely, Jak—but it is sooth."

A guard stirred at the other side of the fire and stalked across. The firelight glinted from his armor and weapons. The smoke wafted away and was lost. We kept a sharp eye out for smoke, down here.

"So these rasts up aloft can survey our progress?"

"It would seem so—although I begin to doubt the fact."

"And there's only one of 'em to each Moder?"

"In all probability."

"Well, I just want to get out of here. I have much set to my hand in Kregen. Time wastes."

"There is, also, Much to be Won Down Here."

"As?"

"You know what I seek. The lady Ariane seeks ways to

topple her fat Queen Fahia. Loriman seeks ways to enhance his standing with and the glory of Spikatur Hunting Sword."

"And Tyfar?"

"He adventures with his father—"

"And what does Prince Nedfar seek in this dolorous place?"

"I am not sure. Mayhap it is pure adventure. He is a great Jikaida player, and will respond to any challenge."

"And Yagno, the Sorcerer of the Cult of Almuensis?"

Quienyin smiled and stretched. "It is obvious, that one. He must read his spells from a book, a hyr-lif. They are difficult to master. But they are effective. Yagno seeks ways to enhance his own sorcerous powers."

"Could he learn enough to make himself a Wizard of Loh?"

"No. By the Seven Arcades—no—I hope not!"

"Yet—you—?"

"I but seek to regain what I have lost, not to gain what I never had."

"Illusion and reality."

"Aye."

I found a stoppered jar containing a little wine and we drank companionably together. Quienyin lowered the jar and spoke reflectively. "San Orien says they go in for magical objects down here. Things that, when possessed, confer special powers."

"My jar of yellow poison—"

"Precisely, Jak."

The yellow light filled the close air with radiance and the fire burned with its eerie blue flames. The sentries prowled, alert, and our gazes kept flickering all about this mausoleum, surveying and noting the shadows in the corners, the corpses on their stone shelves.

"And Strom Phrutius," I said. "What of him?"

"Gold and gems, I think. Treasure of the worldly sort."

"Maybe he has more sense than I credited him with."

"There is a well-known spell which will cause an armband to chain the wearer to the will of the giver. When I say well-known I mean in the sense of its existence being well known. The spell itself is arcane and difficult. With its knowledge a man could spell hundreds of armbands and thus ensure the willing and total obedience of all who wore them."

"Tarkshur!" I said. "That's what he's after."

"It is very likely."

"He'll turn up again, at the exit, you'll see." I clenched a fist. "Katakis are devils at survival."

"So will your two friends, Nodgen and Hunch." Quienyin offered me the wine. I shook my head. He went on, "It is Tyr Ungovich who provokes my curiosity. He is indeed an enigma."

"What he wants," I said, guessing, "will likewise be found on the ninth zone." Then, quickly, I said, "You are confident Hunch and Nodgen will reappear? They went right merrily into their paradises."

"Illusion, as the weapons you bear. They will appear."

I touched the Krozair longsword. The metal was warm—and hard and solid to my fingers. I shook my head. Illusion. . . .

"It is a great pity," Quienyin said, "that Longweill the Fluttrhim* was killed. His gifts would have been useful."

"He's down skating about on the Ice Floes of Sicce now," I said. "May Opaz have him in his keeping, poor Thief though he was."

Shortly after that there was a general alarm as a procession of Green-Glowing Ghoul Vampires wandered past and we had a merry set-to. They were amenable to the kiss of steel, and were driven off. Again I noticed the fine free way Prince Tyfar fought, and, foolishly, I thought of Barty Vessler, and sighed.

When all had rested we set off to explore the nooks and crannies of the various halls containing the corpses. Prowling monsters were encountered and dealt with, each to its own peculiar fashion, and we lost a few more men.

If this was the Necromantic zone, as we believed, the key we sought—the part of the key—lay somewhere hidden. Finding it would take us a long time. And, as we explored, so we drew ever nearer the central chamber and the horrors it would most certainly contain.

There would be a dozen or more cassettes to be filled with my record of the things we encountered in that nine-armed complex before we walked along and reached the place where we had camped. So we had come full circle, had found

_____
* Fluttrhim—Flying man

no way in or out, and must most carefully put our heads together to discover a method of forcing ingress to the center and its mystery.

"To the right, as ever," quoth Kov Loriman. "I will smash a way through the wall, by Lem, and then we will get through!"

He seized a corpse by its arm and pulled and the corpse snapped at once into hideous life and leaped for Loriman's throat. The Hunting Kov was not one whit dismayed. His sword whirled, the corpse's head flew off, and one of his Chuliks swept a broad-bladed axe around and chopped the corpse's legs away.

They kicked the bits of mummified remains of the Kaotim aside and bringing up picks and sledgehammers started smashing into the wall.

"One has," observed Tyfar, "to admire their enthusiasm."

Quienyin touched my arm and we drew a little apart.

"Have you noticed, Jak, that while the vast majority of the corpses are apim, like you and me, there are every now and then a few diffs?"

"Yes."

"There is, I think, a Pattern to be Observed."

So, leaving Loriman and his henchmen to go on smashing the wall down, the rest of us started to inspect the arrangements of the Undead.

In the end, and inevitably, it was Quienyin who spotted the significance. He smiled and pushed his turban straight.

Now, I must of necessity spell the words in English but the final result was the same as the original Kregish. The corpses lay in pattern, as Quienyin had indicated, and their order was thus: Gon. Hoboling. Och. Undurker. Lamnia. Och. Rapa. Djang.

Be very sure I looked long and with choked feelings at the Djangs—most of them were Obdjangs, those clever, gerbil-faced people who so efficiently run Djanduin, and whom the ferocious four-armed Dwadjangs respect with reason.

"It seems," said Quienyin, "we are to find what we seek in the Hall of Ghoul. And it will be the ord* something."

We went carefully through the Hall of Vampires and the Hall of Banshees to the Hall of Ghouls. The yellow light

* Ord—eight

showed us the ranked shelves of corpses. We all expected the Kaotim to stir and sit up and then leap upon us, uttering wraith-like wails.

In this Hall of Ghouls, somewhere, there were seven some-things, and the eighth something would give us the answer.

The sense of oppression enclosed us. We were entombed. Surrounding us lay mile upon mile of corridors and secret rooms, prowling monsters, darkness, and light more hideous than darkness.

The feeling that the domed ceiling would fall upon us choked us with primeval terrors we would not admit. The idea of clean fresh air, and the radiance of the suns, and the feel of an ocean breeze—all these things were gone and lost and buried in the grave. The oppression held us in iron bands. The feeling of hollowness, of dusty silence, of the abandonment of years, choked like skeletal fingers at our throats.

"I—I do not like this place," whispered Ariane.

Tyfar took her hand, and held it, and did not speak.

The tough mercenary warriors looked about with uneasy eyes, drawing together, fingering their weapons.

And then a silly Hypnotic Spider as big as a carthorse fell on his thread through a trapdoor.

"Do not look into his eyes!" yelled Quienyin.

One Fristle, shocked, was too late. The cat-man stood, pet-rified, ridged gristle and fur, and the gigantic spider, dripping venom, swung to take the poor fellow's head into its jaws.

Tyfar and I sprang together. His axe whirled. The Krozair longsword bit.

The Giant Hypnotic Spider burst apart like a paper bag filled with water and dropped from a great height. The squelching stink gagged us all. The spidery arms scuttled away, singly, hairs bristling, and the gross body drooped into a flaccid puddle. The Fristle still stood, petrified.

"If that is the best they can do . . ." said Ariane, shaking herself. She laughed, a shrill tinny sound.

They were all laughing. The reaction after the black thoughts of a moment ago shuddered through them. But the Fristle still stood, unmoving.

"Here," said Deb-Lu-Quienyin. He shuffled up to stand be-fore the Fristle. He did not touch him. "Jak," he said in his casual conversational voice. "Just Take a Look up through the trapdoor. There May Be More Up There. . . ."

If I were a man who laughed easily, I would have laughed then. Obediently, I climbed up a pyramid of men and stuck a torch through the opening. The trapdoor hung down. A fetid odor broke about my head and I spat. The space beyond looked empty, full of ghosts and bones and stink.

"It appears clear, although—"

"Quite!"

Now we took greater cognizance of the configuration of the roof. The dome was broken here and there by bulging cornices, grotesquely carved. From one of these the spider had dropped, and the height, reachable by my pyramid of men, was not too great. We began to study the other bulging protuberances in the roof. The decorations particularly intrigued Prince Tyfar.

"As Hanitcha the Harrower is my witness! I do not discern any pattern! What do you see, Notor Jak?"

Before I answered I killed my automatic wince at his use of the name Hanitcha the Harrower. Ah, Hamal, Hamal, that empire had done great damage to my beloved Vallia!

"If there is a pattern, prince, we must find it."

"True, by Krun!"

"And," said his Brokelsh slinger, Barkindrar the Bullet. "My prince—beware, in the name of Kaerlan the Merciful! There may be more giant spiders. . . ."

We all hopped back a few paces out from under the direct drop-zone in case there might be more Giant Hypnotic Spiders.

"Catch him!" suddenly shouted Quienyin's voice, and we whirled to see the Fristle who had been petrified running, head down, racing madly and with demoniac screams, racing away down past the ranked biers of corpses.

"By Krun!" exclaimed Tyfar. "It's enough to give a fellow a bad heart!"

A group of the mercenaries chased after him and brought him back, calmed him down. He still shook like the leaves of the letha tree. What he had seen in the eyes of the spider no one cared to inquire.

"And have you riddled the riddle yet?" demanded Quienyin.

"No." Arian was short with the old Wizard of Loh.

"Well, we must see what an Old Fellow Can Do."

"Your permission, my prince," said Barkindrar. "There are nine bulges—whatever you call 'em."

The great apim bear of a man, the renowned archer from Ruathytu, craned his thick neck back, stared up. "And only one, my prince, has dropped a stinking spider, by Kuerden the Merciless!"

Quienyin smiled. "You are well served, prince."

"Yes, yes," exclaimed Ariane. "But which way do we count?"

I said, "Widdershins would seem appropriate in this place."

We all moved to the bulge to the left of the one from which the spider had dropped, and stared up, at a loss.

"This is becoming impossible!" Ariane tapped her fur boot against the floor impatiently. "Are all you famous jikais fools?"

"I do not pretend to be a jikai, lady," said Quienyin. He spoke quite mildly; but I, at least, caught the undercurrent in his patient voice. And, I knew, his patience was forced on him by the loss of his powers as a Wizard of Loh. I glanced across at the lady Ariane nal Amklana. She was not wearing well, of a sudden, and I could not find it in my heart to fault her for that.

She was a girl on her own with us. She had left her four handmaids and their bodyguards with the main party. No doubt she missed their loving ministration. Her rosy face stared up, deeply flushed, and her bright yellow hair tangled in disarray, uncombed, with bits of dust and detritus still matting the fine strands. Her dress was in a woeful state.

Yes, I felt sorry for her, the lady of Amklana.

As yet I had not learned her rank; but I felt absolutely certain she was a kovneva. Nothing less would explain her manner and carriage. And, she had been gracious to me.

"It seems to me" I said, and I spoke deliberately loudly, "if these Moder-lords want their fun out of us they won't have much more if we cannot get on."

This was not strictly true. But my words made no difference. Nothing happened as a result of them, unlike the occurrences in that fire-crystal-lit corridor where I had fought Tarkshur and had summoned the key to unlock my chains. Different orders of illusion were clearly operative in the Moder. And I wondered just how the damned Moder-lord watched us—as a Wizard of Loh might do, by going into lupu and observing events at a distance?

Logu Fre-Da and his twin, Modo Fre-Da, were casting worried looks at their lady. The big numim, Naghan the Doorn, was looking at the two hyr-paktuns, and his mane indicated his own concern.

The twins, I had observed with some pleasure, each had the same number of trophy rings from defeated paktuns dangling on their pakais. When a paktun defeats another noted mercenary he takes the ring with which either the pakmort or the pakzhan is affixed to the silken cords at the throat. I had once been betrayed by just such a dangling pakai. But I saw the twins fingering their pakais and I realized they were reassuring themselves, seeking sustenance from their own prowess, the pakais giving them fresh confidence in their nikobi. I have a great deal of time for Pachaks, and these two, it seemed to me, were fine representatives of their fine race.

The intriguing thought occurred to me to wonder how much swag they had concealed about their persons.

An acrimonious discussion began—at least, it was acrimonious from the lady Ariane, although Quienyien and Tyfar remained exquisitely polite. We seemed to have reached a dead end, an impasse, and no one could with any equanimity contemplate going back the way we had come.

For lack of anything better we tramped off around the Nine Halls again, passing Loriman and his men still hard at work. We encountered a few prowling monsters, and lost a Rapa, and so returned to the Hall of Ghouls and stared up at the roof once more.

The answer to the riddle was either so complicated we could not solve it—and with Quienyin with us, despite that he had lost his sorcerous powers, I did not think that likely—or was of an imbecilic simplicity.

Many folk on Kregen are fond of calling me an onker, a get onker, a prince of fools. . . .

"Make me a pyramid of men again," I said and, I own, my voice rasped out as the Emperor of Vallia's voice rasped—or the First Lieutenant of a seventy-four.

At the top of the pyramid I lifted the Krozair longsword and I smote against the roof, savage blows, eight of them, eight intemperate smashes against the prominent knob of polished jet over my head.

The echoes of those vicious blows rang and rattled away along the stone biers.

And the corpses all rose up.

Every corpse rose, and from those ghastly mouths a shrill and ghoulish screaming shattered against our nerves. Every corpse rose up, screaming, and rushed away, ran blindly from the Hall of Ghouls.

They poured in a blasphemous rout through the two side openings to the Hall. We were all gathered in the inner end of the arm, that between the two side passages and the center of the mausoleum complex.

The floor moved.

The floor revolved.

The ends of the side passages and the anteroom at our backs slid swiftly sideways—going Widdershins!—and the floor on which we stood, petrified, turned and carried us around to face into the mysterious heart of the mausoleum.

A few of the mercenaries at last broke. They were not pak-tuns. With shrieks of fear they raced madly for the narrowing slot of yellow light, leaping off the revolving floor, screaming, tearing desperately away, rushing madly anywhere to escape the horrors of this place.

We who were left revolved with the Hall of Ghouls, swinging in to face whatever it was that had caused the Undead to rise in panic and flee.

Chapter Seventeen

Out from the Jaws of Death

We never again saw one of those mercenaries who had fled—not one, ever.

What we expected to see, Opaz alone knows. I do not.

What we did see was a solid wall of darkness. The floor revolved one hundred and eighty degrees, and halted with a shuddering lurch, as though we were suspended by chains over a fathomless gulf. The blackness smote our eyes. The yellow light within the Hall of Ghouls continued; but it remained thin and pale. The stone slabs lay empty of corpses. The detritus on the floor crackled underfoot as we moved. Cautiously, we advanced toward that ebon wall, and it resisted, and we could make no impression on its immaterial substance.

The tall rows of empty biers frowned down. The light smoked somber upon us, and the silence stunned us.

Quienyin said, "The walls. The stone slabs, I think—"

"You are right, Master Quienyin!" Tyfar rushed to the nearest wall and put his foot against the bottom slab. With a slow remorseless pressure his foot was pushed along the floor.

"The walls!" shrieked Ariane. "They are closing in upon us!"

Steadily, with small screeching sounds as of trapped animals, the walls closed one upon the other. The wall of blackness ahead narrowed.

Now we could see that there was a finger-wide gap between wall and floor. And then the full diabolical nature of these stone jaws was borne in on us.

"The stone slabs!" shouted Ariane, and she tore her hair wildly, staggering. "See—they are not opposite!"

It was true. The stone slabs in one wall were set at a

higher level than in the opposite wall. When they met the stone juttings would pass between one another. Useless to jump up and cower in a stone slot so recently vacated by a corpse. The opposite stone slab would crush into that slot and. . . .

We looked about frenziedly for a way out.

"These are the Kaochun," Quienyin informed us, although few of us were in a condition to appreciate the knowledge. "The Jaws of Death."

These Kaochun, these Death Jaws, were going to squash us flatter than an ant under a bootheel if we did not quickly discover the answer. I saw the rock chippings fallen from the stones.

Without shouting, trusting to the others to see what I was up to and follow my lead, I picked up and discarded the chunks until I found a solid wedge-shaped piece. This I pushed point first under that finger-wide slot between wall and floor. I kicked it in savagely. The two hyr-paktun twins were the first to see and copy. Soon we were all ramming wedges under the walls as hard as we could. Some ground to powder, others slipped. But some held.

The chittering noise as of trapped animals faltered, and strengthened as wedges crumbled, and then dwindled again as we went ruthlessly along ramming wedges in as fast and as hard as we could.

The walls shuddered. A thin high whine began.

The walls trembled.

Dust blew suddenly in a cloud from the discarded corpse wrappings. We flailed our arms, heads and shoulders smothered in the gritty dust. We choked and coughed. But the walls did not move in. The tremble shuddered to a stillness, the dust fell away, and the walls stopped.

That high shrilling whine passed away above the audible threshold. We shook, suddenly, each one feeling the pain drilling into his ears.

Slowly, as an iris parts, the wall of blackness opened before us.

When the harsh actinic white light rushed in I saw that we stood in a slot between the stilled walls. There was space left for us only to walk out in single file, so narrow had been our confinement and so narrow our separation from death.

Prince Tyfar was the first to march out.

Head up, sword in his fist, he stomped out onto a black marble floor and into the white light. He stopped. As we crowded out he gasped: "By all the Names!"

Difficult to describe this Mausoleum of the Moder, so many impressions crowded in like a kaleidoscope.

A place of wonder, of awe, and of horror. . . .

The chamber stretched about us, full four hundred paces in diameter. The roof rippled oddly, hung with black insubstantiality, ever-shifting so that it was impossible to estimate the height. And that height appeared to waver and alter and to press up and down.

Positioned some fifty paces in from the walls around the chamber stood fire-crystal tanks, each with a girth of at least twenty paces. In each tank coiled and writhed a monster from nightmare, tentacled octopus-like shapes that slimed and hissed and beckoned obscenely. They would have put the shudders up the toughest of backbones.

Deb-Lu started to talk at once, and I guessed he sought to hold our tattered nerves together.

"We are clearly below ground level here, and I imagine this to be the heart of the Moder—"

"You said there were nine zones and this is the eighth—"

"True. But the ninth zone is not for normal men."

We walked slowly forward between two of the tanks. We did not look again at the gruesome denizens. We all sensed that Quienyin spoke the truth and here was what we had come for—all of us, that is, except the Wizard of Loh. . . . And myself.

Ranged in a circle within the circle of tanks, and crammed close together, stood cabinet and chest, box and trunk, glassed and bound with bronze. Small alleyways led through this circle. The treasures contained within this mass of cabinets defied the imagination. We halted, greedy eyes surveying the wealth displayed there.

Quienyin looked back.

"There will be time to sample these wares—after.". .

No one had the hardihood to inquire of him, "After what?"

What lay in the next circle drew some of us on.

We could not look over toward the center of the chamber, for the brilliance of the light that poured up in a wide shaft from the central floor, lifting and flooding up to be consumed in that shifting darkness of the ceiling.

Around that shaft of pure white light stood a fence, a wall, an insubstantial-seeming yet iron-hard barrier. Passing through alleyways in the circles of displayed wealth and magical equipment we stood before the iron barrier. A silver gate showed immediately ahead, and a golden gate showed to the right. To the left a bronze gate shut off ingress beyond the barrier. Somehow, we all knew there would be nine gates leading onto the shaft of fire.

"I think, my friends," quoth Quienyin, "that is our way out—after."

"Through—" squeaked Ariane. "Through the fire?"

"Yes, lady."

"Well, how do we pass the gates?"

"Climb the fence," offered Tyfar.

"No, prince." Quienyin spoke quickly. "That way lies a sure and ghastly death."

We took his word for it.

The mercenaries were jostling before the cabinets. In there lay unimaginable wealth. I saw a trunk the size of a horse trough filled to bursting with diamonds. At its side stood another similarly filled with rubies. The glitter of gold paled to insignificance in the luster of gems.

"Touch nothing until we are sure!" commanded Tyfar.

The paktuns growled—but even their greed was tempered by our experiences. And, do not forget, these were the hardiest and the toughest of those who had entered, for they had survived.

One quickly showed us a simple way to die.

The black marble of the floor that ringed the chamber gave way to white marble and then to yellow. Where we stood before the flame the floor was broken into patterns, intricate lozenges and heart shapes, circles and half-moons of inlaid stone. This paktun, he was a Rapa, stood upon a crescent of green, without thinking anything of it.

The green crescent swallowed him.

One instant he was standing there, rubbing his wattled neck, the next he was gone, and the green crescent reappeared.

Ariane screamed.

"Test every part of the pattern before you trust it!" called

Tyfar. From then on, every one of us cat-footed about like ghosts.

Remembering Quienyin's ominous words, I looked into the recesses of the chamber, alcoves past the tanks and their hideous denizens. Shadows shifted there, eye-wateringly.

Tyfar was talking, quickly and softly, to the lady Ariane.

The Wizard of Loh said, "Jak, my friend. These things are real. There is no illusion here. Your weapons . . . ?"

Displayed in glassed cabinets stood ranked many swords, many daggers, many different weapons of quality.

"I do not think, San, I will find a longsword like this. Until it vanishes from my fists, I will keep it."

All the same, I did decide to replace the rapier and main gauche when we had the cabinets open.

But—opening the cabinets was the nub of the question.

We all knew that horror would burst upon us as we burst open this treasure.

"My prince," said the slinger, Barkindrar the Bullet. "Let us all stand well away and let me smash a cabinet."

Barkindrar had proved himself on this expedition down a Moder. Tyfar nodded. Quienyin pulled his lower lip and looked at me. I made a small gesture which meant "What else?"

A distant tapping noise that had irritated my ears for a short time now grew loud enough for me to turn, puzzled. The others heard it now. The banging echoed hollowly and sounded like devil-tinkers at work on a yellow skull.

Quickly we ascertained that the knocking noise came from a wall away to our left and we moved back, positioning ourselves, wondering what fresh horror would burst upon us.

Chips of stone facing the wall flaked off. Then a larger piece fell. The noise redoubled. Whatever was forcing its way through the wall was large and powerful. The banging bashed and boomed and rock fell and the wall split. In a jagged wedge-shaped gap the wall split from the floor to a point ten feet above and yellow light poured through with a spray of dust and rock chippings, glinting.

Dark shadows moved within the jagged opening in the wall. They looked black and evil against the streaming yellow radiance.

A form lumbered through, and stood up, and bellowed.

"Hai! I am through!"

We all stared.

More figures burst into this dread chamber, and there was Kov Loriman, smothered in dust, shoving through, a massive sledgehammer in his fist, panting, triumphant. He saw us.

"You famblys! And how many have you lost? Did I not say I would smash my way out?"

Quienyin called across, "Or, kov—*in!*"

To be honest, I could not understand why some horror had not carried off the Hunting kov and all his men sooner.

I could not understand that riddle then. But it was made clear to me, and, I owned, despite his despicable propensities for Execution Jikaida and other unmentionable acts of abomination, Kov Loriman materially assisted me by that bashing entrance through the wall.

We gave him warning about the green crescents, and his men were as wary as ours of the wantonly displayed wealth.

One intereting fact I noticed then was that of these survivors of the expedition there were more hyr-paktuns with the golden pakzhan at throat or knotted in silken cords at shoulder than there were of paktuns with the silver pakmort or of ordinary mercenaries who were not yet elevated to the degree of paktun. But, then, surely, that was to be expected?

Tyfar was your proper prince. However much of a ninny he might be in ordinary life, he was lapping up the marvels and terrors of this Moder. He was punctilious with Lorimer.

"The suggestion is, kov, that my slinger puts a bullet through one of these glass cabinets while we stand back."

Loriman grunted, and glared at his Jiktar, the commander of his Chuliks. This one, a magnificent specimen of the Chulik race, impressive in armor, fiercely tusked, pondered.

"Quidang!" he roared at length.

Chuliks have about as little of humanity in them as Katakis; they have given me a rough time of it on Kregen, as you know. But, at least, they are mercenaries born and bred to be paktuns, and not damned slave masters. And while their honor code in no way matches the nikobi of the Pachaks, they are loyal to their masters. And, they can be loyal even when the pay and food runs out, which is more than can be said for most mercenaries.

As we prepared for this fraught experiment, I realized that the place with all its creepy horrors was actually powerful enough to make me maudlin over Chuliks. By Zair! But doesn't that stunningly illuminate the stark and overpowering impression this Moder was making on me!

So, with Chuliks as comrades, I hunkered down with the rest as Barkindrar the Bullet went through his pre-slinging ritual.

Did he, I wondered, do this in the heat of battle?

Prince Tyfar put store by him, as he put store by his bearlike apim archer, Nath the Shaft who hailed from Ruathytu. And, I should quickly add, neither of these two retainers were mercenaries, as Ariane's numim retainer, Naghan the Doorn, was not a mercenary.

As Barkindrar went through his preparation and whirled his sling another odd little thought occurred to me. As we had penetrated nearer and nearer this Mausoleum of the Moder, so Deb-Lu-Quienyin had grown in confidence. It was as though by merely approaching what he sought he took reverberations from his coming powers, sucking strength from his own future.

Barkindrar let rip. The leaden bullet flew. The glass cabinet splintered into gyrating shards. Splinters and shatters of razor-edged glass splayed out. Anyone standing nearby would have been slashed to ribbons. The smashing tinkles twittered ringingly to silence on the marble floor.

We stood up.

"Well done, Barkindrar!" said Tyfar. He beamed.

"Have a caution, prince," said Quienyin. "There may be a guardian. . . ."

Kov Loriman hauled out his pouch and extracted a small body. It was a tiklo, a small lizard creature, and he held it by the tail gingerly.

"When we were being outfitted by Tyr Ungovich he charged me a great deal of red gold for this little fellow. By Havil, yes! Ungovich said that at the final moment he would prove his worth. Is not this the final moment of this damned maze?"

"Have a care, kov."

"What ails you, Master Quienyin?"

"I do not—rightly—know. It is passing strange."

Old Quienyin looked about, vacantly. I saw his arms begin to lift up from his sides as the arms of a Wizard of Loh rise when he is about to go into lupu. But the old mage's arms dropped and he hooked his thumbs into his belt, and he squiffled around a space before he said, "You could be right."

Loriman laughed and led off to the smashed cabinet.

Barkindrar had picked a cabinet containing crowns. They were ranked on their pegs, brilliant, redolent of power and authority, clustered with gems, shining. Each one would have bought the kingdom its owner ruled.

Loriman picked one out unceremoniously. Nothing happened. He lifted it, with some casual remark that, by Havil, it suited him. He was about to put it on when Quienyin struck it from his hands. It fell and rolled. I noticed, from the corner of my eye, the little tiklo give a twitch in Loriman's fingers.

The crown rolled across the marble. It grew smaller. Rapidly it constricted in size, shrinking, until finally, with a little plop, it vanished.

"Your head, kov, would have been inside that."

Loriman lost his smile and his color. The veins in his nose seemed to strangle into thin white lines. He shook.

"This is a place damned to Cottmer's Caverns—and beyond!"

Tyfar looked troubled and he spoke in a voice low and off key, as though what he had to say perturbed him. "You said," he remarked in that indifferent voice to our oracle, "Master Quienyin, that these treasures were real."

Quienyin coughed and wiped his lips.

"So I said, prince, and so I maintain. Watch."

Deliberately the old Wizard of Loh picked up another bejeweled crown. He lifted it high in both hands. Then, with a decisive gesture, he brought it down and placed it on his own head.

"No!" screamed Ariane, half fainting.

The crown remained on Quienyin's head. It did not shrink. Glittering, it surmounted his ridiculous turban, glowing with the divine right of kings to extort and slay.

"What does it mean, Master Quienyin?"

"Only that Kov Loriman should throw the tiklo away."

"You mean that rast Ungovich tricked me?"

"No. Only that, perhaps, at a distance, Tyr Ungovich was not aware of the true menace of this Moder and its Monsters."

"I'll have a word with him, I promise you!"

Ariane giggled. "Maybe it is your turban, Quienyin!"

"Aye!" shouted Loriman. "Try the crown without that!"

Quietly, the Wizard of Loh complied. The crown remained its true size, a real crown, resplendent with glory.

After that there was an orgy of cabinet smashing.

Some little of the menace of this deadly place seemed to be removed, and yet I do not think a single one of us was lulled. We all knew that the sternest test yet remained—if we knew what it was.

Chapter Eighteen

The Mausoleum of the Flame

A price surely seemed demanded for the wanton looting going on in this awesome chamber. The restraints of reason were broken among these people, the terrors through which they had gone had boiled up insupportably and now burst forth in wild laughter, drunken staggerings, the crazed smashing of glass cabinets and the wholesale strewing of the contents about the marble floor.

The lady Ariane followed by her people was running madly from cabinet to cupboard to chest to box, eagerly searching for the lure that had brought her here. I could only wish her luck if it had to do with unseating poor pathetic fat Queen Fahia of Hyrklana.

We do not always see clearly into the motives of people whom we do not know well, and if they appear to agree with our own wishes, transfer our own desires into their actions.

Fulfilling my promise to replace the rapier and main gauche with a real set of Bladesman's weapons, I saw in the case alongside the equipment I chose a beautiful little brooch. It was in the form of a zhantil, that fierce, proud wild animal, king of the animal kingdom in many parts of Kregen, fashioned from scarrons, a gem of brilliant scarlet and precious above diamonds.

Carefully, I pulled the brooch out. It did not come to life and seek to bite my thumb off. Nor did it come to life and grow full sized and seek to chew my head off.

I put it into my pouch.

A looter, Dray Prescot. Well, I have been a paktun and a mercenary many times, and the paktun's guiding motto is grab what you can when you can. Life is short, brother. . . .

Without discarding the drexer I buckled up a thraxter. If

176

the drexer was going to vanish along with the other weapons of hallucination, then a real blade for rough and ready battling would be a comfort.

That brooch now—for whom else in two worlds would I have taken it?

So that reminded me that when a fellow returns from a little lonely jaunt it behooves him to bring back presents for all the family. Feeling remarkably ridiculous, I toured around the shattered displays seeking items I thought suitable as little gifts. The odd thing was, a little gift from this treasure house of the Moder was worth a fortune.

When Delia said to me, as she would, "And where have you been this time, my heart?" I would have to reply, "Oh, just a little game of Moders and Monsters." And attempt to leave it at that. Of course, I would not be allowed to. I knew full well that after what I told my Delia and after the sight of these little gifts I'd have Drig's own job to prevent her from hopping into a voller and insisting I took her on a little jaunt of Moders and Monsters. By Zair, no! I said to myself, and saw Ariane, holding an ivory box to her breast, the tears pouring down her rosy cheeks, and thought—my Delia? Down here? *Never!*

Well, it just goes to show you that man sows and Zair reaps, that no man can riddle the secrets of Imrien, that—oh by Vox! That I was foolish to imagine what I imagined.

Quienyin walked across to me. He waved an arm about.

"Look at them, Jak!"

Certainly the place was in an uproar. People were staggering about under enormous loads of loot. These were old hands at the game of removing portable property, and the gold and silver were left untouched, the gems and the trinkets which were worth more than the gems of which they were made, these were the objects these ferocious paktuns were pocketing.

"Now, Jak." said Quienyin in a sharpish tone, "here is that which I think you may find of use."

He handed me a thin golden bracelet of linked swords.

"And, San?"

"And just this, young man. When a man wears the Blade Bracelet he is an invincible swordsman. But, wait—it holds its power for one fight and one fight only. After that—poof!"

"And you believe I need this?"

He eyed me with a sympathy I sensed was genuine. "Keep it safe. When you meet Mefto the Kazzur again."

"I give you my thanks, Deb-Lu. But—no, and I mean you no disrespect. Mefto is a great kleesh, right enough; but he is a swordsman and when I next meet him I shall beat him fair and square."

He looked at me as though I were off my head.

"What in the name of He of the Seven Arcades do you want here, then?"

"I," I said, "want to get out!"

The racket continued on about us as he looked shrewdly up at me, his eyes appearing to give forth more light than any human eyes could. "Now that is the most sensible desire in this whole place!"

"We have to get through that wall and up to the shaft of fire?"

"Yes. Look, Jak—" He pulled a belt from one of the many pockets of his robe. "Cannot I interest you in this. If you wear this in a fight your foeman's sword cannot harm you."

"Yes, and is that for one fight only?"

"It is."

"Do these folk know that the magical items they are taking work once only?"

"Oh, no, some of them work for quite a long time."

"I suppose there isn't a device here that will magically transport us out of here? That would be—nice."

"Sarcasm, young man, is cheap. And, no, there is not. At least," he pondered vaguely, "I have recognized nothing resembling such a device. And, I may add, I have felt remarkably young about my lost powers lately."

"I had noticed."

I had noticed, also, that he was not talking in capital letters for most of the time. . . .

"Let us take a look at the wall where Loriman broke in. I am interested." He nodded and we started for the jagged opening in the wall. The wall where the Hall of Ghouls had revolved to bring us—squashing—here was simply another wall like all the other nine. The wall from the Hall of Specters showed Loriman's gap. "The Hunting Kov is a—forth-right—man."

"Oh, aye." I gave a hitch to the lesten-hide belt holding the scarlet breechclout. That had been cut from an immense bolt of cloth here, and the belt was supple and strong. "D'you happen to know if he's found whatever it is he seeks to help him with the Spikatur Hunting Sword? D'you happen to know what it is?"

"He found a gold and ivory casket that gave him joy. Had I my powers—when I have my powers!—I must discern this Cult or Order."

"Well, if it works only once. . . ."

"That is what is so intriguing."

Approaching the jagged opening in the wall Quienyin stumbled on a chunk of the masonry Loriman's bully boys had broken down. He put his hand against my back to steady himself, with a small cry and then a quick apology. Turning, I took his arm and supported him to the gap.

Noises spurted from the jagged wedge-shaped opening, distant and hollow, borne on a foul-tasting breeze that died the moment it reached the central chamber. Quienyin cupped his ear and listened intently.

Presently he looked up inquiringly, and I nodded.

"But how many . . . ?"

A jag of masonry thrust against my side.

"The hole!" cried Quienyin. "It is closing!"

As a wound seeks to heal itself so the walls were growing whole again. I gave a yell at a bunch of shouting Chuliks who, loaded with loot, were making faces at the octopus-like monster in the nearby tank. They ignored me. I started bashing at the walls with a sledgehammer discarded among the rubble. Quienyin at my side helped with a pick.

I bellowed into the hole, that old foretop hailing roar.

"Hurry! The gap closes! Hurry, you famblys! *Bratch!*"

As I smashed away stones so they grew and pressed in. So, although I hate the word, it fitted here, by Krun! and aptly, I bellowed into the hole: "Hurry! Hurry! *Grak! Grak!*"

In only moments they were up the opening and the first face to show, peering through past the glitter of a sword, was that belonging to Prince Nedfar. He looked mad clean through.

"I see you, rast!" In a twinkling he scrambled out and his sword leaped for my throat. I threw myself backwards.

Lobur the Dagger was out, and other fighting men. Quienyin yelled.

"Prince! Prince! Hold! It is us—we are here—this is Notor

Jak and he is a friend. Hurry through, all of you, before the gap closes on you."

There followed a right old hullabaloo before the rest of the expedition tumbled through the opening. The last one through was Hunch, and he shivered and shook as the stones closed up at his rear with a clashing thunk, making him leap as though goosed.

He did not recognize me, for I stood talking to the prince, girded with weapons, clearly one of the lords.

"Jak? Aye—I remember you. You are well met." Nedfar possessed the princely merit of remembering faces. "If your story is as strange and horrific as ours. . . ."

"It is, prince," said Quienyin. He explained as the newcomers with howls of glee threw themselves at the glitter of treasure.

Nodgen the Brokelsh was with Hunch. They did not know me. So it goes with the eyes of slaves. They both looked as though they had spent a continuous month of Saturday nights without a break.

I wished them well of their Tryfant and Brokelsh paradises.

Tyfar welcomed his father and sister with a seemly show of emotion. Also, I noticed the comradely way he greeted Lobur the Dagger. As for Kov Thrangulf, Tyfar welcomed him in the proper style, as befitted a young and untried prince toward a high-ranking influential noble.

The flaunting display of wealth drew the newcomers as a flame draws a moth, and the uproar redoubled in that august and eerie chamber with the Shaft of Flame illuminating all the frenzied moths.

The Sorcerer of the Cult of Almuensis pushed through and stood, feet braced, fists on hips, a glittering figure surveying the mausoleum, the circle of weird creatures in their tanks, the smashed treasure chests and scattered wealth. He nodded, sagely, as though he had planned it all.

"So this is the nadir of the Moder," he said. He puffed out his cheeks. His splendid figure glittered almost unmarked by the desperate adventures of the journey that had turned us into a rag-tail and bob-tail collection.

"Not quite, San," said Quienyin, cheerfully.

But San Yagno ignored the old mage. His eyes lighted on a chest fastened with nine locks shaped into the likenesses of risslacas. The scaled dinosaurs were prancing in bronze. Yagno advanced upon the chest, pushing people and bric-a-brac out of his way. He planted himself before the chest, which was of sturm-wood inlaid with balass and ivory, and bound in bronze.

"I recognize that sign," he said, half to himself. He reached into that sumptuous gown and pulled out a thick book, covered in lizard skin, locked with gold.

"Watch this, Jak," said Quienyin. "It is something worth the seeing."

The Chuliks of San Yagno's bodyguard—there were but five left of the original dozen—formed a ring about their master. But Quienyin and I could still see. San Yagno opened the hyr-lif, thumbed the stiff paper over, found the page he sought. He held the book close to his face and began a long incantatory mumble. Most of it concerned sunderings and breakings and smashings of one kind and another.

The first bronze lock, shaped like a risslaca, snapped open.

The second through to the ninth snapped up in turn.

San Yagno puffed his cheeks out. He was panting. He stowed the book away and motioned to the Deldar of Chuliks.

This one lifted the lid.

"A vast expenditure of thaumaturgical lore," observed the Wizard of Loh. Only the slightest tinge of irony colored his mild words.

"Had it been Kov Loriman," I said. "He would simply have taken an axe to the fastenings."

"Precisely, young man."

And, I swear it, we both laughed.

We did not stop to see what San Yagno found in the chest after the first reeking objects were revealed. But they seemed to delight the sorcerer. He was laughing away to himself and distributing his loot among his followers. I wondered if they would hurl it all away to load themselves down with gems.

Ariane's four handmaids were cooing and aahing over her and attempting to tidy her hair and prepare a quiet corner where she might change into a clean new dress, of which they had a store borne by patient slaves. That made me realize that the arrivals did have slaves with them.

I said to Lobur the Dagger, "How did you fare with the Fliktitors?"

He didn't know what I was talking about.

It turned out that Nedfar's party had followed a vastly different route from ours, once they had branched off, the fortunes of the Moder had treated them as harshly but had spared some of their slaves. They had lost Strom Phrutius.

"He is now being ingested in the guts of some half-invisible creature we could only see in the dark. As soon as there was light he incontinently disappeared."

"San Orien mentioned such a monster. I am sorry to hear about Strom Phrutius. It was a Laughing Shadow."

"Oh, aye, Master Quienyin. It laughed most dolefully when Tobi, a fine archer, shafted into its nothingness. It took itself off, then." Lobur pulled his lip. "Tobi is dead, now. He was engulfed by a poisonous flower that grew from a crevice in the wall at prodigious speed."

We expressed our regrets at the losses suffered by the Hamalese, and it was clear to me, as to Quienyin, that while we might be on the threshold of the heart of the matter, for this short space a sense—a damned false sense, to be sure—of release from tension eased the burdens on the minds and fears of these people. It was cat and mouse. That seemed clear. I asked Lobur the Dagger about his slaves, and he mentioned casually that they had picked up a couple of odd fellows somewhere who had almost been cut down before they managed to convince Prince Nedfar they were not demons.

And then I quelled a quick grimace which might have been misconstrued as a smile as Lobur said: "They were left over from an earlier expedition, wandering about, poor devils."

Hunch and Nodgen had hit upon the same lie as I had to explain wandering slaves without a master. As for Tarkshur—well, that must wait.

I made myself look eager. "By Zodjuin of the Gate! They might be two of my fellows!"

It was now vitally necessary for me to get to Hunch and Nodgen and browbeat them into dumb acceptance before anyone else espied their stupefied reactions when they saw me and, at last, recognized me by what I would say. It would be nip and tuck. Here, in the wider danger of the Moder this small and social-order danger remained just as perilous.

They had dressed themselves up in finery which had been sadly ripped and stained in their struggled advance along the corridors. I found them with a bunch of other slaves, all goggling at the uproar. The slaves were nerving themselves to break constraints and join in the looting.

I took Hunch's Tryfant ear between finger and thumb of my left hand, and Nodgen's Brokelsh ear between finger and thumb of my right hand, and I ran them a way apart, yelling as I did so: "You pair of yetches! You have caused me great concern! But I forgive you! You have done exceeding well! To have remained alive!"

They almost hung on their ears, swinging, as it were, to glare up at me. I bore down on them, bellowing, and, between bellows, I rasped in a low voice, "Yes, you famblys, it's me—and a word will have your ears—no, your heads!—off. Act up. We came here before; but your memories are bad. Say nothing!"

They just looked at me as though a demon had opened his mouth and spat out all his fangs at them.

In a bull-roaring voice I said, "I promised you manumission and manumission you shall have!" I glared about and saw Lobur and Princess Thefi and Prince Tyfar looking at me with undisguised curiosity. "Witnesses!" I raved on. "There are the witnesses. When we are out of the Moder the bokkertu can be concluded, all legally—but, as of now, you are manumitted, Hunch and Nodgen, both—free!"

Had the audience broken into a small and polite round of applause it would have been perfectly proper. In this place it would have been incongruous. But the deed was done and seen to be done, and these two would—if we lived—receive their papers.

The idea of gratitude did not cross my mind. All three of us knew that Tarkshur would turn up—almost bound to—and then our deception would face a sterner task. But these two looked at me, at the continuous looting, and Hunch stood up rather taller than was his usual wont, and Nodgen bristled up in such a way that he looked fierce rather than boorish.

Curiosity touched me as to what exactly they would do. When they launched themselves at the overturned cases and shattered cabinets, I sighed, and went off to see what Nedfar would have to say about the damned nine key-bits we needed.

As Quienyin joined me and we started to move off from the area where the slaves squatted, still quaking, still not sure just how to breach the domination of the lash, we saw an odd—a pathetic—act.

One of the slaves, more bold, more hardy than his fellows, crept cautiously from that shivering group. These were slaves who had been slaves for a long time, many had been born into slavery. This tough one of them inched across to a toppled cabinet and scooped up a brass dish and then, holding it with his back curved and the bowl pressed to his belly, he scuttled back. We watched. He began to hand out chunks of the stuff in the brass bowl. The slaves stuffed it into their mouths and began to chew. It was cham, the great jaw-moving panacea of poor folk on Kregen—and a delicacy for these poor slaves. Quienyin and I exchanged looks and walked on. When the slaves, at last, broke out, would be time enough coming.

From the actions of the group of principals around Prince Nedfar, we judged most of them had found what they sought. Tyr Ungovich, still shrouded in his hooded robe of red and green checks, stood among them. We walked up and San Yagno, glittering, said, "You have a place here, Master Quienyin. But who is this fellow to come thrusting himself in where he is not invited?"

I said, "I leave you to your discussion." I took myself off. There was nothing to be gained by making an issue of this petty business yet; I felt the Wizard of Loh would inform me of the decisions reached. I went off to find Tyfar and Lobur.

Ariane's handmaids had taken her off to the shelter and they would be making her presentable. Slave labor was a mere part of her expectancy, and her handmaids were slave girls, no doubt of it.

Princess Thefi said, "You cannot know how much I am in your debt, Notor Jak! My brother has been telling me of your adventures—"

"You are fortunate to have such a brother," I said, in my best gallant way. But it was true. "And we are going to come through, safe and sound, all of us."

Lobur the Dagger said, "By Krun! I know so!"

Well, he knew more than I did then.

Kov Thrangulf hovered. Somehow, these three managed to have their backs to him. I felt awkward. But Kov Thrangulf, as though bearing a burden to which he was accustomed, went off toward the treasures again.

Presently, Prince Nedfar shouted for Kov Thrangulf, and he went gratefully off to join the conference, along with other second-in-commands. Lobur the Dagger laughed, all bronzed face and flashing teeth. "You have to feel sorry for him."

"Yes," said Thefi. "But if only he wasn't so—so—"

"Did I show you this?" said Tyfar, hauling out a pretty bauble, and thus changing the tone of the conversation.

Among the profusion of treasure and magical items there lay scattered about a vintner's dream. Some of the mercenaries, unable to resist free booze, had been drinking and had, apparently, suffered no ill effects. We four decided not to risk sampling the wines or food. Lobur, with one of his raffish smiles, produced a squat green bottle, and we drank companionably, in turn. It was a Hamalian porter, dark and brown and heavy, and went down with a rich taste.

The sensation was distinctly odd to stand thus in pleasant conversation and drink Hamalian porter in the midst of the scenes caterwauling on about us, in this horrific Moder, and know the three with whom I so companionably drank were avowed enemies of my country. Odd. . . .

The Princess Thefi had outfitted herself in charming style, with tight black trousers and a blue shirt with a darker blue bolero jacket, all in fetching fashion, with a green cummerbund around her waist, which was delightfully slender, by Krun! She wore rapier and main gauche. She looked splendid.

I said, "Princess, my lady—did your clothes come from this place—or did you acquire them within the other zones of the Moder?"

"Oh, we found a veritable storehouse of clothes and weapons."

"Then, princess, best you had don clothes from here. Otherwise," I said, and I did not smile, "you will find yourself stark naked when we emerge onto the outside world."

"Say you so?"

"Aye!"

She gave a little amused squeal and turned her quick lively gaze on Lobur.

"I know those who would joy in that!"

"Princess!" protested Lobur, outraged. "You impugn my honor!"

Well, it was all pretty stuff. But the Moder stretched about us with its dark secrets and we must find a way out—if we could.

Talk of clothes brought other thoughts to their minds.

"You wear deuced little clothes, Jak," said Lobur. "I call to mind stories I have heard—vague, distorted—of a man, a very devil, who went everywhere clad only in a scarlet breechclout."

"Oh?" I said, injecting surprise into my tones. "Can you remember anything . . . ?"

"Only that he was no friend to Hamal," said Prince Tyfar.

"In that case, I shall find something else. When it comes to the fluttrell's vane. . . . Blue, would you say? Or green?"

They began to discuss this with some seriousness and Thefi went off to find clothes that would not vanish to reveal her splendor to the goggling world.

As they talked I wondered just how much they did know from hearsay of that very devil in the scarlet breechclout, that Dray Prescot who was the Emperor of Vallia and deadly foe to the Empire of Hamal, and also the same Dray Prescot who had good friends in Hamal and despaired of a country unjustly governed.

I saw Nodgen and Hunch talking to Quienyin. The two ex-slaves were clad sumptuously and garnished with a Kregan arsenal of weapons. Nodgen held a broad-bladed spear. They went off together, the three of them with Quienyin in the lead, searching among the tumbled magics.

Prince Nedfar called his son over to join the discussion with the chiefs and principals. The princess returned dressed in new clothes, tight black trousers and blue shirt as before.

Lobur looked at Thefi and then at me.

I said, "I have urgent business. . . ." I drifted away.

The situation appeared that we might stay in this wondrous chamber—the Chamber of the Flame, it might have been called—for as long as we wished. When we made our move to break free would be the time when the horrors would pounce.

Yet the object of challenging the dangers of the Moder was to escape with the treasures one desired. Escape was the problem.

Ariane, radiant in a pure-white gown, her hair impeccable, her face rosy-red and glowing, had joined the conference.

"Well, *Notor* Jak——" This was Quienyin, smiling, ironic,

striding up to me with Nodgen and Hunch looking sheepish. "They want you to join them. I have persuaded them that you are not a monster or a djinni or any form of ghoul." He snuffled. "It was a hard task."

"He's a right old devil," said Hunch.

I said, "Strom Phrutius may be dead, Hunch, you hulu—but his chief cook, Fat Ringo, has survived to bring his gross bulk into this place."

"I know. I have kept clear of him."

"Stick by me when we quit this place. We'll win free, have no fear."

Easy words, those—but how were they to be accomplished?

Quienyin and I walked across and joined the enlarged group around Prince Nedfar.

"You are welcome, Notor Jak. I am glad I did not cut you down when we entered through that Havil-forsaken hole."

I said, "Had you not hurried you would have had a puzzle to solve and the Jaws of Death to dare."

"I have been told. Now we need all our wits to riddle the way out of here."

Ariane had regained much of her composure. "The way lies down beside the Shaft of Flame."

"There is a wall of insubstantial iron, lady—"

"There are nine gates!"

"To which we do not have the keys."

Tyr Ungovich's shoulders moved, as though he shrugged in resignation, or laughed quietly to himself.

The red and green checkered hood did not move as Ungovich spoke in a voice like a rusty hinge: "Without the sorcerous power of San Yagno the party would never have reached here. You are fortunate, Notor Jak, that your party is still alive without the aid of so mighty a thaumaturge."

Carefully, I said, "We survived."

"Let me set one of my fellows to climb the wall!" burst out Kov Loriman.

"By all means," said Tyr Ungovich.

We remembered what had chanced the last time he had said that. Loriman hunched himself up, his face bloating with anger.

"Well, Tyr Ungovich. What do you suggest?"

"Do we have all the parts of the key?"

They were produced as though they were precious relics, and Nedfar laid them out on a table which his son quickly turned up the right way. There were eight curiously-shaped pieces of bronze. We all stared at them solemnly.

Well, and by Zair! Weren't they the most precious objects in all this Moder?

And, without the ninth part, they were valueless.

Chapter Nineteen

Of a Gate—and Honor

Much of the rampaging about and the ecstatic sorting through treasures to uncover the finest abated. The explosive release of tensions neared its own exhaustion. Men still capered about, fantastically arrayed in cloth of gold and festooned with gems, they still played stupid silly magical tricks one against another, with spurts of blue fire and whiffs of occult stinks, causing Yagno to twitch. But gradually they quieted and looked toward the group where the decisions of their fates rested.

The hood of ruby and emerald checks drew forward, shadowing all within, as I spoke to Ungovich.

"You sold Kov Loriman the Hunter magics to ward off the magics here. And the others bought trinkets of some power." As the Hunting Kov started forward, clearly about to blaspheme by Sasco over the uselessness of the tiklo, I went on in a louder voice, "Perhaps in view of your knowledge of conditions here, you have knowledge of what it is we need to open these gates."

"It is in my heart to have been with you and witnessed what went on when you were separated from us. Did any of your party find a key?"

"What we have is there on the table." Tyfar pointed.

Kov Loriman subsided, caught up in the importance we all sensed in the words of that rusty-hinge voice, consigning the matter of his tiklo to a Herrelldrin Hell.

"Nothing else?" Tyr Ungovich sounded as though he was becoming annoyed. His rusty voice grated unpleasantly.

These men had talked over and over before I had joined the group, and had settled nothing. We were going to be trapped here if one of us did not come up with the right answer.

"We found a golden key," said Ungovich. "But an oaf lost it for us."

Prince Nedfar drew in his breath. He spoke and all the quiet dignity of the man showed splendidly in that place. "Amak Rubbra, who was a just and honorable man, lost his life with that golden key."

"An oaf, I said," the rusty voice said spitefully. "And an oaf I mean."

"Without a key—" San Yagno started to amplify.

"Here," snarled Kov Loriman. He hauled out the box of a size to take a portion of cham and, opening it, proffered the contents. "A silver key we found. Is this what you want?"

"Ah!" grated Ungovich.

We all craned to look.

Ungovich reached for the silver key. It was left to Yagno to say, startled, "Tyr! Careful! It may be—"

"Quite."

"A silver key for a silver gate, notors?" said Tyfar.

We all moved across to stand before the silver gate in the insubstantial iron wall. The shaft of pure white light lifted blindingly over our heads. Shadows fled away in long fingers of darkness. A smell of ancient decay hung in the air here.

"I do not think the key will harm me," said Ungovich. He lifted it out. Nothing happened. We all watched him as, carefully, he inserted the key in the keyhole and turned, pressing sideways as he did so. The silver gate moved inward a handsbreadth. He paused.

A man shrieked in terror and as we whirled to look back into the Chamber of the Flame other men took up that scream of horror.

This Mausoleum of the Moder was guarded.

From the transparent tank opposite the silver gate the colossal tentacled monster rose, twining those slimy arms and clawing at the sides, lifting itself up. As its gross body climbed to the lip of the tank its eyes, red as fire, large as shields, blazed upon us, and its serrated yellow beak clashed with a champing grating sound that chilled the blood.

I reached forward, seized the handle, and slammed the gate shut.

Instantly, the octopoid monster shrank back into its tank.

"By Havil!"

"May the gods preserve us!"

"To open the gate is to release—*that*!"

Prince Nedfar said over the hubbub: "It seems a perfectly logical arrangement."

Tyr Ungovich's unpleasant voice scratched out. "Well, notors. And what do you suggest now?"

"We cannot stay down here forever!" shouted Loriman.

"Yet if we open the gate—" said Yagno.

"Cannot you spell the beast, San Yagno?"

Ungovich said, "I do not think a mortal spell will affect that beauty."

I looked at Quienyin. He had been keeping silent lately. He caught my look and, in the pause after Ungovich's conversation-stopping statement, said, "This is not a case for spells. This needs the military mind, organization, determination and decision."

Prince Nedfar, Prince Tyfar, I was pleased to see, understood at once what Quienyin meant.

Ungovich said, "I do not see—"

Loriman had grasped it, now.

"Then stand aside, Tyr, and let those who do see—do!"

"Before you begin," I said, "notors, two things." I shouted to Hunch who was standing nearby with his aptitude of overhearing likely conversations. "Did more than one monster climb up its tank?"

"Aye, notor!" shouted back Hunch, quaking.

"And, two," I drew an arrow and nocked it. "Will a shaft perhaps dissuade a monster from climbing—?"

"You delude yourself!" said Ungovich.

"I think not, Notor Jak."

"But more than one monster moves. So we must be quick."

All the same, I held the Lohvian longbow half-bent, the arrow gripped in the old archer's knack in my left fist, as we went about organizing what had to be done.

We allowed half a bur for final preparations. The Deldars—those who were left—bellowed and roared in fine Deldar style and the men formed ranks. The slaves, piled with loot, were positioned and threatened with unmentionables if they stirred too soon and did not run when told to grak. The notables arranged themselves with each party. Nedfar would lead. I offered to be the last, and Tyfar and Lobur said they would stay also, seeing that my party consisted of myself and two men only. Hunch and Nodgen, shuffling up under enormous bundles, looked at me reproachfully.

"Remember," Nedfar called, his voice ringing out for us all to hear. "There is no need for panic. Long before there is any danger we will prevent it. Do not jostle or push. Any man who disobeys me will be cut down."

There spoke your true Prince of Hamal, by Krun!

What we were about to attempt was obvious in the context of the situation. I just hoped the situation would not change. The bastard up there, the Wizard of the Moder, the Moder-lord, could so easily change the rules.

Quienyin stood beside me. "I think I will—"

"You, San, will go out with an early party—as you value my friendship!"

"But, Jak—"

"It will be a pretty skip and jump at the end, I think."

He looked at me with a worried expression. And he was a Wizard of Loh! "The Moder-lord will run us hard."

"Aye."

He nodded. "You are right. I feel strength in the—in the air. Mayhap I can do most good as you suggest."

"I am confident of it."

Prince Tyfar walked to the head of the line to bid his father luck, as I judged, and then he turned to Ariane. She nodded, once, white-faced under that rosy-red, and swung away to speak to her numim bodyguard. The Pachak twins guarded her close. Tyfar, scowling, came back to me.

"Notor Jak—my fellows will swing the gate. Agreed?"

"Agreed." Then I added, "Prince."

"You are a strange fellow—and I see you still wear the red."

"I overlooked that, prince. Still, it is the color of blood."

"Oh, no, Jak! Why, that loincloth is brilliant scarlet!"

"So it is. Well, let us swing the gate and hope it is not stained a darker red."

Ungovich came over. "Get as many through at one time as you can." As he spoke I felt an irrational desire to haul off that concealing hood and have a look at this mysterious man.

He stalked off to take his position in the line, and Quienyin rubbed his thumb under his jaw, scratching. "I think," he said, and he looked meaningfully at Tyfar and me. "I really do think you should not allow the creature to climb out of the tank."

"Once out—?" said Tyfar.

"Indubitably, my dear prince."

I turned away. Deb-Lu-Quienyin was most certainly feeling some tremor of the future, some inkling of the resurrection of his powers. I wondered what kind of a man he really was. The old buffer I knew was certainly far removed from a puissant and feared Wizard of Loh, that was for sure.

All the relaxed air had gone out of the situation. The hullabaloo as the treasures were spilled out wantonly had vanished. Now the men looked anxiously at the silver gate, and cast uneasy glances over their shoulders at the ominous writhing shapes in the tanks. That close confining breathless sensation clamped down on us.

Prince Nedfar called, "In the name of Havil the Green! Open the gate!"

Tyfar nodded to his men, chief among whom were Barkindrar and Nath the Shaft. The silver gate swung open. Nedfar stepped resolutely through, his shield and sword positioned, vanished out of my sight. I swung about, narrowly watching that coiling slimy monstrosity within the tank lifting itself up. The tentacles seemed to be signaling to me, hypnotically waving and demanding my obedience. The tentacles slid over the rim. One red eye appeared, and another. The curved serrated beak showed. Over half the bloated body lifted above the rim of the tank.

"Close the gate!" I bellowed.

Tyfar's men slammed the gate, and others held back the next in line. They halted, sullenly, looking back. The monster slowly sank down into its tank.

I watched it narrowly. Down and down it dropped behind its transparent wall. I fancied, when it stopped moving, it had not dropped as far down as it had been.

"Gate!"

The gate opened and the line began to pass through, inevitably jostling and pushing. Now that the first party had gone on through and had not reported back disaster, the second party were more confident.

When the gate was shut at my shout and we waited for the coiled monster to subside I took stock of the man who came up to stand beside me, breathing deeply. Kov Thrangulf held himself stiffly erect, and his face flushed a dark and painful red. Over in the third group, where we had thought it wisest to include the women of the expedition, Lobur was laughing and talking to the Princess Thefi, who was responding beautifully. Thrangulf bent his lowering brows upon them. Ahead of the princess, the lady Ariane and her people waited patiently.

"By Havil," said Thrangulf. "I am forced to put up with much!"

I watched the monster sinking down. When it came to rest I was convinced it was not as far down as previously.

And—one limp tentacle hung down over the rim of the tank and was not withdrawn.

"Gate!"

The people pushed along. Following the women's group a column of Chuliks waited. One of them was quite clearly incapacitated from the drink and as they moved forward he toppled flat on his face. Some of his comrades were for leaving him; in the end and moving with speed, they threw his sack of booty away and a comrade hoisted him up onto his shoulder, perched precariously along with the swollen bundle of swag. "If he wants his life, we will give him that. But as for his booty—"

"He will never make paktun now," said another. They pressed on. The little check caused them to be tardy, opening up a gap into which they crowded forward smartly, leaving a gap to their rear. I eyed the monster. The tentacles writhed above the rim and a red, shield-sized eye peered balefully down. It seemed to me the damned thing was climbing up quicker each time. I would take no chances. As the serrated beak began to move forward above that gross body, surrounded in slimy coils, I bellowed, "Shut the gate!"

I whirled as shouts broke out by the silver gate.

Tyfar and his men were pulling the gate but three burly Chuliks struggled within the opening, effectively blocking the closure. They insisted on pushing through. The gate hung open, jammed. And the monster began to hiss.

"Out of it, you cramphs!" shouted Tyfar.

I ran. I sped up to the gate and gave the center Chulik such a buffet he took off headlong, his feet flying up. He vanished out of sight and his two comrades were caught, a fist

around each pigtail of coiled hair, and thrust savagely on.
Tyfar's men hauled the gate shut.

I stood back. I felt intensely annoyed by such stupidity.

The monster hissed and began to decend—and the thing
dropped down reluctantly. . . .

"By Krun, Notor Jak! You deal severely."

"Onkers," I said. "Get onkers."

"Next time—"

"Next time teach 'em with steel!"

And I stomped away.

Kov Thrangulf was staring at me as though I was a madman.

"That was Prince Tyfar to whom you had the honor of ad-
dressing yourself—"

"I know. And he'll be a prince in that tentacular beast's inward parts if he doesn't look lively!"

Kov Loriman stumped over. He had elected to stay with
the last party, which did not surprise me. Despite all the horrors of this place I had the dark suspicion that he rather fancied getting his blade into one of those red eyes.

"The prince was given the task because he is a prince and
the son of a prince. But if he cannot manage—"

"He will," I said. "Kov. Do not fret." Then I added ominously, "By the time it is our turn that beast is not going
peaceably back to its tank."

He looked at my bow—I should say that I had put the
bow away once I had taken up my new task—and he
grunted. "I say shaft it, Notor Jak."

That was sweet politeness from the Hunting Kov.

"I think," I said, "I might try a shaft at it the next time it
shoves its ugly snout out."

"Let us all try, by the Blind Archer!"

When next the gate was opened all the archers left let fly
at the flaming red orb of the tentacular monster. If the
shafts hit at all, it was difficult to say. They ricocheted and
caromed away. When that happens to an arrow driven by a
Lohvian bowstave, the archer knows he has loosed at something special.

"The thing is cased in some kind of damned armor!"

"Kov—would you care to try your sword against it?"

He took my meaning at once. The veins in his purple nose
swelled. He looked meanly at me. "When the order to open

the gate is given—I will. . . ." He hesitated, and then said, "I will try."

Kov Thrangulf drew his sword. "If you will, kov, I will stand at your side and smite blow for blow."

"You are welcome, Kov. Let us stand together and smite!"

Although as usual I was amused by all these kovs this and kovs that, here was an intriguing example of etiquette functioning in ways that were universally recognized on Kregen.

The gate opened and the two kovs, positioned and ready, leaped to strike doughty blows at the writhing tentacles. Their swords rebounded. I would not have been surprised had they both been snatched up and ground to pulp in that ugly yellow beak. Kov Thrangulf went on slashing and hacking like a madman, quite uselessly. Kov Loriman dragged him back and a glistening tentacle swept past closer than any fighting man cared to see. A bright blue favor was wrenched from the shoulder plate of Thrangulf's armor.

"By Krun, kov! That was—" Thrangulf swallowed down and looked about. "You pulled me back!"

"Aye! Otherwise you'd be beak-fodder by now—kov!"

Then it was time to bellow the gate closed. The monster was now quite clearly remaining much higher in the tank, and three tentacles hung down outside the rim. As we waited a thought crossed my mind. The Krozair longsword might only be an illusion; it could cut, had cut—would it cut this monster?

I went across. The two kovs were stiltedly polite, one to the other, and it was clear Loriman's opinion of Thrangulf as a fighting man had plummeted. I lifted the Krozair brand.

Loriman said, "You are wasting your time."

"Nevertheless, it is needful I try." And I slashed.

The shock vibrated right up my arms, through my shoulders and exploded in my skull. I was swung around and staggered.

"I told you," said Loriman.

Thoroughly bad-tempered I stomped across and bellowed for them to open the gate. On that occasion we did not get above half the next waiting group through. I began to calculate the odds.

That confounded red and green checkered hood came into view and the rusty hinge voice croaked, "You cannot do it."

"We will try."

"That is the privilege of apims."

So that meant nothing. He could be apim or diff and say that, say the same words with vastly different meanings.

I went down to the gate and gave Tyfar's men a thorough talking to. Then I stalked along the waiting lines and threatened them. The threats were redundant with the looming menace writhing within the tanks. Four limp tentacles hung down outside; those within the transparent walls coiled and squirmed.

And, the tanks farther around in the circle showed their awful denizens at precisely higher stages of movement, as though they were notes in a scale—a scale of horror.

I said to the people at the tail end, "If we all move faster, and do not stumble, we will all get through—just."

Hunch looked ill. Nodgen shook his spear.

Kov Thrangulf came up to me again, puffing his cheeks out.

"They all contume me," he said. He was by way of being light-headed. "I do not have that famous ham in my name. My grandfather carved out the kovnate, and I have held it. Is not that a great thing?"

"Aye, kov." I spoke true words—for I knew of the dangers and difficulties in retaining a hold on lands and titles.

"I am a plain man. I do my best. The Empress Thyllis has turned her face from me." He sounded maudlin. I think at that moment he believed he was going to die, that he was facing certain death and not the possibilities of death that lurked in the Moder. "I am a plain man," he said again. "Not fancy. I try."

"I'm sure," I said. "Kov."

"My grandfather, the kov. He lived too long. My father never forgave him for that." He choked up and wiped his mouth. "My father showed me his displeasure, knowing I would be kov."

Another batch of fugitives went through and I narrowly surveyed those remaining, measuring the length of the lines against the height up the tank of the nearest monster. And, as I thus watched the lines and the monsters, and listened to Kov Thrangulf, I was aware of another thought itching away, a trembling suspicion that we would not get away as easily as all that, even from here.

I felt sorry for Thrangulf. What he said added up; but the

urgencies of the moment supervened, so I contented myself with saying, "All men have a purpose in life, kov. Find yours."

He looked at me as though I had struck him. I stared back, and he took a step away from me as though blown by an invisible wind. I suppose my ugly old beakhead carried that demoniac look.

"Take your place in line, kov, and go through quickly. . . ."

"I shall not forget you, Notor Jak—even if I die!"

He resumed his place in the line. The process of escape went on, a remorseless logic of attrition. Now there were a dozen tentacles hanging outside the tank. Limp when the gate was closed, they wriggled to squirming life when the gate opened, hauling up that gross body. The red eyes glared malevolently. The serrated beak clashed.

Hunch and Nodgen looked at me appealingly. I showed them a stony face. Someone had to bring up the rear. I could have wished it was someone other than them, though.

No prowling monster wandered through, gibbering. Had one done so I believe we would have roared with laughter at the inconsequentiality of such an apparition at this time.

Many of the nearer monsters hung close to the tops of their tanks, and bunches of tentacles hung down outside.

When but three groups of people remained I said to Loriman: "Let us leave the gate closed for a longer period, kov. Mayhap that beast will slip down."

"We can try. . . ."

So we waited, apprehensively, in that gruesome chamber among the overturned treasures. The tentacles of the monster hung limp. It did not, as far as I could see, drop down an inch. We waited.

Presently, Loriman swore. He said, "By Hito the Hunter! It is no use. Open the gate and send the next one through."

We did so.

The monster balanced on the very rim of the tank, swaying and clacking its beak. That beak could grind stone to powder.

I believe the very remorselessness of the whole process, the gradual approach of the monster to escape and our destruction, the logic of it all, wore us down more than any screaming screeching monster-charge could ever do. And something of that feeling must have permeated the Moder-lord, watching us, no doubt, and giggling and mumbling soggy toothless jaws. A piece of discarded gold in the shape of a dancing Talu, beautiful and abandoned, stood up and began to dance toward a cabinet that righted itself and shuffled its legs into the position it had occupied before. The glass joined together over the Talu.

With a scraping whispering furtiveness the strewn treasures began to replace themselves within healed boxes and cupboards. Chests turned upright and refilled with spilled gems. The whole mausoleum filled with the glint of gold and the glitter of gems and the rustle of scuttering treasure. As for the magic items—ghosts, wraiths, call them what you will, the cabinets filled and resumed their accustomed places.

"The cramph of a Moder-lord considers we are finished," said Loriman. He spat and hitched up his shield and sword.

"There is still a chance," I said. "There were two men in Jikaida City reputed to have returned from the Humped Land with treasure and with magic. Can they best us?"

"It is not they who will best us—"

"No. I think the monster will climb out of the tank the next time we open the gate—"

"Agreed!"

"So we must open wide and all press through, fast—fast! It must be done."

Kov Loriman the Hunter, a rough, unpleasant slave-owning man, a player of Execution Jikaida, said, "I shall, of course, go last."

I said, "Kov, tell me. What did you say to Master Scatulo when you lost at Execution Jikaida?"

He stared. "You were there?"

"I was there."

"I told him that he had one more chance and then I would send him to take the place of the Pallan of the Blacks."

"Very good. I shall go through last."

"Do you wish to fight me for it?"

And then the incongruousness of the situation came to my rescue. I didn't give an adulterated copper Havvy for him. Did I? Whatever path his honor made him tread, my path lay in the light of the Suns of Scorpio and of the well-being of Vallia.

"Of course, of course. With my compliments—you may go last."

"As is right and proper." And he fingered his sword and looked back with a black look at the octopoid monster.

Other intrepid adventurers had come here and gone through the gates loaded with treasure. Mayhap this Moder was different from others, and those two successful men of Jikaida City had plundered an easier tomb. For, of course, we were all grave robbers—although the stakes were raised to a rarefied level. But, still, other men had succeeded here, I felt sure. The tentacled monsters could be outwitted. That could only mean worse things awaited down the Shaft of Flame.

"Now?" said Loriman.

I couldn't say I liked him. But he had been—useful—in his uncouth way. And I didn't know from whence on Kregen he hailed. He had carefully not said.

I looked at the last men waiting. I shouted. "When the gate opens—run! If any man stumbles he must be pushed aside and tail on at the rear! So, doms—do not stumble!"

Loriman shouted, "I shall stand at the gate. If any man attempts to push out of place, him I will strike down!"

Prince Tyfar looked a trifle green about the gills. I walked across. "Prince—go out with your men first—we will close the gate."

"But—"

"*Do it!*"

He looked crestfallen, like a chastised child. I turned away and gave him no room to argue further.

"All set?"

"All set!"

The gate swung open. The men began to run through, quickly, plunging out of view, shooting like peas from a pod. Tyfar went. His men followed. The lines ran up, men panting, frightened, pushing on, keeping in line, shouting. Loriman stood at one side of the gate, his sword raised, his face hateful.

I prowled the other side, urging the men on, encouraging them.

With a monstrous hissing the tentacled octopoid, immense, writhing, slimy, toppled from the tank and scuttled for us.

"No brainless bunch of guts is going to beat us!" roared Loriman. "No matter that it is invulnerable to honest steel. Run, you hulus, run!"

Shrieking, a man stumbled and I seized his neck and hurled him on. Out of sight through the silver gate they crashed, two by two, hurling on. Hissing, writhing, the monster raced swiftly over the marble toward us. No treacherous pattern of that floor engulfed it. The tentacles swirled, slimy, reaching out. . . .

Only a half dozen more . . . Nodgen and Hunch were through . . . Two more—then the last two . . . I swung to face Loriman.

In that moment he stood there, exalted, his face a single ruby flame, his eyes murderous. I thought he would stay and challenge the monster out of the sheer joy of hunting.

I grabbed his arm and pulled as a clansman pulls a vove up over a fire-filled trench. Together, we roared through the silver gateway and I slammed the portal shut. Its clang sounded like sweetest music.

The shaft of fire rose before us, lifting from a stone-walled pit. Men were running forward, following the one ahead and vanishing out of sight down between flame and wall.

"We've done it!" exulted Loriman. He swaggered toward the pit from which rose the Flame. "The cramph of a monster has been beaten!"

A gigantic hissing belched up behind us, like a volcano bursting. We swung about. We stared up, appalled.

Tentacles appeared over the top of the insubstantial iron wall.

A gross form rose into view. Red eyes like flame, the size of shields, stared wickedly down upon us. A yellow serrated beak clacked. Deliberately, the monster lifted over the wall, balanced, fell clutching down toward us.

Chapter Twenty

The Fight over Vaol-Paol

Dread of that primeval horror exploded in my skull. Two thoughts clashed in my head. The monster was impervious to steel. And other men had escaped from this awful place.

Squirming with coiled animate energy the monster rushed swiftly across the stone toward us as we fled for the Shaft of Flame. Between that supernal white light and the lip of the stone pit a narrow opening offered the way of escape. Stone-cut steps spiraled downward within the confines of the pit. Another monster flopped over the wall and, hissing, propelled itself on those wriggling serpent-like tentacles toward us.

Men pushed on down the steps. The slot between wall and flame was perhaps just wide enough for my hulking shoulders. A man toppled. Screaming, he pitched from the steps. His body entered the flame. Spread-eagled, his pitiful bundle of loot flogging free, he drifted down as though suspended against a blast of invisible force, and as he fell he dwindled and burned. We shuddered and hurried down the stone steps, treacherous with slippery moss and slimy with fungus.

Looking back past Loriman, who thumped down with a look of ferocious distaste on his florid features, I saw the monster's red eye appear, festooned with coils of slimy writhings, saw it lash futilely down after us.

Loriman bellowed, jerking his head back. "The thing is balked! Ha! We have bested the monster!"

But the monster launched itself into the column of pure white light.

Like thistledown, it floated. It sank. Its arms writhed and its eyes glared, its beak clacked, and it dropped down and down within the Shaft of Fire.

Loriman switched up his sword.

"If we are to die," he shouted, hard and venomously. "I will strike and strike until I am dead!"

I thought of that poor devil who had fallen through the Flame. "Look!" I shrieked. "Look—the thing shrinks!"

And it was so. As we hurried down and the monster sank within that supernal radiance, so, we saw with thankfulness, it dwindled in size and shrank until it was no larger than a coiled mass of rope such as would be found on the deck of a swordship.

That shrunken bundle of horror still held menace. It drifted in to the steps and as we hurried down so it fastened upon the arm of a Rapa. He shrieked, his feathers all stiff with horror. He slashed with his sword, and the steel bounced, and the dwindling monster pulled him free of the stone steps, and he sank with his death into the shining whiteness.

Up there other monsters launched themselves into the Shaft of Flame.

As we hurried with desperate caution down those slippery steps I knew that no magics we might have found above would preserve us from this danger. And, also, I was convinced that nothing the Moder-lords with all their thaumaturgical arts could provide would prove of any use to me in my dealings with the Star Lords or the Savanti. The Moder-lords dealt in illusion and horror and fear. But they were mortals. Their reach of dread power had its limits.

Looking down the spiral stone stairs one could see only the bobbing heads of the men in front, curving away out of sight beyond the radiance of the Flame. The stairs went down Widdershins. How far the pit sank into the ground, no one could tell.

To our left the shrinking monsters drifted down through the Flame. Their hissing ceased. The only sounds were of men's breathing, and the slip and slither of feet upon the stone. Down we went and then I saw the men below me turning into a low stone opening, arched in the wall at our sides. The steps down trended on and down and out of sight. Thankfully, Loriman and I ducked into the opening, to stand erect in a wide chamber and see the rest of the expedition waiting for us.

The babble of greetings and the quick question and answer as the fate of comrades was disclosed went on like a surf roar. Light of a sickly green fell from a roof away behind the dazzle.

"Thank Havil we are all safe—save for those poor unfortunates who succumbed." Prince Nedfar betrayed determination. He issued his orders in a hard voice. "We have discovered a passageway and a long corridor leading upward. This must be the way out. But—we go carefully." That, we all knew, was a remarkably redundant piece of advice and betrayed the state of our nerves no less than those of Prince Nedfar's.

"We go on in the same order." He looked meaningfully at Loriman and Tyfar and the rest of us latecomers. "It has been a long and trying wait down here."

I looked about among the people.

"Where is Master Quienyin?" I shouted, pushing through the throng.

But Quienyin, Ungovich and Yagno were missing.

"I believe they went on ahead, to spy the way," said the lady Ariane. "Let us go on!"

Her face had lost a great deal of that high color. But what she said made sense, although Nedfar might have thought differently. We started up the corridor, and all of us, from time to time, cast apprehensive glances backwards.

"By Tryflor!" panted Hunch. "This place has scared me witless." He shook with fear.

Nodgen tried to bolster his courage with a bellow. "You Tryfants are all the same. Only good for running!"

"True," moaned Hunch. "Too true!"

We pressed on and soon we recognized that the sequence of corridors and rooms matched those through which we had first passed when we entered the Moder. Nedfar shouted that this was a good sign. "The way out mirrors the way in! Courage! Onward!"

We trended upward and when we reached a chamber draped in solemn purple we stopped, dismayed. No doorway broke those somber walls.

Men rushed about pulling the purple curtains aside. All they found was a small secret door beyond which stood a lever. The lever was fashioned of ivory and bronze, and it looked ominous.

"Pull that . . .?" said Loriman. "It is a riddle."

"We have no time for riddles." Nedfar looked outraged.

Tyfar stood near me, and Ariane leaned on the shoulder of her numim.

"The three who went ahead," I said, "they must have riddled this riddle aright—or where are they?" I looked at Ariane. Her face flushed, bringing her color back to that rosy red. She stamped her foot. I said, slowly, "Did they go ahead, lady?"

"Yes!" she flared. Then: "No—I do not know. I did not see them. I think they went on down the stairs of the pit."

The transparency of the lie could not soften my feelings.

"I shall go back for Quienyin."

"I shall come with you, Notor Jak—" said Tyfar.

"No, prince. Better not—you should stay to take care of the lady Ariane."

He looked at me. His spirit was up. The diffidence had gone, at least, for a space.

"No, Notor Jak. I think not."

"Pull the Havil-forsaken lever!" roared Loriman, "and have done!"

Nedfar snapped out, sharply, "Not until we have examined everything thoroughly, three times over!"

"There is," put in Kov Thrangulf, swallowing, "the matter of the ninth part of the Key—"

"Yes, kov," sang out Lobur the Dagger. He stood very close to the Princess Thefi. "You are right, by Krun! Now how could we have overlooked that weighty matter?"

I turned away sharply. I went back along the corridors through which we had just toiled. The scene I left was not to my liking.

Through the corridors I hurried and crossing a nine-sided room with curlicued marble floor inlaid with the symbol for vaol-paol, The Great Circle of Universal Existence, I stopped stock still. Against three of the walls stood tall glass cabinets. In each cabinet and plainly visible through the glass glowered a Kildoi warrior. On each, the four arms and tail hand grasped weapons.

Now I could have sworn those cabinets had not been there when we hurried past this nine-sided room. Then, with a resounding Makki-Grodno curse, I pushed on. Mysteries, mysteries. . . .

The quick shuffle of footsteps in the corridor a few rooms

along heralded Deb-Lu-Quienyin. He looked different. And, yet, he was the same.

We turned together to hurry back, exchanging news.

"The three mages went on down the pit of the Shaft of Flame. I warned Yagno; but he said he was a Sorcerer of the Cult of Almuensis. Well——" Quienyin sounded genuinely aggrieved. "What I saw down there, on the ninth level, I will not say, young man. It is not for ordinary mortals."

"Did you regain your powers, San?"

He gave a half-despairing, half-amused laugh. "Yes and no. I found what I sought, as San Orien had promised. The Moder-lords do not allow Wizards of Loh into their Moders. That is a fact. But I was no longer a real Wizard of Loh. So I found that which was needful."

"Wonderful——but, in this place, there is a catch?"

"There is a catch, Jak. I will only regain my full powers when I am safely outside the Moder."

"Then that is all right. They are searching for the last part of the key now. They have found a lever. We will soon be out." Then, I said, "And Yagno? And Ungovich?"

"Yagno was——no, better I do not reveal that. As for Ungovich, he disappeared, and I fear he shares the same fate as Yagno."

"So——unhappy though it is, we do not wait for them?"

"By every Queen of Pain whoever reigned in Loh," he said, and surprised me by that word, "no. It is useless to wait."

We entered the nine-sided chamber with the inlaid motif of vaol-paol in the floor. Quienyin halted. The three glass cabinets opened. The three Kildoi stepped forth. They glared at us.

No time to think. No time to understand that these three were Kildois, just as Mefto the Kazzur was a Kildoi, with four arms and a tail equipped with a fist, superb fighting men, tremendous in their strength and skill. Mefto had bested me at swordplay. No time, no time. No time even, with the flashing memory of Seg Segutorio heartening me, to bring the great Lohvian longbow into action and shaft the first of them as he rushed upon me.

Quienyin shouted something, and I caught the tailing words: ". . . the Kazzur!"

The Krozair longsword ripped free.

In my two fists and gripped in that cunning Krozair hold, the brand gleamed in the unwavering beams of the black candles in their golden holders. . . . The Kildois hurled themselves on.

The first gripped thraxters in his right upper and right lower hands. His lower left hand slanted a round shield. His upper left hand wielded a spear. And in his tail hand that wicked daggered steel glittered as his tail swept in high above his head.

No time to delay. No time for fancy work. As I had fought the overlords of Magdag on the swaying deck of a swifter I would have to fight now. It was all hard, merciless, practical fighting and none of your fancy academy fencing. . . .

The thraxters slashed for me. The Krozair brand blinded, whirling like a living bar of light, chunked through the shield, bore on to score a deep wound all down the Kildoi's chest. Before he had time to yell, before he had time to fall, I bounded away and swung into action against his fellows. They bore in from each side, cunning, clever, supreme fighters. And as these superb Kildois attacked they did not understand they faced an old Krozair Brother, a Krozair of Zy—who knew more tricks than the Krozairs, by thunder! The longsword swept dazzlingly. A thraxter scored across my right shoulder and then the first Kildoi was down, minus a tail he had flung unavailingly across to protect his throat. Tail blade, tail hand, throat, vanished in a welter of purple blood.

The second flung himself forward, shield up, spear aiming for my eye. I slid his blow, brought the Krozair brand around, quick, quick! Ah, the Krozair Disciplines teach a man how to stay alive, by Zair!

Whether they were real Kildoi retainers of the Moder-lord or whether they were illusions, I did not know. But their steel would kill.

The fight was over. Three dead Kildois lay on that inlaid representation of the symbol for vaol-paol, and their purple blood dripped thickly. I stood back. I panted only a little.

"By the Wizard of—!" said Quienyin, shaking.

"By the Black Chunkrah! Now that opened the old pores a trifle! Let us, San, hurry on—and get out of here!"

As we came up to the purple-draped chamber and the

noise of the people of the expedition arguing away at the top of their voices—as usual—I said, and I admit rather slyly, to Quienyin, "San, tell me—that Bracelet of Blades you wished me to wear—how would it have worked there? For all three Kildois? Or the first one only?"

He gave me a look along his nose. "You are a hard man, Jak."

"Aye—to my sorrow."

Hunch and Nodgen appeared glad to see me and the Wizard of Loh still alive. They told us that the lever had at last been pulled, that a wailing pack of Lurking Fears had writhed out, that the warriors, although quaking with super-naturally-induced terror, had managed to slay all the Lurking Fears.

"And," shouted Hunch, "the lever did two things—"

"The ninth part of the key in a secret cavity!" shouted Nodgen.

"—and the keyhole in an onyx wall—there!"

"And now," said Nodgen, "they are fiddling about putting the bits of the key together. That is brainy work."

A triumphant shout racketed down from the far wall. Ned-far waved the completed key aloft, his face radiant. "We have it!"

Everyone felt that we must hurry. Urgency drove us on, for we were all confident that at any moment fresh horror would prowl down upon us. The purple draperies were pushed aside to reveal the onyx wall and the keyhole. It had to be a keyhole! There was no other way.

"Something dire will happen when that key is turned," said Prince Tyfar. He looked excited and wrought up in a way far different from his usual diffident manner.

Ariane shuddered and drew away from him.

Lobur the Dagger held Princess Thefi close. Retainers and paktuns held their weapons ready, a forest of steel blades. We looked about the chamber and back to Prince Nedfar and the onyx wall with the keyhole. He placed the key in the lock. He paused. Then: "In the name of Havil the Green!" He pushed the key in and turned it.

The purple draperies vanished in puffs of smoke. The odor of charred flesh gusted. The solid wall peeled back to reveal a colossal statue of Kranlil the Reaper, a full hundred feet tall, crowned, ferocious, malefic, wielding his flail.

Between the mammoth columns of his feet a narrow door groaned open, bronze bound, crimson, double-valved, the door slowly opened.

A long upward slope was revealed. And—at the far end, tiny and distant—light! Daylight! As our eyes made out the drifting shapes up there we saw clouds and the streaming mingled radiance of the Suns of Scorpio.

And then, as the first mobs broke through, shrieking their joy, a whirling darting maddening cloud of stinging insects broke down about our heads. They poured from the opened casket in the claws of Kranlil the Reaper. They tormented us as we ran, stinging and lacerating and driving us mad.

The vial of yellow poison kept my skin partly immune, so that I felt the stings as light prickles, like nettles.

Men were screaming, and flailing their arms, and running, running, tearing madly up that long narrow corridor.

Tyfar screamed and caught at his collar. I grabbed him and twitched out the little horror that was clinging to his neck. It was banded in yellow and green, gauzy-winged, and its sting was black and hard and tipped with a globule of moisture. I threw it away. I could not see Nodgen and Hunch in the bedlam.

We pushed on and Logu Fre-da and his twin, Modo Fre-da swiftly assisted Ariane along. Her hair was covered with insects. She screamed, trying to beat them free. Modo let out a yell and fell, clasping his legs. Both limbs crawled with the insect horrors. Logu bent to him.

"Leave him, you fool!" screamed Ariane. "Help me!"

Shrieking, Ariane stumbled. Tyfar caught her, helped her up. He was covered with the stinging insects. He choked, trying to go on, and fell. Quienyin grasped my arm, shaking, beating at the air. Tyfar was on his knees, looking up imploringly, still gripping Ariane's white dress which crawled with banded green and yellow.

"Ariane—princess—"

"Let go, you rast! I do not care a dead calsany's hide for your life! *Let me go!*"

She struck Prince Tyfar. She wrenched free and ran screaming and sobbing up the slot, pushing and beating at the backs of the people struggling on. The two hyr-paktuns watched her go.

Quienyin said, chokedly, "Let—let them go—the insects will follow—" He let go my arm and beat at himself. "I am on fire!" The hideous uproar persisted, a cacophony of torture.

Barkindrar the Bullet and Nath the Shaft sprang to the side of the prince. All three hummed and buzzed with insects.

"We must go on!" I shouted.

We staggered and stumbled on. We were the last. The two Pachaks struggled along side by side, helping each other.

Our little group fought a way through the swarming clouds of insects. Hunch and Nodgen, trying to shout and making mewling noises, lurched on up the slope. Up there the daylight showed, bright and welcoming. The glory of the ruby and jade light fell into the opening, and irradiated the walls, and we fell and crawled on, afire with the poisonous stings from the winged furies.

We neared the top and the way to freedom.

Slaves, paktuns, retainers, notables, passed out through the opening and faintly we heard their yells of exaltation and triumph.

We pressed on.

Almost—almost we reached the opening.

Then the slab fell clashing down, stone on stone, and the blackness descended upon us.

We were shut in, denied life, trapped within the Moder.

Chapter Twenty-One

Of the Powers of a Wizard of Loh

Trapped. . . . And all that ghastly catacomb of the Moder as our tomb. . . .

"Back!" I yelled, savagely. "Out between the legs of Kranlil before that door closes!"

Scrambling, shouting, we raced desperately for the lower door. We came shooting out into the purple-draped room, and the double doors, crimson, bronze bound, groaned shut at our backs.

"But it is no use!" cried Tyfar. "We are doomed—"

"The insects are gone," I said. "We have our lives still."

Quienyin looked at me and shook his head.

"It is a long way—"

"Yes. But the only way, now. We must return through the Moder and make our escape the way we came in."

We stared one at the other with frightened eyes. We knew what we had been through. . . .

"We are a choice band," I said. "We can win through if we bear up and trust in ourselves."

"But, think of it . . ." whispered Hunch. Then he shouted, "I will not think of it! It is too frightening."

"It is," agreed Nodgen. "So best think of something else and just come along."

Yes, they were a choice band. Prince Tyfar and his men, Barkindrar and Nath. Nodgen and Hunch. Logu and Modo Fre-Da. And Deb-Lu-Quienyin, a Wizard of Loh whose powers would return only when he was safely out of here. A choice bunch, indeed, to venture back through this Castle of Death.

They were all scratching themselves. My vial soothed away their stings; but we still itched uncomfortably.

"It is a mortal long way," observed Barkindrar.

"Look," said Nath the Shaft. "I wager you I can shoot out the right eye of that damned statue before you can sling out the left. Is it a wager—for an amphora of best Jholaix when we sit in The Scented Sylvie?"

"Done," said Barkindrar.

Sling whirled instantly, bow bent at once—leaden bullet and steel-tipped bird flew. Both of those staring green eyes clipped out, sparking, tinkled away somewhere.

"Mine, I think—"

"Ha! Mine, of a surety!"

I said, "I am surprised they allow ruffians like you in The Scented Sylvie. By Hanitch! What Ruathytu has come to!"

They gaped, then, and Tyfar suddenly burst into a laugh.

"You know the Sacred Quarter, then, Notor Jak of Djanduin?"

Nodgen and Hunch stopped arguing to stare at us like loons. The two Pachaks gave up hunting for the fallen eyes of Kranlil.

"Well enough to know I intend to spend a pleasant evening and night there again. You may not be a Bladesman, but I wager your axe sings a sweet tune."

"And I shall share that evening and night with you!"

"Done!"

"Now we must make our way back," he said, airily. "There is a charming tavern on the Alley of Forbidden Delights— The Sybli and the Vouvray, it is called." He started to walk out of that dolorous chamber and along the corridor. We all followed. "I shall have great pleasure in taking you there, Notor Jak."

"You do me the honor," I said, walking on.

Well, at least, this was one way to anchor the mind to sanity. What we faced was like to test us to the utmost. And there was an intriguing fact I had not overlooked. As we marched on I counted us again. Yes, I was right.

Nine.

We were nine adventurers, challenging the sorcery of the Moder.

As we walked the twin Pachaks talked to each other and then, respectfully, they addressed Prince Tyfar.

"Prince, we request that you witness our formal severing of our nikobi to the lady Ariane nal Amklana."

Tyfar's face pinched in. But all he said was, "I so witness."

We went on toward that spiral stair up the pit of the Flame. I took the opportunity to say to the two hyr-paktuns. "You would do me a favor, and confer honor if you were to look out for Master Quienyin. Is this acceptable to you?"

They nodded solemnly. They did not give their nikobi—not yet. But I felt a little easier for Quienyin. We were going to need stout hearts and hard fists to get out of here. Hunch was a weak link, possibly, but I fancied Nodgen and I would handle him.

I do not propose to detail all our struggles and torments as we battled our way back up the Moder. I will say that we found Kov Loriman's discarded picks and sledgehammers and simply bashed our way out, as he had bashed in. We did take a number of magical items indicated to us by Quienyin in the spirit that we had earned them the hard way. We plodded on, encountering monsters and vanquishing them by sorcery or by steel, and so went on and up.

We found ourselves taking a different way fairly soon, and we saw no sign of the lake and the sunken ships and the quicksands.

Corridor after corridor, room after room. . . . They blurred after a time into a continuing progression of horrors. But we went on. We were nine adventurers and if we were not hard-bitten when we began, we were hard-bitten enough at the end, by Vox!

Another interesting fact was that, going up as we were instead of down, we ran into traps from, as it were, the rear. Monsters, too, seemed a trifle put out that we did not appear from the right direction. I can say we left a trail behind us that would have done credit to a raging boloth in a potter's yard.

We came to a corridor which curved gently out of sight ahead. Low golden railings separated each side from the main passageway. Within these golden railings stood or lounged or reclined on sofas hundreds of the most beautiful women of many races. They smiled seductively. Their eyes lighted on us brilliantly. Lasciviously they beckoned to us. Some played harps and sang. The whole impression was of a single gigantic offering to passion.

Hunch and Nodgen stopped. They licked their lips.

Most of the women were half-dressed in exotic and re-

vealing costume, attire calculated to drive a man wild with
desire. I pointed at the long rows of carved skulls set back
from the golden railings, each some four or five feet from the
next.

"You are not in the Souk of Women now, you famblys."

"No, but—look at that one!"

"And look at her!"

"Look—that is all."

A Kaotim prowled along just then, a figure of a skeleton of
a Rapa with his big beak glittering. He seemed surprised to
see us. Quienyin whiffed him into ashes with a sprinkle of
powder from a jeweled box taken from the Hall of the
Flame. "Over a hundred pinches of powder left, friends," he
reported.

The Undead drifted away in a dribble of ash.

Kao is only one word for death in Kregish, which is a language rich and colorful.

"But," said Hunch, "only to look. . . ."

"You are in a Moder. You know what mod means,
Hunch?"

He shivered, and took his longing gaze away from the sylvie who smiled lasciviously, beckoning, sweet.

"Yes. I know what mod means."

"Then let us go on."

So we went along between those wanton women and heard
the mewling slobbering cries ahead. We proceeded cautiously.

A man came into view. He had clearly not heeded the
warnings implicit here. The women near him were all laughing and displaying themselves and taunting him. From the
mouth of one of the skulls a long, thin, prehensile line, like a
whip, fastened about this man's tail. The two whip-tails
linked and held, fast locked, knotted.

The man kept trying to pull himself away, and crying, and
shrieking, and then falling to his knees. In his hand he held a
knife. He was, we judged, insane.

"A Snatchban," said Quienyin. "He will never cut that."

On the floor lay two swords and a dagger, sundered into
halves.

Hunch and Nodgen started forward and then, as the im-
prisoned man shrieked and swung his knife down and so
withdrew it, they halted, as it were, on one foot, and stood
staring dumbly.

"If there is one thing they fear above all else," said Tyfar, "it is to have their tail cut off."

"Yet, if he doesn't cut if off, he will perish here, miserably."

"Would you cut it off—for him?"

"Me?" I said. "Well—I might."

Quienyin did not say anything.

Nodgen and Hunch came to life. Each took out his knife.

"We will cut it off for him, notor." Then Nodgen said, "Perhaps it would be better if you went ahead a little?"

Hunch said, "He may be—violent."

I said, "We will walk on."

So we seven walked on between those beautiful women until the curve of the corridor closed in at our rear and the next chamber opened up ahead. Muffled mewling sounds drifted up from the way we had come. We entered the next chamber and set ourselves to read its riddle—backwards. Once we were through the riddle, the way out would be clear, for that was the way in. Presently Nodgen and Hunch rejoined us.

"And?" I said.

They kept their gazes down.

"We talked about it, notor. We felt it would be—undignified—for him to lose his tail. He would probably prefer death."

"You put him out of his misery?"

They shook their heads.

"Oh, no, notor. It would not be seemly for two ex-slaves to slay him."

I screwed my face up. I did not blame them. But, all the same. I started for the way we had come in, saying, "Then I will cut his damned tail off." The entrance closed with a snap.

"There is no way back to him now," observed Tyfar.

"No. . . ."

"Poor devil," said Tyfar. "I do not like them as a rule. I wonder who he was?"

"You did not recognize him?"

"No, should I have?"

"I do not think so." He had—changed. The experience had altered him profoundly. But Hunch and Nodgen and I knew him.

Thus was Tarkshur the Lash left to his fate.

I wondered if they had left him his knife.

We were now running low on food and water; but we made a camp and rested up until we were refreshed enough to continue. How we managed our escape at the top occupied a deal of our conversation, but I found I was going beyond that in my own black thoughts. A very great deal further, by Vox!

The thought that the beautiful Krozair longsword would vanish when we reached the outside had to be faced. I was conscious of the privilege of having it in my fists once more. The Eye of the World, Grodnim and Zairian, seemed a long long way away now.

We were nine. One Tryfant. Two Brokelsh. Two Pachaks. Four apims. Nine.

Chance had brought us together. And we used chance to our own ends. We nine battled our way through the horrors until we stood in an echoing hall where the screams of lycanthropes banished away still lingered, and recognized where we were.

"Through that door, yonder," said Quienyin, pointing.

"The first thing I do," began Nodgen.

"That will be the second thing for me," quoth Hunch.

"I think, my friends," said Quienyin, "it will go something like this." He drew himself up and took a breath. In a strong voice he called, "Answer no is there."

From the room where I had last eaten a chunk of doughy mergem we walked out as the doors opened of themselves. We stood in a hall and the dust coated the floor. I studied the many sets of footprints. Then I began to walk quietly off to a corner.

"Beware, Jak!" cried Tyfar. "Look at those stains at the ends of footprints which end—abruptly!"

"Yes. But we are not the ninnys who entered here."

"That is true, by Hanitcha the Harrower!"

"I am not sure I know what you are about, Jak," said Quienyin, "and if I suspected what it was I am sure I would not want to know. But, let me see. . . ."

He walked across and halted well before the end of the line of footprints I had chosen. The ceiling curved into a bulge here, and the shadows clustered among the cobwebs. Quienyin took a small crystal object the size of a shonage from inside his robe and turned it about. Presently in its pale depths we saw a blue-green glow and the outline of a humped shape. Quienyin turned the crystal until he had the blue-green glow responding most strongly.

He nodded his head and then pushed his turban straight.

"Yes. A Trap-Volzoid. Nasty—serrated teeth that will fasten around your neck—that explains the stains. He'll lift you straight up. He's lurking up there somewhere and spying on us."

"A Volzoid—but—"

"This is a Trap-Volzoid. He can leap for perhaps three or four paces. He is waiting for you to walk into range."

"Let him wait, notor!" called Nodgen.

Hunch said, "The door is this way." He started to walk to the portal through which we had entered—a long time ago.

I said, "Will the harpy with the golden hair open it for you?"

The torches still burned above the gates. But they were fast closed, and the iron bars and studs did not look rusty.

"Oh, by Tryflor—have mercy!"

The others went across to the door. They banged on it. It did not open. Nothing happened.

"Right," I called. "You've had your fun. Now scoop up handfuls of dust—large handfuls—and when I yell cast them up into that corner. Make the dust thick."

"You think to blind it, Jak?"

"Long enough for me to reach the corner."

"You take a terrible—"

"That is what this is all about. Now, doms, ready!"

I yelled, the gathered dust flew up in a thick black sheet, and I went hurtling forward for the corner expecting to feel a fetid breath envelop me and razor-sharp fangs encircle my neck and find my head inside the capacious mouth of the Trap-Volzoid.

The dust smothered everywhere and I crashed into the wall.

Winded, I clung to the dusty stone. After a space I could see the other's faces like full moons rising through the dust cloud. I began to feel for the catch in the wall and found the right knob after a space and pressed. The door in the wall swung inwards.

I turned back.

"The last one—"

"I will go last!" declared Prince Tyfar.

"Wait!" I said crossly. "Logu and Modo. You next. We will go up and deal with the Trap-Volzoid. Then the last will cross in safety." The two Pachaks nodded, pleased I had selected them for their superb fighting ability in confined spaces.

We went up a narrow stone stair and crept out into a hollow and stinking place filled with detritus and bones. The Trap-Volzoid crouched on the lip of the bulge, looking away from us, ready to leap the moment an unsuspecting man walked within range.

The Krozair longsword bit, the Pachaks swung—and the damned thing, wounded and hissing, leaped out into the dusty hall.

In the end Tyfar and his men finished it off. It lay, a leathery ball, fanged and vicious and stinking, and the men stood back and looked up at us in the bulge and shouted.

So, up the winding stair we all went, and I led over the protestations of Tyfar, and we went with naked steel in our fists.

"I am beginning to think, my dear Jak," said Quienyin as he puffed up the steep and narrow stairs, speaking over the heads of the two Pachaks who followed me—Tyfar brought up the rear—"that this may count as being Outside the Moder."

The others would not guess the significance of that. But, if he was right!

"I pray Djan you are right, San."

"Mind my foot, you fambly!" came Nodgen's indignant voice, followed at once by Hunch, saying, "This is too scary for me!"

They were good fellows. . . . We went on and the narrow stair gave onto a tiny landing where a skeleton leered at us and an arched lenken door with its bronze studs all green shut off the way.

"This is not a case for magic, I think," said Tyfar, and Quienyin closed his mouth. Hunch stepped forward and looked at the door and the lock. He pursed up his Tryfant mouth.

"Looks normal enough. Nothing to fear there—" He started working his dagger about in the lock and, after a surprisingly short time, the catch snicked back and he pushed the door open.

When we were all inside the room, which was harmless, I said: "You showed skill in opening the lock, Hunch, but—"

"Oh, well, notor," he said, spreading his hands, "everyone has to have a trade."

"Maybe so. But, next time, do not push the door open so recklessly—else!"

Hunch the Tryfant went green.

We eased out into a passageway. It was paneled in painted wood, carpets covered the floor, there were exotic vases with flowers, and paintings and carvings against the wall. The air smelled sweet and yet there hung in the warmed air the faintest smell of tangs, as of sweet rottenness.

What followed I would prefer to pass over swiftly. But my narrative would be incomplete if I did not attempt to convey the sense of disgust which pervaded us as we investigated that palace. For it was a palace. We were prowling among the luxurious chambers of the towers perched atop the Moder. Yes—we had penetrated to the lair of the Moder-lord himself. Or—itself. . . .

The sights we saw there made us realize that our stomachs were not as tough as perhaps we had thought.

We spoke in hushed whispers.

"I am uneasy, Quienyin. It seems to me we have gained entrance here too easily. A mere Trap-Volzoid? A skeleton that did not move?" The air carried that sweet smell of putrefaction. "We are being sucked into a trap."

"Oh, yes, my dear Jak. Indubitably."

I glanced quickly at Quienyin. He stood by tall curtains of thick dark blue damask. He looked—different. The air of being an old buffer fell away from him. Although men on Kregen do not materially alter as they age through over two hundred years of adult life, until the very end, the change in him was profound. His eye was clearer, the lines around nose and mouth fined away. He walked with an alert step.

"Your powers—?"

"Not all. Some. Enough to bring us here and not notice what the Moder-lord had spread for our destruction."

I let my breath out. I have said that the powers of the Wizards of Loh are very real and very terrible. Perhaps this very exhibition of them, unconscious as it was, chilled me most.

"What—?" said Prince Tyfar.

Quickly, on a breath, I said, "We have come far enough. We must find a way out. A normal way."

"If there be such a normal thing in this devil's cauldron," growled Nodgen.

"Bound to be," said Hunch. "Got to be—hasn't there?"

We had crossed through most of this palace from the entrance we had found and so I said, "A stairway down near the outside. There has to be one somewhere."

Walking along the corridor, warily, we entered a chamber through draped crimson curtains. The room glittered with gold. Everything, it seemed, was fabricated of gold. A golden cage stood in a corner, with a golden statue of a creature none of us had ever seen before. Then Tyfar started, pointing.

"Look, by Krun! So one of us had the same idea. Perhaps he knows the way out—?"

The figure in the red and green checked cloak turned.

The hood fell back.

We all gasped.

The head was hairless—and lipless and noseless and earless. The skin was of a gray-green marbling, deeply fissured by furrows that turned the whole head into a ghastly parody of humanity. The face looked as though decay and dissolution, well advanced, had been halted and petrified. Thick green sinews stretched between the chin and the neck of the checkered robe. And the eyes—black and read, and demoniacal in their intensity of hate!

"You are welcome," said Tyr Ungovich. "I had not expected you, but here you are—"

"You did not expect us," I said. "And, Ungovich, tell me a riddle, as you love them so. Why should you live?"

No readable expression crossed that gruesome countenance.

"Surely it is you who should answer that?"

I put my hand to the hilt of the Krozair longsword—and it was not there.

Nothing remained of what I had taken from the fire-crystal opening that provided what I lacked. But those replacements I had taken from the Mausoleum, the Hall of Flame, these remained.

I touched the hilt of the rapier.

"Steel will not harm me." The red and green checks stirred as Ungovich swung about, sharply. "And now you die!"

He put a golden whistle to his mouth and blew.

No sound issued.

He blew again, the ghastly gray-green marbling of his cheeks pulsing. Again and again he blew. He swung to face us, and the eyes blazed in unholy anger—demoniac.

"I am the Wizard of the Moder! You will die when my pets—"

Quietly, Deb-Lu-Quienyin said, "I do not think they heard your call, San."

The exquisite irony of that formal salutation of San was not lost on us—nor on the Wizard of the Moder.

He peered closely at Quienyin.

Then he moved back, sharply, and—from nowhere—a sword appeared in his left hand.

"You—" he said, and his words were a thick choke. "You are—"

"Yes."

"But none enters here! None! It is not permitted!"

This—thing—had caused us great grief. It had set traps for us, riddles, hurled occult monsters upon us, tortured us. Now it stood there, slashing a sword about, mewling, fiery-eyed, and helpless in the grip of those awesome powers of a Wizard of Loh.

"Let me shaft it and have done," said Nath.

"Let me put a bullet between its yes," said Barkindrar.

Hunch goggled.

Nodgen hefted his spear.

The two Pachak hyr-paktuns set themselves, as ever, ready for what might befall.

I said, "We came here of our own free will. We have taken treasure from this thing. Let us not slay it."

"No?" breathed Tyfar. He was shaking.

"It protected its honored dead," said Quienyin, "and the protection turned ugly, became a game, a game of death."

"I didn't come here of my own free will," said Hunch. "By Tryflor, I said as much at the time!"

"By the Resplendent Bridzikelsh, nor me!" quoth Nodgen.

"Nor did I," I said. "But most of us did. We agreed to this thing's terms for its abominable game. We have exposed it. I think that wounds it sorely."

"Wound it!" said Nath the Shaft. His bow lifted, the arrow nocked. "I'll wound it past the Ice Floes of Sicce!"

"Together, Nath," said Barkindrar. His sling swung suggestively.

The thing that called itself Ungovich hissed at us.

"Should we kill it?" whispered Tyfar.

"Men kill things they do not understand. Do we understand this thing, this Moder-lord? Do we descry why it does what it does?"

"You have the right of it, Jak," said Quienyin. "Let us be-gone!"

Silently, we left the Wizard of the Moder hissing and slash-ing his sword about. We left that golden room. We were per-fectly confident we would find the way out.

Ungovich, green and marbled with arrested decay, slob-bered after us. He sobbed in the agony of his spirit. As we reached the crimson curtains of the doorway, Nodgen turned back and spoke.

"The next time we come here, old Wizard, we may not be so magnanimous!"

"Come back!" squeaked Hunch. "Come back *here*! You off your head?"

And so as we went out we laughed.

But I felt again that dark sense of dread that, one day, I *would* return. . . . If not to this Moder then another of the many dark death traps of the Humped Land. . . .

We found the stairway, we found the door, we opened it with an ordinary handle.

We stepped outside.

We stepped into the clean fresh air, and into the glorious streaming lights of the Suns of Scorpio. . . .

The dark and ominous bulk of the Moder brooded at our backs.

By Zim-Zair! But it was good to be alive, and on Kregen!

DRAY PRESCOT

The great novels of Kregen, world of Antares.

Fully illustrated.

If you wish to order these titles,

please use the coupon on

the last page of this book.

Presenting JOHN NORMAN in DAW editions . . .

- [ ] **EXPLORERS OF GOR.** The latest novel in the exciting saga of Tarl Cabot. (#UE1449—$2.25)
- [ ] **SLAVE GIRL OF GOR.** The eleventh novel of Earth's orbital counterpart makes an Earth girl a puppet of vast conflicting forces. The 1977 Gor novel. (#UE1474—$2.25)
- [ ] **TRIBESMEN OF GOR.** The tenth novel of Tarl Cabot takes him face to face with the Others' most dangerous plot—in the vast Tahari desert with its warring tribes.
  (#UE1473—$2.25)
- [ ] **BEASTS OF GOR.** The twelfth novel of the Gor saga takes Tarl Cabot to the far north to confrontation with the Kurs' first Gorean foothold! (#UE1471—$2.25)
- [ ] **HUNTERS OF GOR.** The saga of Tarl Cabot on Earth's orbital counterpart reaches a climax as Tarl seeks his lost Talena among the outlaws and panther women of the wilderness. (#UE1472—$2.25)
- [ ] **MARAUDERS OF GOR.** The ninth novel of Tarl Cabot's adventures takes him to the northland of transplanted Vikings and into direct confrontation with the enemies of two worlds. (#UE1465—$2.25)
- [ ] **TIME SLAVE.** The creator of Gor brings back the days of the caveman in a vivid lusty new novel of time travel and human destiny. (#UJ1322—$1.95)
- [ ] **IMAGINATIVE SEX.** A study of the sexuality of male and female which leads to a new revelation of sensual liberation. (#UJ1145—$1.95)

DAW BOOKS are represented by the publishers of Signet and Mentor Books, THE NEW AMERICAN LIBRARY, INC.

THE NEW AMERICAN LIBRARY, INC.,
P.O. Box 999, Bergenfield, New Jersey 07621

Please send me the DAW BOOKS I have checked above. I am enclosing
$_____ (check or money order—no currency or C.O.D.'s).
Please include the list price plus 50¢ per order to cover mailing costs.

Name _____

Address _____

City _____ State _____ Zip Code _____
Please allow at least 4 weeks for delivery